MERGATROID

RIVERS OF TIME

BY

RAYMOND WALTER SEIBERT

Published by Advanced Concept Design
Lago Vista, Texas

Copyright © 2012 by Raymond Walter Seibert
Published by arrangement with
Advanced Concept Design
Library of Congress Control Number
to be assigned
International Standard Book Number
ISBN 13: 978-0-9826162-3-9

For information, address
rseibert@advancedconceptdesign.com
axlerod@peoplepc.com

First paperback printing December 2012
Printed in the United States of America
derek@kustomkwikprint.com

First Edition December 2012 10 9 8 7 6 5 4 3 2 1
Second Edition May 2025 10 9 8 7 6 5 4 3 2

Table of Contents

Dedication

This second work in the "Rivers of Time" series is gratefully dedicated to my older brother Burt, who helped look out for our father, as we watched Star Trek together. Dad threatened to throw a shoe through the television set, if he caught us watching 'that nonsense' again.

The title of Dr. Burt's master's thesis on binary stochastic variables was used in "Supernova" the first book in the "Rivers of Time" series. Burton was the first of us to find the science fiction magazine, "Analog", and generous enough to bring it to me saying, "You are not going to believe how good this story is", as he showed me the first issue of "Dune" in serialized form. We haunted the bookstore magazine stand together, waiting for the next installment of Frank Herbert's stunning classic of science fiction, quite beyond anything that we had ever read before.

Thanks Burt!

Acknowledgments

There are so very many people to give thanks to, I hardly know where to start. First, let me thank Derek at Kustom Kwik Print in Dallas for years of effort in helping me with my own and other publications. Their untiring effort has made it possible for me, and many others to find their way to print. Thanks to Billy and Pop Day for the effort on behalf of all of the ACD authors printed at their shop.

Editing credit goes gratefully to my senior editor Norma Melrose, and helpful friends, Don Van Slyke, Philip John Brooks, and many others, and most of all my wife Jean. Thanks goes out to Michael Hearne for use of part of the lyrics to his song "New Mexico Rain", which is like an anthem of the Santa Fe area. Credit goes to Rosario Carelli of Taos New Mexico for his tutoring in African drumming, which gave insight into the correlation of this early form of communication and human speech, with the psychic component of togetherness that exists within a drumming group. Rosario, a big 'Gum-baa' to you.

The sources of inspiration are many. I have tried to include a little bit of every science fiction writer that I have ever read. Direct influence and research for this work has come from many sources. The works of Plato in his recount of Socrates to begin, to "Visions of the Future", edited by Pickover and inclusive of almost every major science writer in the world, if not as contributor, then as source material for that book. Pertinent articles have come from my sister Dr. Karen Farmer's leading edge magazines on genetics and scientific research, which seemed to yield just the article that I needed, at the point that I needed it. Also Ray Kurzweil's works, especially "The Singularity Is Near" must be credited. I would like to mention a special *thanks to Kristy Keffer for showing me around the town of Los Alamos, and showing me what she was able of the Los Alamos laboratories, and for discussions of the genetic mutating effects of alpha particles. I would like to think Chris O'Brien for his "The Mysterious Valley", and work on cataloging the unusual events and goings on in the San Luis valley. I was led to Chris's work through a suggestion by Mike Addington of Red River that I notice the story told by Tom Reed of Questra.*

Near future science fiction is the hardest to write, and the most risky, as it is easy to go wrong and be left behind, or entirely miss the twists and turns that the near future may hold. Human genetics, computer consciousness, nano-technology, political intrigue and scientific advancements on every front have been considered. I am sure that I will miss in many areas, but I am sure that we will take horses to the moon, and so cowgirls on the moon is a sure thing. Cowgirls on the moon, what a great idea!

Raymond Walter Seibert
Red River New Mexico August 2012
May 2025 Lago Vista

Chapter One The Sisters of the Second Sight
Hungary/England/Scotland

She was listening at the door. "As long as Macbeth," she heard her father say. She edged closer to the door, pressing her ear against the thick oak. It pushed in and rattled. Her uncle opened it and scowled at her.

"It is only Margolia," he told his brother. This was her nickname, "Pearl". She retreated to the garden.

She thought to pray. Her troubled, ten-year-old mind sensed the changes all around her, the hushed adult conversation and the arrival of men from England. "Lord," she began. "Protect us from the pagan evil," she crossed herself as she had seen Father Andrew do.

The year ten-fifty-six had many changes, and the Princess Margaret, daughter of The Exile, had been fasting and praying for days, as Father Andrew had instructed was the way our Lord Jesus sought the heavenly Father. She sought the Heavenly Father. She was committed, in her mind, to be a Nun. She knew her father had other plans. That was why she was in the garden praying, praying fervently to be protected by her Heavenly Father.

There was a flash of light. She could see it behind her closed eyelids. The fasting was putting her in an ecstatic state, she felt the presence of her Heavenly Father. This sudden flash of light filtering through her closed eyelids filled her with ecstasy. She opened her eyes in the ecstatic moment and beheld two suns in the sky. One big one and one Supernova, like a small and very bright sun, bursting out a sublime light.

People began to shout to one another, and soon the garden area was full. Her father and his brother both came out of the doors leading to the garden and began to point up and gesture at the new sun in the sky.

"It's a sign from God," Father Andrew told her father at the supper table. "Maybe the return of Christ," he held his hands palms up.

Margaret almost swooned with the lack of food, an ample supply hidden in her lap, where she had pretended to eat. A thrill coursed through her, and she was almost overcome by the thought of the final judgment. "We'll be going back to England," she heard her father say.

The second sun in the sky lasted for two weeks in the year ten-fifty-six AD and then, as quickly as it came, it disappeared. No scholar could give an honest answer to the cause of the event. It would not be until the year of 1972 before the Neutron Star in the tip of the horn of the bull in Taurus, the source of the phenomena would be understood. This was a Supernova explosion. The opening of the Dragon's Door.

Ten years went by, and Margaret grew to be a lovely woman with high cheekbones and a noble bearing, reflecting the linage of her family. She was a pious girl, and rose in the night each night to pray, as she had done even before they had returned to London some ten years earlier. She prayed for her father, or rather his soul as he had died the month before of pneumonia.

She was deep in prayer for her departed father when she became aware of sound and movement. Her mother opened the door and entered flushed.

"Get up Marg," her mother roused her from her prayer.

"Yes, mother?" She questioned.

"Harold has been defeated and was killed. William is on his way to London. We must leave."

"Where are we going?"

"Back to Hungary," her mother told her.

The servants came in to pack her things and dress her for the trip. There was haste and everyone was moving at twice the normal speed. The castle was in great

2

turmoil, with shouting and people running in the courtyards and through the halls. The servants quickly packed all of their belongings.

As they hurried to the river to depart to the boats that would ferry them to a waiting ship, a figure moved from the darkness at the portcullis door. Her mother stepped in front of Margaret. "Who are you?" She questioned sharply.

"You know me, Milady," a smooth voice soothed. "It is Archbishop Stigand."

"You startled me Archbishop," her mother chided. "This is a night filled with fear." She gripped a small knife hidden in her skirt and demanded straight out. "Do you mean us harm?"

"No, Milady, not at all," he took a step back, noticing her hand calmly poised, knowing a pocket was in the fine dress and what was in that pocket. He moved discretely out of striking range.

"You opposed Edward," she accused.

"That is long past, and I placed the crown on your brother, Harold," he countered, and then crossed himself. "God rest his soul."

"You had your hand on the crown when the Archbishop of York crowned my husband's brother," she informed him in disgust. "What is it that you want with us on this dark night of misfortune?" He stepped closer but seemed to not know exactly how to begin. "What is it, man?" She questioned him with impatience.

"I beg to speak with your daughter Margaret," he exclaimed. "I," he stammered, "I must tell her," He began to explain.

"Most strange, Stigand, what is going on here?"

"Milady, I have been instructed in a dream to convey certain trusts to Margaret."

"What trusts?"

He pulled back his hood and assumed authority. "I am Archbishop of both Winchester and Canterbury, and I have instructions for your daughter Margaret." Her mother stepped to the side. "Alone," Stigand demanded. "These instructions are for her alone."

Margaret watched as her mother passed through the portcullis and out of hearing. Stigand moved closer to Margaret.

"Come here child," he coaxed, as he brought a box about the size of a man's hand from a cloak pocket. She could see the glitter of the gilding even in the dim morning light.

Margaret felt she was in a dream, as Stigand's voice echoed from the damp walls. She hypnotically moved a step closer. He opened the box lid. "You must kneel, child," Stigand instructed her. "You are looking at part of the cross of Jesus Christ our Lord." Margaret fell to her knees in wonderment as she stared into the dark center of the box he held in front of her eyes, "and more," he continued. "With the True Cross, is the lance point that pierced the side of our Lord Jesus as he gave his life for all mankind."

Margaret's eyes grew large in wonder as she stared into the gilded box. Her pupils grew accustomed to the low light, and she began to see the two objects inside the ornate container. She instinctively reached for the box, after Stigand motioned it toward her. He handed it to her. She was electrified in every atom of her body.

"Bless this child to your purpose, Amen," she heard him pray over her. "Margaret," he came close and peered into her eyes, "God has commanded me to entrust these sacred Holy Relics to your care to keep them from the hands of William. You are to establish a church with the Holy Rood, stained with the Blood of our Lord. You are never to allow the spear point to be carried or used or known in your lifetime and beyond. Never let it be known

4

how you came to have these, Relics. This is God's will for you," his voice boomed out above her. "Now go to your mother, and go with God," Stigand dismissed her.

As he watched her pass the portcullis, he shook his head in wonder at what he had done. He had spent a lifetime, and most of the fortune garnered from the two rich sees of Canterbury and Winchester, to obtain the Relics. They had come as a chance during a sojourn to Hungary some years earlier. The negotiations had gone on for years, but finally he had them. The piece of the cross was the largest ever sold by the Holy Roman Emperor, and the spear of Longinus had cost as much. The piece of the Cross was from the find of Helena, and her son Constantine had held the spear in his hand during the Council of Nicaea, in which the Holy Scriptures were canonized. The effort had caused him to seek and gain control of two rich dioceses and had led to his excommunication by the next Pope. This could very easily lead to his expulsion from the church in England, and even his execution, certainly a dark cloud would descend over his political career. Would William support him? It was unknown at this point. Certainly, he would be an outcast among the English Bishops. His only hope would be to support William's claim that Edward had promised William the throne of England when Edward had passed to his Heavenly reward.

Margaret had risen and walked as in a trance, taking the Relics and secreting them in the sleeve of her coat, and joined her mother. "You've a strange look to you Margaret," her mother questioned. "What did Stigand want?"

She pulled the gilded jeweled box tight under her cloak sleeve. "I am sworn by oath to secret," she said, as she concealed the relics.

"Did the Archbishop give you something," she pressed her," a note to Father Andrew in Hungary, perhaps," she prodded.

"No, nothing," Margaret lied, to keep her secret, which she now considered a vow.

Stigand watched from the shadows of the portcullis, as the two and their attendants boarded the boat that would take them to the waiting small ship. He was still stunned that he had given up the relics, after spending a lifetime in their pursuit. The cost alone, the accumulated wealth drained off the church coffers of two rich dioceses, Winchester and Canterbury, had given much to the purchase of these Holy Relics. The spear point had been lost when Charlemagne was thrown from his horse and killed, but up until that moment had been held in the hands of every would-be emperor since Constantine's mother Helena had brought it from its hiding place in Judea. Gained by the torture of several Rabbis, Helena had obtained the three crosses of the crucifixion, from under the pagan temple of Venus in Jerusalem, after it had replaced the Jewish temple on the Temple Mount. The True Cross had been determined by the miraculous healing of a sick woman lain upon it and cured.

Constantine had held the spear in his hand as the Second Council of Nicaea had argued the Cannon of the Scriptures in front of him. It had passed into the hands of Attila when he sacked Rome, but he had thrown it at the feet of a group of Roman Commanders saying that he did not believe in the spear or the One it had stabbed, and he had no use for it. The spear had passed into Muslim hands for centuries, but in one-thousand -nine AD had been recovered and passed to the Church, but by ten-sixty-five, only one year earlier, Stigand had purchased it from a corrupt Pope, and it had come to him in Hungary at a church confab of Bishops, just a short time earlier. He had meant it as a means to establish a Saxon hegemony in world order. Now, that dream was dead. William the Bastard must not have the spear. Stigand's vision was clear, very clear on this, and now it was in God's Hands.

From the shadows, he watched as Margaret and her mother were rowed out to a waiting ship. He watched until the bark was underway down the Thames to the ocean. He pulled his heavy cloak tighter around him as a nip was coming in the air, and a wind was starting to blow out of the north.

The captain was glad for a gust coming from behind. He was being well paid for this charter, made ready with haste in the middle of the night. A fair wind would make an easy sail to the channel, but by the time they had rounded the coast and headed for the Flanders side, the sea was rising strongly out of the northeast, and the craft was beaten back to a more north-only course, with no headway being made eastward. Without star sighting, for it was totally cloudy with squalls coming on them out of the east, they were carried far to the north. They fought for two days and nights to make the continent to the east. Then the weather really got bad, and they let out the sea anchor, but still were driven before the storm, helpless to make progress, with the sails totally reefed and the masts threatening with creaks and groans to splinter at any moment, as waves washed the deck and threatened to take anything not lashed over the side into the sea.

The three women huddled on the shore dressed in foul weather black capes. They sat around the fire built next to the shore. One stood and sniffed the air. "I kin the storm akomin," Megan pulled her shawl up around her head over her bonnet and tight about her shoulders. The wind suddenly changed and blew out of the east directly down the Firth of Forth where the women warmed by the fire. The increase in wind fanned the flames and they searched for more driftwood from the shore and threw it on the fire to build it higher. The fire crackled and roared.

It began a misting rain. The women hunched under their cloaks and waited. "We must wait," Megan told them. "Keep the fire high so that they may see the way to us," she yelled above the shriek of the storm fury.

The storm howled and tried to put their fire out. The wind tried to rip the cloaks from their bodies and the tightly strapped bonnets from their heads.

Megan stood slantwise against the wind. "It is komin," she pointed out into the dark mist. The others hurried to the shore. They strained to see.

"We see nothing, sister," they shook their heads.

"It is komin," Megan insisted. "I see the boat, just as in my dream," she yelled against the wind.

A form materialized from mist and fog. A shape grew clear and the frantic movements of people aboard a ship being driven onto the rocks on the southern side of the Firth of Forth near the mouth of the channel could be seen from the shore. Suddenly, the wind stopped, dead calm, and the boat's momentum guided it to the rock where the women were waiting.

Margaret came on deck to find the three women just in front of the prow of the little ship. Megan held her hands toward her, "Welcome Queen Mergatroid," she boomed out the greeting, and then all three bowed low to the ground, as Margaret stood in shock at the events of the last three days.

Chapter Two Moon Base

Where the Hell is Stark Raven?

Striker Rich ambled in his rock and roll easy manner across the open space of the central dome. His six-foot two frame moved in a graceful gait. He always looked as if he owned the world and hadn't a care. He ran a hand through his dark and long hair to loosen the tangles of the night's sleep and tied it back in a long ponytail, as it was still a little wet from his morning shower. His gray-blue eyes scanned the vast field of the containment dome.

A lush and green lawn of well-manicured grass surrounded the outer edges of the dirt clay mixed with sawdust of the central arena. Intense lighting, powered by solar collectors, lit up the area furnishing the photons needed for photosynthesis. Margaret Hartman, the twelve-year-old granddaughter of Herman Hartman the billionaire real-estate developer, exercised her favorite barrel-racing horse, tearing around the central barrels at breakneck speed, turning and racing back to the starting barrel. She pulled up and waved at Striker and then reined her horse Trixie toward him at the edge of the dome. She pulled back on the reins hard and made Trixie stand on hind legs and hop, and Trixie could hop high in the low gravity. She had a school-girl crush on Striker Rich, and she wasn't the only one. She stopped short of the railing surrounding the practice field. "Hello, Striker," she called and waved, hoping that he would come over to her.

"Hi, Marge," he hallowed her back. He turned and walked on across the lawn to the exit. Margaret got a pout on her face at being so ignored, but Striker had pressing business this morning. She turned the horse and raced around the edge of the railing the entire distance of the large circle. The dome had been constructed by a Waxahachie Texas Dome Company, and because of the low gravity of the moon, was immense. It was six times larger than any dome that had ever been constructed on Earth. The windows around the edge were of a thick annealed quartz glass with special thermal properties, and Striker looked out across the Sea of Tranquility at the Earth on the moon's horizon. He could see The Sea of Japan was in sunlight. America was in darkness on the other side of the world. The bright jets of a Virgin Space Transport plane were settling softly onto the moon's surface, just at the left hand corner of the visibility he had out this window. He quickened his pace, as the government attaché of Senator Samuel Omar Prickle was on that transport, and here on the moon discussing several projects with Striker. They were valuable contracts, if they came to fruition, and Striker Rich liked to make money, and he made it often and easy. He just seemed to have the Midas touch of being in the right place at the right time.

Thinking of Senator Prickle brought to mind his sometimes-partner Stark Raven. They both disliked Prickle, and Striker laughed to himself at a joke Stark liked to make of Prickle's name. He had not heard from Stark Raven in more than three months, and this was very unusual. He made a mental note to send him a text message soon to find out what was so important that they had lost touch for this unusually long time.

He made the door at the edge of the huge containment dome and entered a corridor that would take him to the lounge that was made of a clear plastic at the disembarkation area of the Space Port landing area. He passed by several doors with air locks leading to smaller concrete domes with special insulated outer skins that were used for the support functions of the 'Port' as it was called. It was early, as moon time was organized around Earth time in Beijing, although the place never really slowed down, but the sleep cycle was geared to the dominant political and money center on Earth. He met only a few people heading the other way, but several people were headed toward the 'Port', and the arriving transport from Earth. There were sometimes several a day, and sometimes none for several days, as was needed, scheduled, and paid for by the immensely rich men that used the moon for the myriad reasons that had been found profitable or desirable for just the plain fun of it.

The port dome was a geodesic with steel girders and thick plastic panels giving a stunning view of the stars and the arriving space plane, with giant V swept back arms over the top of the rest of the name. Dust had risen all around the arriving shuttle and was slow to settle in the low gravity. The hatch opened between the shuttle and the port and people began to disembark.

The first ones off the ship were the disabled. Those late baby boomers that had lived long lives and had the money to purchase homes or lease in the assisted living area of the complex. Some were in wheelchairs and others on walkers, which as soon as they had entered the port signaled the nurses that were helping them that they wanted to try to stand and walk. Most were able to abandon the wheelchairs and walkers and take unassisted steps for the first time since they had become invalids.

Striker watched as pleasant smiles broke across many of the faces as they took their first tentative steps. An old song from the previous century came to his mind.
"Arms that can barely lift a spoon,
Everyone's gone to the moon."
Next came the first-class passengers in the front cabin, with business men from all over the world in every type of clothing from caftans and turbans to the standard

pin striped suit and tie. He spotted his man and approached. The man had a picture of Striker and was looking around the port for him, saw him coming toward the line of travelers, put on his best smile and stuck out his hand as Striker arrived. "Roderick Axtel," the man introduced himself. The two men shook hands and exchanged the common civilities. Striker suggested that they take a table in the commissary while waiting for the luggage. Axtel acceded to the suggestion and motioned for Striker to lead on. They settled into the stiff backed, poorly padded chairs around a small table.

"Axtel," Striker questioned?

"Yes," the man confirmed. "Call me Rod."

"Been with Senator Prickle long?" Striker continued.

"About two years. I came on after the last mid-term elections, but I've only been in Washington a little over a year."

"Is this your first trip to the moon?"

"I've been here twice before," he surveyed the surrounding structure, "but parts of this look new. He gazed back toward the large Dome some distance away. Several smaller domes were visible branching off from the corridors that led out from the port like spokes of a wheel. "The large dome was still under construction when I was last here. Looks like it has its PI thermal coating. Is it finished inside?"

"All complete, and very impressive on the inside. It is set up for a rodeo right now, and when I came through a few minutes ago Marge Hartman was practicing for the barrel racing event."

"Is that right," Axtel shook his head in disbelief. "Horses on the moon, it is just hard to grasp." A waiter came over to see if they needed anything, and Axtel ordered a hot chocolate. Striker ordered coffee with cream and sugar.

"Well," Axtel began, "we have a lot to discuss," he set a briefcase on the table and opened it, taking out the small and new computer that had come into style. He removed several manila folders from the flap in the top of the computer case and looked them over for a few moments to refresh his memory about the topics that he wished to take up with Striker. "Things are changing fast. With the end of 'Operation Sundrop', NASA will need a new mission to keep it funded and moving forward. This new linear accelerator technology that launched the Apollo station is going to change everything up here. We see many new opportunities, and much of the old way of doing things, such as the older launch systems are going to go by the ways in a fast pace. Companies like S. G. Raven Enterprises are going to be left behind, as the new technology is implemented very quickly," he paused to watch Striker's reaction to this news.

"I suppose that is true," Striker arched an eyebrow. This was the second time today that he had thought of Stark Galileo Raven and company.

"I know that Rich Explorations has always had a close relationship to Raven Enterprises, but with the new cryogenic linear accelerator technology taking over many launch tasks, much of the rocket technology will be unnecessary."

"That's the way it is shaping up," Striker had to agree.

"The concession for building and shipping the magnets has been granted to the Santa Fe Group," Axtel's body language assumed a new confidence. "Much of the development has come out of Los Alamos and Albuquerque, from government laboratories, and The Santa Fe Group has been awarded the contracts to begin development of applications. Moon launches by linear accelerator are seen as the natural place to start with the practical use of the new technology. There will be, in time, robotic missions to Mars and its moons, and to the asteroid belt to assess the mining potential. We know that this has always been a dream of yours. You have written numerous papers and published them on the subject. Also, the pharmaceutical industry has an interest in the development of new drugs using zero gravity and deep space to develop some of the anticipated advances. Your company with its mining explorations and robotic expertise is foremost in the potential to make money from these future projects."

"What type of business applications are you anticipating for the near term," Striker questioned?

"Well just for starters, you saw the many feeble old rich people that got off the shuttle with me. They are going to eventually die here on the moon."

"I suppose that is inevitable," Striker agreed. He could still see some of the new arrivals trying to learn to walk again in the moon's low gravity. Some walked with the help of nurses, while some that were in better shape literally sprang up in the air and kicked their heels together like young boys at a picnic, from the sheer joy of being able to stand upright and walk.

"The cost of returning bodies to Earth is enormous, and the governments of Earth are trying to reduce expenditures for those types of rocket ships, and the refueling that has to take place in orbit is more expensive than the launches in the first place. Several governments are requiring the feebs to sign agreements to be buried on the moon." Striker narrowed his eyes at the man's unfeeling use of a new slang term that had lately been making headway as a new word in the English language. "It is foreseen that a cheaper alternative is going to be able to be offered to the heirs, which will want to save money on burial of their loved one and put that money in the estates."

Striker could see where this was going. "So you want to use the new linear accelerator technology to launch the bodies?"

"Yes."

"Where," he asked, but knew the answer already. "Into the sun for cremation."

"Yes."

"Sounds like a plan."

"There are movements afoot to legislate this type of burial as a precondition for the advantage of living out their final years on the moon, in what is partially government funded housing."

"Sounds like this has been thought out for some time."

"It has been foreseen as a possible option and talked about in committee in the Senate."

Striker thought that somewhat macabre, as those Senators would one day be old people themselves. The human animal always thought in terms of those unpleasant things happening to someone else. He held his peace and tried not to let the disgust that he was feeling show in his face.

"We want your company to be the contractor of record for the building of the launch system."

"Who is we," Striker asked, matter of fact?

"Well, it will come as no surprise that Senator Prickle is a very good friend of The Santa Fe Group. He is chairman of the Commerce Department's guiding executive staff in the Senate, and this development will come through his committee."

"That is a big assignment. Why my company?" Striker could see clearly that this was a separation between S. G. Raven Enterprises' interest and that of Rich Explorations. It was really obvious to him as he knew that Stark had made an enemy out of Senator Prickle on several occasions.

"It is a good fit," Rod Axtel smiled his best and most beguiling smile. "Plus, after the experience that you will get with the installing of the magnets and support systems, your robotics division will be in a position to launch explorations into the asteroid belt. Mining is your thing, is it not? And, you have, as I have already stated, cherished the dream of exploring the asteroid belt for rich pockets of minerals. Up until now, that has been an impossible quest, as rocket fuel has proven to be harder to manufacture on the moon than hoped for when moon base was first conceived and built. With the experience that you will get and the contract to build the first of the linear launch systems you will be in the lead to build the system to explore the belt."

Striker tilted his head slightly with this thought. Axtel had him there. His dream of exploring the asteroid belt was well-known in magazine articles and other interviews on radio and television talk shows. He made no secret of his great dream of mining the asteroid belt with robots directed from moon base.

It was at that moment, as his gaze wandered to the Earth in the distance, that a tremendous flash of light came from just above the ionosphere of Earth, spreading and growing more brightly than looking into the flash of an electric arc welder, until Striker was forced to close his eyes, and even hold his hands over his face to stop the intensity of the light that was coming at them from over the Earth's horizon on the night side, just above the United States. When he could force his eyes open a crack to look, the Earth had developed a corona that glowed a myriad of colors that seemed to dissolve the very atmosphere of the planet. People all around him screamed, and many fell to the floor. Some fell to their knees, with mouths wide open, and some placed their palms together in fervent prayer.

"What the Hell," Striker said under his breath to himself, and then looked at the astonished face of Rod Axtel. Without another word to the man, Striker rose and ran toward his quarters, where he had communication equipment that he could use to find out what had just happened. He ran back along the corridor the way that he had come that morning a few minutes earlier. Everyone along the way was in dazed confusion or dashing about in frenzied manner. When he entered the large dome, Trixie was dashing about the arena kicking and bucking. Marge Hartman had been thrown and hit her lip on one of the barrels which lay on its side next to her. Striker climbed the arena rails and ran to where she was trying to get up. She had a cut lip, which had hit the rim of the barrel.

"Wha..What happened," she managed to say through the blood pouring out of her mouth. A tooth was turned back part way from its alignment, and she was dazed. Trixie continued to circle the big arena, whinnying wildly, with terrified eyes.

"Don't talk," Striker cautioned her, and pulled off part of the sleeve of his shirt and began to try to compress the cut in her lip to staunch the flow of blood.

"What's goin' on," she questioned again?

"I don't know," he told her. He sat on the ground and gathered his feet under him and tried to lean her back upright on his leg. She propped herself up against him, and he held the torn sleeve against her lip. Two men that usually watched her had been some distance on the other side of the arena, and they came on the run. They had gone to get coffee, and Striker had been the first to reach her, but he let them take over and slowly shifted her weight to them and then tore out on the run, climbed the arena fence rails and continued to run toward the portal that led to his office and housing in the distant far side of the space port compound living area.

Striker walked quickly back to his office and rooms in the compound, refusing to be stopped by the people that he met along the corridors, people in confusion seeking anyone that might know the answers to what was happening. When he reached his rooms, he tried to think of who on Earth might know what the explosion was, and kept coming up with the same answer, S. G. Raven Enterprises. Communication was totally jammed and all he got from the phone company was a recorded message: "All lines are out of service at this time". He turned on the television, but the Earth cable channels were nothing but static. Local broadcasting on the moon gave little better with the commentators speculating that a disaster had occurred. The Chinese and Arabic stations had nothing more to add.

Eventually, reports began to surface that a prominence on the sun had sent an incredible number of charged particles out that had reached the Earth in a historic Aurora that was seen around the world. He recognized this as pure propaganda and nonsense, as that would have triggered an alert on the moon to take shelter.

There was nothing more he could do to try and find out what was happening on Earth. He called the port to book on a shuttle and was told that everything was grounded at present and for the foreseeable future, and that it was unknown when that would be changed. He thought next about little Margaret Hartman. He made his way to the medical section. The corridors were strangely empty now. Out the window along the way he looked out at the Earth. The planet looked normal again. He shook his head in puzzlement and went on toward the medical dome. At the nurse's station, he got information about the room in which Marge had been placed. Herman Hartman, a very worried grandfather, was hovering over his granddaughter when he entered. Marge brightened a little when she saw Striker.

"Mr. Rich," Herman came to shake his hand. "I know who you are, even though we have never met, Marge talks about you all the time."

"Very pleased to meet you," Striker returned the man's firm handshake.

"Thank you so much for tending to Marge right after her accident. Those sorry guards have been sent packing. They were both in the commissary and I pay them well to never leave Marge alone," Hartman's jaw clenched in anger as he spoke.

Striker went to Marge and gently stroked her forehead and hair. "How you doin', Marge," he asked? She tried to smile a weak smile but only grimaced beneath the bandage on her lip.

"She is going to have to go to Earth for medical treatment," Herman told him. "Her front tooth is ruined, and she will have to have a root canal to replace the killed nerve. The sooner the better to keep the tooth from discoloring."

"That is too bad, a tough break for her," he brushed her hair gently. "What do you hear from Earth," Striker asked?

"Not a thing, a complete black out on phone service, but some nonsense about a high energy discharge coming from the sun is starting to come in over the television. Have you heard anything?"

"Nothing, the same as you," Striker shrugged. "I tried to book a return shuttle with Virgin and was told that everything was grounded for the foreseeable future."

"Well, I'm not grounded," Hartman informed him. "I have my own private transport in my hanger and it's being fueled right now. I'm taking Marge back to Earth immediately, and you're welcome to come along with us."

"I'll take you up on that offer," Striker accepted. He looked over at Marge. Her eyes sparkled.

"Well get your gear and meet us at hanger twelve. We're leaving. You know where it is?"

"Yes," Striker affirmed. "It won't take me fifteen minutes to get ready and meet you there."

"Good, because that's about how long it will take for me to get Marge over there. Damn the clearance."

Striker hurried back to his room and threw the few things that he would need into a small case, along with his laptop and arrived at hanger twelve as Hartman rolled up in an electric cart with Marge.

They were under way in minutes, in spite of a warning from the clearance and control tower. Two other private shuttles could be seen lifting off. They circled the moon one time to take the advantage that was gained from the pull of the moon's gravity as they accelerated by falling around the planet. They passed close to the surface as they headed for a point that would let them be captured by the Earth's gravity and would allow them to gain orbital speed by the time they reached Earth. From there controllers at a New Mexico spaceport near Clovis would guide them into a re-entry trajectory for the landing. It was a two-day trip, and Herman and Striker talked of numerous things and Marge tried to hang close, but was soon sleeping in a reclining chair.

They had just been served a nice meal by an attendant with pretty blue eyes and long lashes that she batted at Striker, when the pilot came back to the passenger's section with a worried look on his face. He came to Herman's chair and stood silent for a moment.

"What's the problem," Herman could see the uneasiness on the pilot's face.

"I'm not sure, sir," he started slowly. "We have been getting continuous alerts and warning from the controllers on Earth. They have been warning us to turn back to the moon, but I haven't told you as I knew that you were committed to making it to medical attention on Earth as fast as possible. I couldn't see any reason for the warnings, but something is coming on the forward radar. You had better come forward and take a look at this."

Herman and Striker followed the pilot back to the cockpit of the space plane, where the co-pilot was intensely studying the radar screen. The pilot stood close by and pointed out the two shuttles that had left at the same time as they had. "See, here is the two other shuttles that left the moon a little ahead of us but look at this."

The two men leaned in close. There were patches of what looked to be static on the screen. "That looks peculiar," the pilot observed. "It looks to be a field of debris of some type spread out across our path."

"It's coming toward us," the co-pilot said. "I've been watching it for several minutes now, and it is spreading and also coming this way." They all watched as the specs on the radar merged with the two shuttles in front of them. Suddenly, there were bright flashes coming through the windshield observation port directly from the place where the other shuttles had entered the path of the objects. The blips that marked the two shuttles disappeared from the screen and more static like debris appeared where they had disappeared.

"This is bad," the co-pilot said with obvious panic in his voice.

"Can we change course and avoid it," Herman asked?

"We're pretty much committed," the pilot told him. "If we expend very much fuel in an effort to avoid it, we won't have the fuel for the retro re-entry."

"Can we use some fuel to avoid the field, and then burn off some speed in the upper atmosphere," Striker questioned?

"To a certain extent, that is possible, but it is a dangerous way to perform re-entry, as the atmosphere can be of varying densities. Once committed to a re-entry angle we can dive too deep too fast, and to correct at that point it becomes possible to skip like a stone on a pond and end up marooned, without fuel, and needing help that we might or might not be able to get."

"We have to do something soon," the co-pilot pointed at the fast approach of the unknown debris field.

"This is going to have to be done by computer control," the pilot warned, as he sat back into his console and made frantic adjustments to allow the computer to attempt to guide the ship through. "Get the 'Dutch Boy' meteorite patches out and give them to everyone. We're bound to get some punctures. Everyone strap in and then be ready to slap a patch on any holes that hopefully will be fixable."

The co-pilot went to a locker just behind the cockpit and got patches and gave some to each of the men and the stewardess, whose eyes were big with fear. Striker had an empty feeling and nervous butterflies churning crazily in his stomach like he had just dropped down a roller coaster incline. Marge was still asleep, and they quickly strapped her down and raised her seat to a sitting position then strapped themselves into their seats.

Marge tried to speak around her bandaged mouth with a sleepy, "Wha........," as the computer took over guidance and the rockets began to fire, lurching the ship one way and then another. She screamed as small particles tore through the ship from one side to the other, and the hiss of escaping air was all around.

Several seconds passed until the ship settled into a straight trajectory and the men were able to get up from their seats and plug the number of holes that occurred when debris passed entirely through the ship. They were placing patches over the last two obvious ones when the captain came back to the passenger cabin.

"Are the little Dutch Boys plugging the holes," he asked? He used the term that had become popular among the pilots that had used the plug patches before. "Is everyone all right back here," he asked?" The two men affirmed they were good, and so did the stewardess who was shaking uncontrollably. Marge nodded her head up and down with eyes wide with terror.

"So far the holes are tiny, and the patches are holding," Striker told the captain.

"That is good, because a bigger hole and the tiles would not be thick enough to withstand re-entry without a spacewalk repair, and we are not prepared to do that," the captain was thinking ahead. "I've got red lights all over the control panel. We had two hits through the fuel tanks, but they are self-sealing for small particles, so I think we're not in trouble there. The other two ships that took off in front of us were not so lucky."

The co-pilot came into the cabin. "We're still registering a loss of cabin pressure from a puncture somewhere captain," he informed.

"Get the smoker," the captain ordered. The co-pilot left and returned in a few moments. "Please be as still as you can be," the captain requested. He let loose a trickle of smoke from a canister and everyone held their breath and stood stock still. The thin trickle of smoke slowly headed in a thin line toward the back of the shuttle. It dispersed and the captain moved toward it and let out another trickle and watched again. A thin line of smoke headed for two areas and when they saw the smoke disappear into a floor and ceiling area, they were able to pinpoint the last holes in the fuselage.

"We've been lucky so far," the captain told them. We seem to have holes in the frame but we won't know what damage there may be to the heat shield tiles until re-entry. Everyone strap in again until I have made the course corrections that we will need to put us back on target for Earth orbit."

They did as they were told, and for several minutes the rockets fired on and off several times to position their trajectory to the proper orientation. Small talk ceased after the trauma.

In a little while, the stewardess had her shaking mostly under control and she offered hot chocolate all around. Striker accepted, Hartman declined and went forward. Marge settled and slept again. Striker got a magazine and read. After the cup was empty the stewardess picked up the cup. She was still nervous and came back to where Striker was sitting. "Mind if I sit by you," she asked?

"Not at all," he made leg room for her and she settled beside him. She made a deep sigh and then introduced herself.

"I'm Calley she said, "Calley Stevens."

"Striker, Calley from the galley," he joked, and shook her hand. "Where do you call home?"

"Yeah," she smiled, "I'm the galley slave," she smiled at the joke. They could both use the relief that a little humor brought. "I'm based in Los Angeles," she told him, "but I'm assigned all over. This was only my second trip to the moon." They exchanged small talk for a while and then her eyelids began to droop as the adrenaline left her system, and she closed her eyes, and sat back in the seat.

Striker began to thumb through a journal of mostly advertisement, and in a few moments her head nodded against his shoulder and when he looked over at her, she was asleep against him. He held still and let her sleep. After an hour of so, Striker was tired from the shock and he slept also.

When he awoke, they were in Earth orbit, and Calley was roused also. They could see the Earth outside the port side windows.

24

Hartman came back to the passenger's cabin. "We're getting ready for re-entry," he said. "I tried to get an intact space plane up here to get us, but there is none available for days, and we lost so much air from the punctures that we can't wait days, so we are going to have to chance it."

The ship began to position for re-entry. Small rockets fired in the nose to get the alignment correct, and then the big engine fired up for the slow down needed to start the entrance into the upper atmosphere. Calley reached over and gripped Striker's hand. She was white as a sheet and shaking again. He smiled at her and gave her hand a reassuring hug. Tears of terror ran down her cheeks. Everyone knew of and remembered the fate of Columbia.

The ship slowly slid into its downward angle and began a smooth decent into the atmosphere. Calley gripped Striker's hand harder with the first jolt as the craft began to bump off the atmosphere, as it entered more dense air, hitting pockets of varying humidity, she began to squeeze Striker's hand harder and harder. He looked over at her and she had her eyes closed tightly.

Flame began to show out the portholes as the heat tiles became red hot and then white hot, showering sparks out from the force of the friction of passing through the thickening air. The space plane tossed and bumped in its transition.

In the cockpit, the pilot watched his gages nervously and the co-pilot talked with the Las Cruces New Mexico spaceport. "We're on a good path," he told the pilot. "Las Cruces has given us clearance for landing on runway number one north."

They came smoothly into a glide path and the rocky ride straightened out. The cabin pitched upward as the craft's nose came up for a landing orientation. There was a slow turn, and then in a few minutes the whirring whine as the landing gear came down.

When they were near the ground and almost landed the "Dutch boy" patches began to loosen, as the atmospheric pressure near the ground become slightly greater than the cabin pressure, and some of them began to bulge inward, only held to the fuselage by the adhesive coating on their sticky side.

"We're down," Stark told Calley and gave her hand another squeeze.

"I don't know if I can ever stand to go back into space," she confided through tight and white lips. A little color began to come back into her cheeks.

They touched down and rolled to the runway end and then came back to the disembarkation area at the assigned gate. Striker bid them all farewell and Calley had a little pout going like a small child who was losing a favorite toy.

He found a lounge area where he could get a good cell signal. He called S. G. Raven Enterprises' number and got a strange message stating that no calls or messages were being accepted at this time. Next, he tried the number at the ranch in the foothills of the Sierra Nevada between Los Angeles and San Francisco. It was a private number for Stark Raven's home, and it rang and rang, and rang.

Finally, someone picked up and said, "hello", very low and somewhat tinged with sadness. He recognized Carlo's voice. His stomach tightened. He hadn't talked with Carlo since the explosion that had killed Angelina and so many others several years earlier.

"Carlo," he started tentatively, "this is Striker Rich." There was a long silence at the other end. "Carlo," Striker asked? "Is that you?"

"Yes," came a short reply.

"I was so very sorry to hear about Angelina," he finally stammered.

"Thanks Striker," the voice replied low. "That was a long time ago, and I've had to make my peace with it."

"That's a tough one, man," Striker was at a loss for words. After a long pause, he questioned, "Is Stark available?"

"That's a good question," Carlo said. "Enrico is here, and I'm going to let him try to answer that," Carlo continued the mysterious dodge. The phone went on hold for a few moments.

"Enrico Rameriz," a voice said. "Who is this?"

"Enrico, it's Striker Rich. I just came in from moon base. We saw a tremendous explosion above the United States and then a black-out of news. What's going on?"

A long pause followed, and Striker checked the cell phone to see if the connection was lost. Finally, Enrico spoke slow, "There are security issues, and Homeland Security is monitoring phone calls with a automatic system. Understand? Why don't you come on up to the ranch and stay a few days, it would be good to see you here." He emphasized the word "here".

"Well, whaa........," he was stunned. Then got his wits about him. "I will have to catch a plane to Ontario and then rent a car and come out. It will take some time."

"That's right," Enrico told him. "Come on out to the ranch, and we will be expecting you. You can relax a few days, and we will all catch up." That was it. He gave no farther hint.

"That's what I will do, then. Expect me sometime tomorrow."

"See you then, Striker," the phone went dead.

Striker scratched his head and put his cell phone away. He turned back toward the ticket counters and was crossing the kiosk area with the food courts when he saw

Calley, Margaret, and Herman Hartman sitting in an eatery. He waved and they motioned him to join them, and he went to see what they had found out.

Calley flashed a bright smile as he approached and moved a chair out for Striker to sit beside her. "Any news that has any truth to it?" He directed the question to Herman Hartman.

"Nothing," Hartman told him. "The story is a solar prominence caused a huge Aurora around the world. Have you learned anything?"

"I called my friend Stark Raven at his ranch in the Sierra's north of Los Angeles. A close employee answered, and it was just more mystery."

"How so," Herman asked?

"Well, he couldn't tell me where Stark is and he said that I would have to come see him before he could tell me anything else."

"Why was that?"

"Some kind of security clamp down by Homeland Security."

"Huh," Hartman was puzzled. "This just gets stranger all the time."

"I will have to take a commercial plane to Los Angeles Ontario and then rent a car to get out to the ranch."

"I've got a private jet being serviced and fueled to take Marge to a dentist and plastic surgeon in Los Angeles," Hartman told him. "We're all headed there as soon as the jet is ready. You can come along with us, if you like," Hartman invited.

"I'm in your debt again," Striker was glad to get the ride.

"Think nothing of it," Hartman assured him. "Glad to do it."

It was after dark when they arrived in Ontario airport. He shook Hartman's hand and hugged Marge.

"I'll keep in touch if I find out anything from Enrico at the ranch," he told Herman.

He and Calley looked long at each other. "I have to rent a car; can I give you a lift to your place?"

"That would be nice and save me an expensive taxi ride."

They made their way to the car rental and Striker got a mid-sized compact. She guided him out to the airport, and they took the freeway and drove to her apartment in Pomona.

"It's pretty late to drive any distance," she was tentative. "I can offer you a place to stay at my apartment. I've got a spare room as my roommate is on a flight to New York and won't be back until tomorrow night."

"Are you sure that will be alright?"

"Very sure," she coaxed.

He parked the car in the slot she pointed out and followed her inside. "Make yourself comfortable. Want some tea?" She asked him.

"That would be good," he sat on the couch. The living room was separated from the kitchen by a counter. He looked around the room. It was very tastefully decorated with quite a few photographs of landscapes, some with sunrises or sunsets in brilliant color. Some were seascapes, some were mountain scenes.

"Would you like hot tea or iced," she asked?

"Hot sounds good."

She came back to the couch and sat a tray with cups, sugar and milk down on the coffee table. He fixed his tea with sugar and milk and sipped the brew. "Earl Grey," she told him as she fixed hers the same way. "I hope you like it."

"Very much," he sipped again. "Did you take the photographs?"

"I did," she smiled.

"Very nice."

She began to tell him where each one was taken. He listened and drank his tea. When she had gone all the way around, he took a final sip and emptied his cup. There was an awkward moment as their eyes met. She placed her cup on the tray on the table and took his hand. She stood and squeezed his hand and pulled him toward her. He followed her up the stairs to her bedroom without saying another word.

He was up very early. Calley was still asleep when he wrote her a note and quietly left.

It was early, before daylight, and he took I-10 west to the big intersection with the coast highway, then took California One north. There was traffic. There was always traffic, but by the time the sun was coming up over the coastal range, he was well north of the metropolis and pushed the mid-sized compact around the curves and over the high bridges. The surf pounded on the rocky cliffs below, and the smell of salt air from the Pacific mixed with evergreen and then redwood as he got some one hundred and fifty miles north in two hours. He was making good time as most of the traffic flow was going south toward the big cities.

He took a small two-lane road east and the going got slower. The sun was high enough not to be blinding, and the golden pastures of the western side of the coastal range rolled by. He began to pass orchards and nut trees, rice fields, interspersed with condominiums whenever he neared and passed through a small town or city. Not far from a large intersection, he came by a huge roadside fruit market. It was filled with apricots, cherries, peaches, avocados, plums, and every imaginable fruit and nut. He chose from among the perfect fruit and added a small bag of mixed dried fruit and nuts and a cold can of guava juice, paid and continued east.

The Sierra Nevada came in sight and just short of entering the mountains, he took a small, paved road north.

He came to a large gate with cross member set in rock columns made of redwood logs. A large, black, metal raven adorned the top beam and he turned in and pushed the button on the intercom. A voice said, "Yes?"

"Striker Rich," he identified himself, and in a few moments the motor activated and pulled a chain which slowly slid the gate open. He drove through and about a mile later, after fording a couple of nicely running streams on concrete low water crossings, came around a low hill to find the ranch house and barns in a pretty bowl of a valley, nestled against the backdrop of the rise of the Sierra range.

As he pulled up to the ranch house, he recognized Enrico Rameriz. Everyone called him Nacho, and he was Stark's right hand. He watched Striker unfold from the small car and wave, pulled off his gloves. He instructed the men around him, pointed at a group of Hereford Bulls in the coral, tucked his gloves in his right rear pocket and walked toward the house.

"Hey, Nacho," Striker greeted him and they shook hands.

"Come on inside, Striker, I could use another cup of coffee. How about you?"

"Sounds good to me," he followed Enrico into the large ranch style kitchen that formed the heart of the ranch house. There were double ovens, stainless steel refrigerators, a double sink island in the center, and a huge fireplace with a spit capable of roasting a half carcass of a full-grown steer. Black coffee was in a full carafe on one end of the kitchen island.

"Cream or sugar," Enrico asked?

"I'll take it black this time of the day," Striker told him. They sat on stools across from each other and sipped the strong piñon, chocolate, coffee mixture. Striker broke the silence. "We saw a huge explosion from the moon," he started. Nacho waited him out. "Some bullshit story about a solar prominence." Nacho just sipped his coffee.

Exasperated, Striker blurted, "What the hell is going on here on Earth, and where the hell is Stark?"

There was a long pause as Enrico studied his eyes. "There are aliens here," he stated flat.

"You mean like wetbacks?" Striker looked around the kitchen thinking maybe a maid was listening, or something he wasn't understanding.

"No," Enrico told him, "Like from another galaxy."

Striker felt a cold tingle go down his spine, and the little hairs on the back of his neck and on his forearms stood straight out.

"Bring your coffee, and let's go for a walk in the woods," Enrico rose and led him out the door at the back of the kitchen. "There's too many electronics around here." Striker rose and followed him in what seemed like a dream like trance.

Chapter Three Stark Galileo Raven

Cold, intense cold was his first sensation. He was freezing, miserable, freezing. 'Cryogenics' was his first thought. Memories flooded him. Strange creatures, like giant ants, washed in front of his mind's eye. He fought to remember who he was. It eluded him at first, but soon he decided that he was Stark. He reached for more. Yes, he was certain. He was Stark Galileo Raven. He flew jet planes. He built communications systems, and he had a rocket launching facility called Tres Negras. He sailed a ship. That brought back memories of Uris and Kurege on board the ship. Then he remembered the pain from a liquid pumped into his veins, that had come to demand every trace of memory that he had of Uris and Kurege.

Slowly, he ceased to be so miserably cold. There was an audible pop, then light hurt his eyes, even though he thought he had them shut tight. He tried to force them open, but there was pain as if some cruel optometrist had put drops in his eyes to dilate them. He forced them open a slit, then shut them tight. The nightmare was still there, the big ants staring down at him. He was lying down in some kind of container. He felt lifted and placed on his back on a soft cover. Soft towels began to dry and massage his entire body. He felt oil, warm oil being rubbed on his body, like he was getting a full body massage. He was rolled over and oil was rubbed all over his backside. His sense of smell came back, a pleasant, sweet scent with a slightly antiseptic hospital smell.

The rubbing stopped and he sensed that he was alone. He began to try to move his arms. Feeling came back slowly. In a few minutes, he was able to push himself up and then roll over like he was an infant. His tongue seemed to be stuck to the roof of his mouth.

Eventually, small amounts of saliva oozed from his glands and with several efforts, he was finally able to sit up.

Slowly, slowly, he was able to swing his feet off the large, padded table and slumped to a sitting position. He forced his eyes open a narrow slit and thought he was in some sort of hospital examining room. He felt that he was being watched. He realized he was naked, and he felt exposed, so when he spied a blanket like cover laid out on the table, he was able to pull it around his shoulders, but he still couldn't stand yet but gathered it to cover himself the best he could. He wiggled his feet and rubbed his legs with his hands to start some feeling in them. He smacked his mouth open and closed, and his tongue came unstuck. His jaw hurt on both sides. He heard small sounds outside the room. He was alone for some time and eventually was able to get up and walk around the room and stretch. He began to pace and looked for a way to open the door. He examined the room entirely, and there was nothing in any way that he could see to use. Light came from a ceiling that gave off a soft glow, but no heat. Whatever had been the intense light that he felt when he had first awakened was absent. He could find no ventilation. Only the table in the center, and there was no sign of the containment that he had felt himself lifted from.

Suddenly, a door opened in the wall, and six of the large exo-antlike creatures entered and confronted him. They were armed with some type of weapons that looked like they were in the form of a taser, and they were in uniforms alike. They had a serious posture to them and they obviously meant business.

Urme's eyes were wide with delight as her mother carried her in the crook of her right arm as she rode securely over the closely manicured grass of the peaceful Louisiana cemetery. Uris carried a small cypress tree in a pot in her other hand. The two, mother and child, had gone ahead to the graves they were searching for after Kurege had driven the car to the closest approach, then found a shady parking spot to leave the car.

"We won't be long, mother," he said to Amy Hodge, who settled herself into the back seat to wait. The day was humid as Louisiana late spring days always are in the delta country. He rolled down the car windows to let the pleasant breeze blow though, then got out and opened the car trunk, removing the shovel they had brought with them from Kansas for its intended purpose. He gathered flowers in a basket, shut the trunk of the car, then gave his mother a look to make sure she was settled.

"Michael, I'll be alright, "Amy told him. "You take all the time you wish. We've come all this way. There is no hurry, and I will be fine."

Satisfied that his mother would be comfortable, Kurege shifted the shovel to a balanced position and strolled after his child and his lover. He could smell salt in the air, as the coast was near, and he looked to his left, and south toward the water, hidden behind a cypress forest in the distance. He noticed the black Ford Expedition discretely parked some distance away with two men in dark sunglasses watching. Thoughts of that night, a little over two and a half years ago, flooded back to him, brought to mind by the ocean smell in the air. He caught up with Urme and Uris at a grave site. The marble coffins were on the raised platform that was necessary in this type of marsh ground. Carved into the marble were the names:

Loving Brother, Henri Usay, and on the other next to it, Loving Sister, Danielle Usay.

As Kurege approached with the shovel, Uris let Urme to the ground. She delightedly raised herself and began her toddling walk using the raised marble sarcophagi to help support herself.

"Where do you want to put the Cypress tree?" Kurege asked Uris.

"Between the two gravef, where the mowing makhinth cannot get at it," she still had trouble with the s, and j sounds in English. Kurege used the shovel to dig a hole between the two marble platforms. Uris became very quiet and felt along the inscription on Danielle Usay's name and the dates March 31, nineteen-sixty-nine-June 19, twenty--. The date was already being overgrown with moss from the humid environment, and Uris scratched at the discolor to reveal the year. She remembered that fateful day and was suddenly overcome with grief for the only mother that she had ever known. This was the first time that she had visited the grave, and her own part in the death of this good woman suddenly filled her with remorse. She lay her head against the top of the marble sarcophagus and copious tears ran down her face and splashed onto the cold stone.

Kurege had a hole dug and looked up to see Uris's shoulders shaking as she cried and went to her and placed his arm lightly across her shoulders. Urme, too, saw her mother in grief, and moved closer and grabbed her leg with both hands and began to squall and cry in empathy to what she felt, partly with the non-understanding of a child in fear.

Kurege picked Urme up and hugged her against his chest, and she buried her head on his shoulder and wept. Uris saw the child's distress and forced herself to accept things as they were, wiped her eyes, and smiled and cooed at the child until she looked up from where her head was buried in her father's neck, and seeing her mother had stopped grieving, smiled back at Uris.

Uris picked up the Cypress tree from the top of the marble grave and pulled it from its container and lovingly placed it into the hole and carefully filled in dirt around it. She rose and looked around the cemetery, looking at the black Expedition. "Where is Oh Le Blanc," she still could not even come close to the 'j' sound in English.

"I think this way," Kurege led off into the cemetery. They walked for some distance, examining the inscriptions on some of the graves. Kurege referenced a paper that he took out his pocket. They noticed a one-armed man among a family plot with flowers in his hand, who noticed them. A scornful look crossed his face, and he began to watch them searching among the graves with a furious intensity on his face.

Uris and Kurege, with Uris carrying the shovel, and Kurege carrying Urme, consulting the map of the graveyard, found the plain sarcophagus of Joe Foy La Blanc, and stood quietly together reading the inscription. "True Friend."

They heard the sound of someone moving toward them. "Hey," a man screamed at them. "I know who you are," the one-armed man approached with an angry body posture, shaking the flowers in his one hand at them. "Look what you did to me," he held up his amputated arm, with the missing hand.

Uris held the shovel cross ways in front of her in a defensive posture and stepped toward the approaching man, coming between him and Kurege and Urme. The car doors of the black Ford Expedition opened, and three men emerged from the front and back seats, and came on the run, drawing nine millimeter pistols and cocking them as they ran as fast as they could toward the confrontation.

"I know who you are, you bitch," the one-armed man screamed. "You cut my arm off, you inhuman witch," he threw the handful of flowers at her head. Uris ducked and the flowers went over her and hit Kurege in the chest with one or two striking Urme harmlessly on the legs. She began to whimper and hugged her father's neck, tightly.

Uris came out of a crouch and lunged at the man with the point of the shovel, trying to take his head off. She guessed that he would move left, but with a fifty-fifty chance of losing his head to a trained fighter, he got lucky and moved right. The point of the shovel just missed his neck and the edge cut him, but not deep enough to reach the jugular. Blood poured from the wound, and he yelled in surprise and shock at her quickness and determination to kill him.

"I know you," she pulled back and circled for another thrust. "You are Etienne, the 'udath that cauthed the death of my friendth. You have given my fatherth data to Metatophilith," she screamed at him. "You have dethtroyed thith planet."

He moved back from her fast as she circled and pursued him cat like, searching for another moment to lunge with sure effect. At that moment, the three running men arrived and two of them grabbed Etienne on either side. The third man was John Gavin, holding his hands and gun up in a surrender position came between Uris and her intended victim.

"Whoa, little lady," Gavin coaxed. "We have him. Stop. Stop," he told her.

She respected John Gavin, and she relaxed her posture and lowered the shovel and took a step backwards.

"I'll get you for this," Etienne screamed at her, shaking the stump of his arm, as the dark suited men in sunglasses dragged him away. "I'll get you, if it's the last thing I ever do," he continued to yell threats at her.

Gavin looked nervously around the cemetery. Amy Hodge was standing in an alarmed position at their

car some distance away. "I think you should go now," he
told Kurege over Uris's shoulder. He was unwilling to
look Uris in the eyes and knew from experience with her
that she responded very poorly to orders. He understood
that she still thought of herself as Queen, not used to
taking orders, but giving them.

Kurege patted Urme reassuringly on the back, and
the little girl was soothed enough to take a peek at her
mother in a sideways look from the shelter of her father's
arms. "It's time to go," he told Uris. Mother is worried,
and Urme has had enough trauma that she can't
understand." Uris looked back at him and inclined her
head. Her fury was somewhat abated, and she followed
Kurege as he rubbed Urme's back and carried her toward
the car, where Amy Hodge stood with worried expression.

They were delayed while local police took Etienne
into custody from the FBI men, and he was loaded into an
ambulance and taken away. They drove out of Cutoff
Louisiana along the coast, through Beaumont Texas and
on to Hobby airport in Houston. The black Expedition
followed close behind. At Hobby airport, John Gavin
arranged for first class seats to the Topeka Kansas airport.

They boarded the flight last as it was getting ready
for departure. There were no other people in first class, as
Gavin had purchased and pre-emptied the entire section.
Uris sat alone and seemed to be brooding over the events
of the day. She had expressed sorrow and anger during the
car ride that she had not killed Etienne. Amy watched and
played with Urme, who fussed at being strapped in for take
off but now toddled around the cabin and sat on the floor
playing with her favorite toys, Stanley Snail, and Boots the
Alien from her favorite book, *Snails and Aliens*. Kurege
and John Gavin sat side by side, with John in the aisle seat.

"Ahhme," John eased into the conversation that he
wished to have with Kurege, after the small talk ran dry,
and Kurege had explained who Etienne was to him and

Uris. "Now that Urme is walking and will go to kindergarten soon," he began, "the President and other advisors were hoping that you two would be agreeable to make a contribution to national security," he stated.

"How so?" Kurege asked.

"Well, there have been several ideas put forth. We know that you are very interested in computer work, and from what I hear, are progressing very well with the systems that you have at home in Lawrence."

"Yes, I spend much time on the Internet exploring."

"We would like to send you to a special school for training," John continued.

"What type of training?" Kurege was intrigued.

"Well, Dr. Ruben McAuley is coming down from Washington to talk with you and Uris about the specific proposal, so I think I will leave the particulars to him."

"Where do you think I would be trained?"

"New Mexico is the most likely," he revealed a little. "It will be an excellent position for you, that I can assure you."

"That would be hard on my mother, as she is very fond of Urme."

"We can bring her out often, or she can move with you."

"She has many friends and a life with her church," Kurege reflected. "I don't know." They were silent for a few minutes. "Uris is very bored with Lawrence. She is not happy and longs for her own people. She speaks of it often. She is very worried about what may be happening on Saphos."

"That's understandable, but we have no way to help her with that," he paused. "On the other hand," this was his salient point, "we would like for her to help us to understand her ship, the robot, and perhaps the ship that

40

was captured in the Pantex fight, and the Probe that Uris disabled. Do you think she might be amenable to that?"

"I can never speak for Uris," Kurege told him. "She makes up her own mind, but if it gets her back with the Pearl and working to repair Andro, I am certain that she will consider it."

They left it at that and passed time with magazines and watching the progress of the flight. They landed at the Topeka airport in a little less than two hours after attaining altitude.

There was another large, black, Ford Expedition waiting for them as they came out of the airport. John Gavin carried the heavier bags and opened the hatchback for Kurege to place the ones he carried. Dr. Ruben McAuley got out of the driver's side and opened the back door for Amy Hodge and Uris, who carried Urme, asleep. They settled in, and John went to the front passenger's seat. Dr. McAuley reached over the back seat and shook Kurege's hand. "Hi, Uris," he nodded to her, but saw the sleeping child, then remembered he should have acknowledged Uris first, saw her frown and tried to make himself a mental note to observe protocol next time. "John," he shook Gavin's hand.

"How are things in Washington?" Gavin asked McAuley.

"It was raining when I flew out," Ruben told him. "How was the trip to Cutoff," he asked?

"Uris had a run in with an acquaintance," he told him. "Unanticipated, and a total coincidence."

"Really," Ruben looked alarmed. "What happened?"

"She almost cut the man's head off," Gavin shook his head back and forth incredulously.

"What was that about?" McAuley showed genuine concern.

"Something that as Chief of Extraterrestrial Contact, you should have known about in a debrief at some point. If I had known, I would have had him watched and known his whereabouts before the trip. He damn sure would not have been at the cemetery."

"As head of the FBI, John, you've debriefed her too," Ruben defended himself. "Why didn't you know about him?" he challenged. "What was it?"

"A man that was in the fight at the shrimp shed in Cutoff. He and Uris have personal grudges against each other, as she cut his hand off, and she blames him for the deaths of the Usays and Joe LaBlanc. Somehow, we both missed it. You know, we never did figure out who some of those agents were that were there, or who it was that killed the Usays."

"I'm going to want to go over this again and I want a full report on this," McAuley said as they pulled away from the airport.

"So am I," said Gavin, "as soon as I get a report from the questioning of him, I'll let you know what we find out."

"Good enough," McAuley agreed. He accelerated on the highway toward Lawrence. He got with the traffic flow and began to pass other cars, as he came up to speed a little faster than the traffic.

"I thought you weren't coming to Lawrence until later in the month," Gavin questioned the change in the plan.

"The President asked me to try and step up the timetable, if possible."

"It's going to be best to let them settle down a couple of days."

"Have you broached the subject with them," Ruben asked?

"I've talked with Kurege about it, but not in detail," John shrugged. "I told him that you would be coming with the particulars at some point soon."

"Good," McAuley nodded. "I'll just hang around a couple of days and get a hotel, get the feel of things with our tired little group." He was watching in the rear-view mirror. The passengers in the back were relaxed, maybe dozing, but not listening or aware of the conversation in the front seat. "I am very curious as to why Amy Hodge was chosen, and her son was kidnapped and taken from Earth. There must be some reason, and maybe there is something in her background, some clue in her family history." John didn't respond as he had his own mystery that was puzzling him as to the incident at the cemetery and why the people were killed, or why his agents could not tell him how it was that the Usays and Joe LaBlanc had ended up murdered. It was making him nervous, and caution seemed to be in order.

It was almost midnight when they pulled into the outskirts of Lawrence. Amy unlocked the door to her house and was a bit put off when John Gavin insisted on checking the house for intruders before letting the others inside.

"Ridiculous," Amy told him as she crossed the threshold. "This is Lawrence Kansas." Uris carried Urme, who had slept much of the day, and now wiggled loose from her mother's arms and ran to her room. She was fast ceasing to be a toddler, and on her home, ground had her feet well under her. Kurege and Ruben carried in the baggage and set it down.

"I will be around for a few days," he told Kurege.

"Thank you both," Kurege shook the men's hands, "for watching out for us." Uris had sat exhaustedly in a chair. She was all in as the adrenalin from the fight had left her, and the emotional drain of the cemetery had fully taken effect.

The men pulled away in the government car, and Kurege shut the door. Amy went into the kitchen. "Would anyone like a cup of tea," she called. Uris shook her head 'no' and Kurege relayed, "No, mom, we're both tired." Urme returned at that moment carrying a handful of her books. She handed her very favorite to her mother, who just looked at it tiredly.

"Read," she requested. Uris looked at the cover. "Stanley The Snail and The Aliens", it said. Uris just looked defeated. "Read," she insisted, wide awake, now.

Amy came back from the kitchen, and with her mother's non-response, took the book to her grandmother. "Read," she begged.

"Alright," Amy sat down and set her tea on a table beside her, picked up Urme who settled into her lap. She opened the book and Urme placed her finger on the first words and image. "Stanley the snail," her grandmother read, "lived in his snail's place, and lived life at a snail's pace, which was slow indeed." Urme giggled and turned the page.

Uris rose from her chair and went toward hers and Kurege's room. "Mom," Kurege inquired, "can you put Urme to bed?"

"We will be just fine," Amy told him and then continued reading. "The Aliens had never seen a snail before," she read on, and Urme turned the pages in delight. They read the book through three times and Urme wanted to start over again. "No, three times is my limit," she told the little girl, and let her carry the book as she took her in her arms to Urme's room.

She pulled back the covers and placed the little girl on her bed and undressed her and then dressed her in her favorite cotton pajamas. They, of course, had snails all over them. She tried to take the book away and place it on the shelf, but Urme put up a fuss and would not turn it loose. Urme placed it under her pillow, and would not give it up to her grandmother, stubbornly refusing.

Amy gave up as the fuss was getting too loud and let Urme keep the book beneath her pillow. She turned out the light, leaving a low glowing night light on at a plug that shone through a stained-glass flower, filling the room with a soft color. "Go to sleep now, young lady," she admonished her, as she kissed her forehead goodnight. Urme settled down on her pillow with one hand closed around the book.

She was soon asleep fast. Stanley The Snail was there and so were all the Aliens, the green ones with trumpet ears, the blue ones, with eyes on stalks, and the fat, brown, squat ones, that squinted. She played and played with them almost all night. She lived the story in the book, and she laughed and played and passed the night away, but she could only do this when the book was under her pillow.

It was three days later that there were footsteps on the porch and the doorbell rang. Kurege looked out to see Dr. Ruben McAuley at the door. Kurege let him inside. "Dr. McAuley," he shook his hand. Uris and Amy Hodge were working in the kitchen, dried their hands, and came to the front room. Urme heard the door and toddled in holding her favorite book.

"Hello, Uris, Mrs. Hodge," he greeted them, then keeled down and spoke to Urme. "Hi, Urme, what'cha got there?"

"Book," she told him. "Read?" She asked, holding it out to him.

He took it, "Stanley Snail and the Aliens," he read. My niece loves this too," he told her.

Amy picked Urme up and started to leave the room, sensing that Dr. McAuley had something important to say to the other two. "Wait, Mrs. Hodge," he stopped her. "This will involve you too."

45

"I'll put Urme in her room to play," she said and took her to her room and distracted her with some toys and then came back. They had all sat down in chairs in the front room which was the living room area. She took a seat next to her son on the couch.

"Los Alamos," she heard McAuley say. "It will be a great position in a new building that is opening. It's the Chemistry and Metallurgy Research Replacement building. We call it the CMR facility.

"Dear me," Amy said, with a worried look.

"The housing will be very nice, and Urme will be enrolled in the best kindergarten in the United States. She would be in day care to start, for another year, and Uris would only work part time. Amy," he turned to her concerns, "you can choose to move with them, or we will see to it that you are flown out to be with them as often as you wish."

"What will we do there," Uris questioned?

"Your ship is at this facility," Ruben told her, "So is the robot."

"Andro?"

"Yes."

"And my Pearl?"

"Yes," he was selling her, he could feel it. "We need your help in a number of areas in understanding these devices, and also the Probe and the other ship captured in the fight."

"The fight ith not over," she told him. "They will come."

"That is our thinking too," he told her. "We need to know the things you know. We need your expert understanding of these technologies to be prepared."

"What will I be doing," Kurege could see that Uris was convinced. This change would reunite her with the things from her own life.

46

"Los Alamos is on the forefront of supercomputing. We want to train you to help us with the next advancement in computer science. It's leading to the advent of artificial intelligence, AI. You've already had experience with computers beyond anything that we have. Your knowledge will be invaluable to us in this field."

"Will Uris and I work together?"

"It's a large facility, and you will be in the same complex of buildings, but not in the same department."

"It sounds like a good fit," Kurege told him. It was a slang expression that he had heard.

"It is a great fit," Ruben told him. Kurege looked over to Uris and then at his mother. He could read both their faces and saw reactions that he expected. Uris was sold; his mother was anxious.

"We will have to discuss it," he told Ruben.

"Of course," McAuley agreed. "Mrs. Hodge," he turned his attention to Amy. "I have been trying to understand why Kurege was chosen, and why this happened to you."

"I've often wondered," she told him.

"In doing some background checking on you, I see that your heritage is Scot," he stated tentatively. "Is that correct?"

"My grandparents were immigrants from Scotland in the nineteen-twenties," she reflected.

"Kurege told me that he dreams of the future on occasion, and this was the reason that he was taken. Are you psychic?"

"Heavens no, not that I'm aware of," she shook her head. Then thought a moment. "My mother's mother was said to 'have the sight', if that is what you mean," she remembered.

"Hmmm," Ruben reflected. "That might be the key. It certainly seems to be the reason for Kurege, or

Michael's kidnapping. Somehow that must be a part of the answer," he puzzled it out loud.

"It was in the records on Pandamon, the ones that I saw," Kurege told him.

"There's something to it," he reflected. "Well," he stood. "You young people have a lot to discuss. Here is my private cell number, give me a call when you've reached a decision," he moved toward the door, then turned. "We didn't discuss money, but in addition to the free housing and food, and medical, they will offer pay of over one hundred thousand a year each." He looked from face to face. It made less of an impression on Kurege and Uris, who were just beginning to understand the need for money, than it did on Amy, who placed both hands on her cheeks with her mouth open in amazement.

Dr. McAuley returned to Washington. He was able to call President Logan Wilson very shortly to tell him that they had accepted the offer.

"I'm not sure that I fully trust Uris," Wilson had his misgivings. "I was there at Tres Negras when she used that laser knife on the attack force that was sent."

"She was under attack, and no one knew then or knows now what happened to Stark Raven, after the penetration of Pantex." Ruben hedged the President's doubts. There are still many mysteries that surround that day, as to who could intercept encrypted messages, and obtain nuclear codes, in an attempt to wipe out Tres Negras and both Uris and Kurege."

"That operation put me on the inside, and was the spark that sent me into politics," Wilson recalled the sequence of events. "I want her working in the lab on those machines, helping us to understand those technologies, but I can't trust her, as she has a different agenda, all her own, I suspect." Wilson twirled a trophy of his military career on the top of the oval desk. "I can't let her take the knife out of the lab, but I know that she will need it to open the Pearl, so she will have to have possession of it when working in the laboratory." There was a silence as the men looked at each other.

"With the funding now coming out of Prickle's senate committees, we will be able to afford to increase the research at Los Alamos National Laboratories, and I think that I have located the proper person to handle the de-engineering of those strange machines," Ruben looked on the positive side.

"I'll leave you to make those decisions," President Wilson stopped the twirling and moved on. "But she is not to take anything out of the lab, especially that knife."

Los Alamos is situated on a high plateau north and west of Santa Fe some thirty-five miles as the Raven flies. As the jet came in for a landing on the long concrete strip poured out on top of the ancient erosion of volcanic tuft, almost as red as blood, Urme's eyes were closed, but popped open when the thrust reversers were engaged in the jet engines, with the slight bump as the wheels touched down. She raised up and looked over her father's shoulder and was curious to see a crowd of thousands of people lining the fences at the left side of the runway just beyond the tall chain link fence that lined the landing field on that side. "Protesters," Kurege observed to Uris. "Did you see the article in the paper," he asked her.

"I muth have mithed it," she lisped. "Whath the futh about?"

"They are protesting the opening of the new plutonium manufacturing plant here," he told her. "They are going to make pits of plutonium for the detonation of hydrogen bombs. It is a modernization upgrade of the United States' nuclear arsenal."

"Really," she marveled. "How do you know about thith?"

"It's been in the papers and on the news here in New Mexico for months. Don't you ever read the paper or watch the news."

"Not really," she gave a disinterested shrug."

"It's been under construction for over twenty years, and longer for some parts of it, since back in just after the beginning of this century. Today is the ribbon cutting ceremony. That's the new building that you are going to work in. Didn't you know?"

"I knew that it wath a chemithry and metallurgy rethearth building. That ith what they told me."

"Well, the metal is plutonium. They are building what is called PITs, and it stands for Plutonium Ignition Triggers. They are for the compression of hydrogen in the starting of implosion fusion bombs, Hydrogen Bombs. There is intense opposition to the opening of the facility. That's why all the people out there," he pointed out the port of the jet.

"Oh," she said, and looked a little more intently past him at the crowd, waving placards, wearing gas masks, and some in full environmental hazard suits.

Urme was happy to be taken out of her seat belt, and Uris carried her, while Kurege gathered luggage from the overhead compartments. Amy got her carry on and the baby's bag of diapers, lotions, powders, and toys. Ruben McAuley had ridden in the back, the only other passenger, and he came through the curtain and helped move the little group to the door.

There was no extending off ramp as at larger airports, and they disembarked down a stairway that was brought to the plane by truck. As they descended the stairway, they got a good look at the protesters. A squabble of some type was occurring just at the perimeter fence line as a dozen octogenarians on walkers tried to cross the police line at the entrance to the Los Alamos base. They were immediately stopped by uniformed guards and Los Alamos police, handcuffed to their walkers, with the walkers placed sideways on the ground. The old protesters were placed face down on the ground next to the walkers, to which they were attached. An ugly yell came up from the crowd and batons and tasers came out for show and ready to use. The crowd surged forward and a short melee ensued. Most of the crowd fled the force of the blows, but some faced it and were bloodied or tasered to the ground. Reinforcements came on the run.

McAuley came out of the plane behind them, saw the trouble at the perimeter, and moved around the little group and down the stairs. "Come on," he encouraged them, and they followed him across the tarmac and into the main terminal building. They were close behind and entered a secure section from the door. A guard at the counter became aware as they approached. "Dr. Ruben McAuley," he showed his credentials to the man, who immediately called a supervisor from an adjoining desk. The supervisor took one quick look.

"Right this way, Dr. McAuley," he motioned them around the security and led them inside.

Once on their own, he turned and informed them. "I'm going to take you to your quarters, which will be a small house in town, but until security cards can be made, you will stay within the facilities of the city. I'll get you settled, and then we will go shopping at the commissary. This afternoon, Kurege, you and Uris have appointments with base doctors for physicals, and Urme has an appointment with the base pediatrician.

They followed Ruben to an elevator, down several levels to a long corridor. "I have found a house near the center of town, not far from the Bradbury Museum and near enough to walk to work if you wish Kurege." There were several electric golf cart type conveyances with seats for four passengers, and Amy held Urme for the ride to a waiting black Expedition, and on to their quarters. They drove to a small single residential house on 40th street. There was an upstairs, with one bedroom downstairs. It was a barracks house that had been moved from the World War II base and located in town when the base was modernized some seventy years earlier. It was small with one bath, two bedrooms, one down and one up, and a detached garage to one side, but the hardwood floor had been sanded and finished to good effect. Also, the kitchen had been modernized.

Kurege was concerned that his mother would have no place, but Amy quickly told them that she had plans to head back to her home in Lawrence Kansas. She assured them that the hid-a-bed in the living room would suffice until then. It had a motif of desert colors orange, brown and turquoise, which she said were here favorite colors.

Not far from the house on 40th street where Urme played and Uris tended to some details of the house, Kimberly Kirkendalll was seeing her new lab assignment in the basement of the new CMR building. Kirkendalll's laboratory was at the end of the hall, and a loading dock and giant overhead door led to the outside. Inside the laboratory, which was over one hundred feet of free span, was stored the Pearl, Andro, and the ship captured in the fight at the Pantex plant some years earlier, along with the galactic Probe. They had been sitting from lack of funding ever since Senator Prickle's committee had blocked the appropriations year after year, so that only a small staff of technicians had been hired, mostly to keep the dust off.

She wandered over to the work bench against one wall and turned on the bank of fluorescent lights. She noticed a curious object that turned out to be a knife in a scabbard. She drew the knife and looked at the blade. The tip seemed to have a tiny hole in it.

As she looked at it, a tiny blue slit appeared across the cowling of Andro, the battle robot that Uriah had built to protect Uris. A turquoise scan bathed the room in a barely discernible glow. It lasted only a microsecond, but Kimberly Kirkendalll noticed it and turned to see what had caused the slight glow. She couldn't see where it came from, but she noticed Andro and walked to him and peered closely at his cowl. She turned away and felt along the smooth skin of Uris ship. The Pearl was so smooth and yet a luster glowed from its incredibly hard skin. That blue glow again, and this time she turned swiftly around with an eerie feeling that she was being watched. Still way too slow for Andro. He had seen all he needed to see in a nano. She moved on to the other ship, the more saucer shaped ship. She would need a staff member for this work, too much for one scientist. She would need a staff of electrical, mechanical, and others, she thought. People with drills. There must be some way to get inside these things and find out how they worked. She had always been incredibly adept at taking things apart, even as a tiny baby. She laughed at some of the stories she had heard from her mother. She would get inside these things, that blue glow again, and a feeling she had of being watched. Must be the cool mountain air, she rubbed her arms, walked to her office and began to make plans for getting to know the mysteries in her care.

Once she began to make inquires, it wasn't too long before she got a visit from Ruben McAuley. He gave her a background on the objects around her laboratory. Not too much, but the essentials of the Pearl, Andro, the Probe, and the other, the Pandamon fast attack ship.

Kirkendall looked questioningly at Ruben McAulley. "You mean that we have the people that brought this ship and this robot to Earth?"

"You now seem to have a need to know."

"You are damn correct about that. I am going to need them to help me untangle this technology." She held her hands up in exasperation.

It was some weeks later, after President Wilson had considered and given limited approval, Uris came to visit the Kirkendalll laboratories, she brought Urme, and her father. Kurege shook Kirkendalll's hand, as Ruben McAuley introduced them as, "Michael Hodges, and this is Uris and her daughter, Urme. McAuley had been spending time at Kirkendalll's lab whenever he was in Los Alamos. There was chemistry between the two of them, as Kim was glad for the attention. Ruben had chosen her for the job, after all. That had been an interview that had somehow been very special to Ruben.

"Ruben tells me that you two may be able to help me make some sense of these machines," Kirkendalll gestured to the warehouse sized laboratory's contents. "There has been no money for research or personnel to work on any of this for years with the crash of the American economy last decade, and the extended recovery, well," she shook her head, "it's just lucky that there was money for storage. So, I am going to be very grateful to any help that I can get."

"You realize," McAuley instructed Kimberly, that the existence of these persons is top secret, and of extreme importance to the nation, Miss Kirkendalll?"

"Of course, Dr. McAuley," Kirkendalll assuaged his concern. "I was placed under oath and warned before I was allowed into this laboratory." Uris had begun to look around the room. She saw her knife on the workbench, and made a delighted sound, as she went to it and picked it up. The two women eyed each other warily.

"My knife," Uris explained. "A gift from my father."

"Oh," Kirkendalll said. "It seemed like it might be a weapon."

"That and a great deal more, in Uris' hands, but nothing that anyone else can manipulate," Ruben told her. Uris continued to look at the knife. She approached the Pearl, felt of its skin lovingly. She pulled the handle and turned it to a position so familiar to her even after this long, spoke what sounded like "Gleeeeem."

There was a momentarily turquoise flash in the room. Uris looked knowingly at Andro. A seamless door began to open in the side of the Pearl, and a boarding ramp came out to meet the floor. Another flash of turquoise blipped on and off for a microsecond. Andro was stealthily watching the progress.

Urme saw the flash and she instinctively knew where it was coming from. She pretended to turn away, but in a moment turned toward Andro the robot with her eyes. She caught the quickest blip of a blue line across the cowling. He held her gaze there. Andro knew that he had been seen. The turquoise blue line appeared razor thin on his cowling, and he and Urme made eye contact for several moments. Urme continued to be fascinated with Andro, as she wrapped her arms around his metal bulk and pressed her ear to his cold skin.

Andro, for his part, recognized a new generation of the house of Ur and accepted his prime directive to protect Urme at all cost. This was a brand-new addition to his directives, that registered in a moment's time.

"Amazing," said Kirkendalll. She followed Uris into the inside of the Pearl. Uris set about doing a check out on the ships systems.

"Not all working but repairable," she told Kurege and Ruben when she emerged. Andro blipped again, but it seemed like a fluorescent light blinking that no one noticed other than Uris, except for Urme, who was still examining every part of Andro.

"What is the metal man that Urme is so intrigued with," Dr. Kirkendalll asked?

"That is a robot," Kurege told her.

"He ith warrior," Uris informed her.

"Really?" Kirkendalll looked at Andro. "What about this other ship?" She was really covering some ground while she had them in the lab.

"That is a Pandamon fighter, captured some years ago in an earlier incident. "The door was open when it was captured, but little has been able to be learned about it with Prickle blocking funding and no research has been done on it," McAuley told her.

"I am going to need your help if I am going to be able to determine much myself, it's a complicated machine," Kimberly addressed Uris, and Michael.

"I can probably read some of the markings on the controls," Kurege added.

"Is that so, Michael," she questioned?

"Yes, I am proficient in the language."

"I will certainly welcome any help in that department. What about the other device at the far end?"

"That is a disarmed universal probe droid," Ruben told her. "We have been advised to not touch it."

"Why," she asked? The President had been suspicious, and had conveyed the sentiment to Kirkendalll, 'what was she hiding'? Wilson was cautious. He thought Uris unpredictable and dangerous to the interest of the country if it conflicted with her own interest. Yet, they needed her help, and in the end, had given access to the artifacts from the Pantex fight. The two women stared at each other without blinking. No one answered the question Kim had asked.

Uris eyes wandered to the Pearl and a grin came on her face. She walked to it and touched its skin so smooth and cold and hard. Memories flooded her and she closed her eyes and stood there.

"I think we can handle it from here, Ruben," Kirkendalll could sense that Ruben wanted her to take control.

"I'll leave it in your hands then," he turned. "You have been schooled on this, correct?" He questioned.

"Fully briefed on her, Thanks." She led him to the door.

This was the beginning of Uris's work with the artifacts from her Pearl, and the Pandamon craft, which brought Uris and Kirkendalll to work each morning. Dr. Kirkendalll's efforts went into drawing, defining, and she cataloged all the work Uris did to restore the Pearl to working order. They would lack the Helium III to activate the cryogenic anti-gravity coils, but other systems could be restored and recorded. Kim spent time filming Uris's actions in bringing the Pearl to working order. Several months passed with this work, while Urme went to pre-school, and Kurege was given advanced training in Quantum Computer theory.

Time went by in this way, until Kurege was finished with the preparatory courses. The following morning, after Kurege's completion, he was to receive a new assignment. Uris had been doing her job at the Kirkendalll lab, but she too had received a notice that new routine would be added to her work schedule.

Ruben had a pleased look on his face that morning. Some months had passed with Uris at work in the Kirkendalll lab and Kurege working in orientation for Dr. Chen Ching's lab at AI. Dr. McAuley had been dropping in every few weeks to make sure there were no problems, and to see Kimberly Kirkendalll again. They laughed and stood very close to each other when they were 'working'.

Eventually the go ahead was given to introduce Uris into the theoretical physics department. Dr. Chen Ching had put in a request for someone with Kurege's training to work in his laboratory. And, more good news, in addition to Uris work in the Kirkendalll's laboratories, she has been offered a bonus to spend time in the theoretical physics department of Dr. Hans Beckman. "I will get her in the morning and take her to that department," he had telephoned. True to his word, Ruben was at the house on 40th street early the next morning to take Uris to her additional assignment in theoretical physics.

Ruben arrived a little after seven, and after taking Urme to her pre-kindergarten across from Ashley's Pond, escorted Kurege and Uris to a section that had a security door, and a dragon lady guarding it. "Can I help you," she asked Ruben suspiciously as they approached her desk.

"I have an appointment with Dr. Marcus Black," he informed her. "I am Dr. Ruben McAuley." She punched a number on the phone console at her desk.

"Dr. Black," she said in a moment, "A Dr. Ruben McAuley is here to see you." She paused for a moment. "Yes sir," she put the phone down. "He will be right out," she told them.

They sat in a group of chairs nearby. "Uris will continue in the lab where her Pearl is stored," Ruben told them. "You will work here in this building, the CMR where Uris is working is just down the hill. Later, today, we are hoping that she can find a place in the theoretical physics department, where she would be working under Dr. Hans Beckman there. Can you find your way back to your quarters when your day is complete," he asked Kurege?

"I think I can. There are maps at the elevators and the corridor junctions."

Dr. Black came through the secured door, "Dr. McAuley," he greeted Ruben.

"This is Kurege," McAuley did the introduction. Black took his hand.

"Kurege," he questioned? "Is that a last name?" Kurege just grinned.

"That's his chosen name, Dr. Black. You'll find him listed as Michael Hodge on your paperwork, but we all call him Kurege."

"I see," Black said, not really understanding, in a world where everyone was a doctor of something. "Well, follow me," he took Kurege in tow and they disappeared through the secured door. Ruben took Uris to the theoretical physics department in a nearby building around the corner and got her introduced.

It was several hours later, shortly after lunch, and Kurege had been interviewed by several department heads. He had seemed to best fit with a Dr. Chen Ching, who was experimenting with Bose Einstein Condensate, as Kurege was familiar with nano gate processors on Pandamon, and had trained as a technician in the field, gaining access to the core, and programing his escape. He informed Dr. Black that he was familiar with the architecture of that type of system, as Black brought him in to bring him up to speed.

"Well, now that we have you introduced to the computer and artificial intelligence geniuses around here, let me give you a little refresher course in the history of AI," he indicated a chair in his office, and Kurege sat. "Let's see, where to start. OK, let's start with a summary of the history of AI research. I guess the first real beginning would be the Church-Turing Test. This is the criteria that is still used today to determine the threshold of Artificial Intelligence.

"The Turing Machine," Dr. Black continued is a hypothesis yet to be proven, but generally accepted, that the insights that are the creative, driving force of the human brain, may be duplicated by a machine with the proper algorithm," he absentmindedly drummed a pencil on his desktop. "Of course," Dr. Black began to digress, "early machines using linear computational methods, made some progress in speech recognition, and were able to solve some problems encountered in industrial manufacturing, but basically failed in many areas to form creative solutions to problems that the human brain was easily able to solve."

"That brought on the theory of connective-ness," he continued, "and the neural networks of hugely interconnected supercomputers. Computer vision seems to be a kind of key, and we are working toward the understanding of the brain as holographic, and able to experiment holographically with real world solutions," he drummed the pencil faster. "With terabytes of Random Access Memory and google bytes of storage, we are expecting the long anticipated breakthrough," he smiled. The Church-Turing Test will be realized, and a truly creative, thinking machine will exist."

He stopped drumming and sqenched up his mouth into a doubtful pout. "That does not necessarily mean that the machines will have self-consciousness. That really doesn't matter, if they function creatively, then they are problem solvers," here he stopped and drummed two more explicative beats with his pencil and laughed. "I leave that type of conjecture to the lawyers, tree huggers, and science fiction writers," he laughed again, a self-assured and derogatory chuckle.

"I think I am following most of what you are saying," Kurege told him. "My command of English is still not as good as I would like."

"Really," Dr. Black sat back. "Where are you from?"

"Kansas," Kurege told him, "But I was away for many years."

Dr. Black assumed he meant Europe, perhaps Vienna. "Where did you get your education?"

"Mostly a corporate background," Kurege dodged the question.

"Well, you must be brilliant from the way you are being brought aboard." He paused. "Are you well versed on the programming side?"

"Yes," Kurege thought this a good answer. Ruben McAuley had carefully made he and Uris understand that they were not to divulge their history to anyone. "I see one difference that you have not discussed," Kurege offered.

"Yes," Black perked his ears, "and what is that?"

"The humanoid brain dreams. Machine brains do not dream."

"This is true," Black admitted. "We dream but dream analysis has shown that early sleep is a mere classification of the day's experiences in long term memory, and also memories are being relegated to the trash can and forgotten as unimportant. Rapid Eye Movement dreaming has been shown to be problem solving, by the brain fishing through previous experiences to find anything applicable to a problem that it wishes to solve. Sometimes this is very fruitful and creative, and sometimes meandering, frustrating, wandering through symbols and events with little to no relationship to the problem at hand. This can have the person in a confused state upon awakening." Black was smug and cock-sure of his analysis.

"What about dreams of the future?" Kurege inquired.

"Nonsense," Black was emphatic. "The so called deja' vu experience is a kind of brain fart. Any psychologist worth his salt will confirm that these types of experiences are the brain mistaking a previous event and superimposing it on a current one, with the mistaken impression that the current event is from a dream. It is false memory. The word deja' vu means 'seen before', and that is exactly what it is. An event seen before and mistakenly identified by the brain as seen in a dream," he was very sure.

"Huh," Kurege remarked. He knew different but also knew that it was useless to argue the point. If it happened, it was known. If not, there was no rationale that would convince.

It was at that moment that the phone rang. "Excuse me," Dr. Black picked it up. "Yes, he is with me. Certainly," he hung up. "Dr. McAuley needs you back at the AI entrance desk," he rose and led Kurege through the maze of doors to the entrance. "I trust that I will see you tomorrow morning," he shook Kurege's hand and left him to usher himself through the door.

Ruben was frowning this time, unlike earlier in the day. "It's Uris," he told Kurege. "There has been some trouble. Please come with me, and let's see if we can salvage the situation."

"What has happened?" Kurege asked as they walked on down the hallway and got into one of the electric cars.

"I'm not sure of the details," Ruben told him, accelerating the car. "There has been some kind of altercation, security was called, and Uris resisted security. She was subdued and is being held. That is all I was told. They saw you listed as husband and me as liaison agent, and I was called and asked to bring you to security as quickly as possible.

Kurege frowned but said nothing. Uris could fight in a dozen ways. She had a great deal of training. Many fearful thoughts went through his head. He only hoped that she had not killed. She would have no compunction to refrain. They made several turns at corridors and arrived at the security section after a considerable distance.

As they entered security, Uris was sitting on the floor. Her hair was tangled and covered her face, and her hands were tied behind her back with a thick plastic pull tie. Her legs were also bound, and she was very blue in color. "Dr. Ruben McAuley," Ruben introduced himself to a man behind a desk in one corner. Two big, burly men in security uniforms stood alert near Uris. "This is Kurege, Uris' husband," Ruben told the man at the desk. Uris looked up at the sound of Ruben's voice and the mention of Kurege's name. Her face told a horrific story, as it still registered rage and hatred, but there was something around the eyes that was defeated, sad, and hopeless. She was blue and in need of her Xenon inhaler.

"Quite a little spitfire, young man," the officer addressed Kurege. "You have my sympathy. She put three grown men, strong men, on the floor, before we tasered her and strapped her. One men in the hospital. I have never seen anything like it," he shook his head.

"Uris," Kurege knelt by her. He had to say her name again before she looked at him. "What happened?"

It was a long moment before she spoke. "It wath lecture on unified field theory. He had out paper. It wath full of error. I tried to talk. He made fun of my talk. I hit him with hith idiot paper."

"Where is your Xenon inhaler, you are in need of it," he asked. She only shrugged that she did not know.

"Do you know what happened?" Ruben asked the man in charge.

"I didn't see the original incident," he replied. "I only arrived after security was called. I was called to the lecture hall in the theoretical math department. From what I gather, Dr. Hans Beckman was lecturing the gathering when the lady joined them. She was given a handout, rather thick, and sat down near the back. Dr. Beckman was lecturing and writing formulas on the blackboard when she approached the board, rubbed out some of his writing, and to quote Beckman, 'began to talk gibberish and write meaningless symbols over the work'. At first, he made light of her. He said to joke it off, and she turned on him, screamed he was an idiot, and hit him hard on the head with the workbook of his work, that she had been given when she entered, knocking him almost senseless." The security chief raised an eyebrow and looked from Ruben to Kurege and Uris. "Dr. Beckman called security and me and two men went to the lecture hall. She was at the board waiting and talking in a fury. Dr. Beckman was cowed behind the podium. He signaled to remove her, and my two men approached. When they reached her and began to try to lay hands on her and remove her, well, all hell broke loose. She flattened them both in a few seconds. She had all the moves. I called in four more men, this time with tasers. She still did damage. We had to taser her twice to put her on the floor. I've seen big guys high on meth, and they were handled easier. It was amazing. Even after being tasered to the floor, she was somehow managing to use her feet. That's how one of my men went to the hospital. Usually, the muscles are in rigor, and my man approached her. She caught him square in the face with a heel and broke his nose. He was really lucky the bone wasn't driven into his brain," he shook his head.

"Uris?" Kurege asked. "Will you control yourself?" She looked with fury at him, then the fight just drained from her in defeat.

She shook her head up and down, and mumbled, "yeth."

"Let's cut her loose," Ruben told the security.

"You've got to be kidding," the security man looked at him incredulously.

Ruben pulled out his cell phone and called up a number and punched the dialing. "Mr. President," he said. "There has been a mix up. Uris is in custody, and I want her released to me," he said, then listened a minute. "No, not that bad, no one is dead. I think I can handle her now. I want to take her back to her quarters. OK. Explain it to this security man. Here," he said, and handed the phone to the security chief.

His eyes got big with wonder, "Yes sir," was all he said, and handed Ruben his phone back. "Say," he said in puzzlement. "Who the hell are you?"

"Need to know, only," Ruben told him, "And you don't need to know."

The man shook his head from side to side and raised his eyebrows. "This place just gets stranger and stranger. Cut her loose," he instructed his men, taking a pair of diagonal wire cutters from his desk and handing them to the closest officer. "But she better be OK, cause any more trouble, and I'm going to personally shoot her," he threatened, with complete assurance in his voice.

The officer cut her bonds, and Ruben and Kurege sat her in a chair. She rubbed her hands and arms, while Kurege massaged her legs. She wouldn't look him in the eye. After she got feeling back enough to walk, they supported her on either side, and the security chief held the door open. They led her away, and her head was bowed in defeat, something that she had never known before.

****

Kurege arrived at their quarters as the sun was beginning to hide behind the Jimenez Mountains and throw long purple shadows on the mesa and the desert below, in the distance. Kurege looked out the apartment window to the east. It was a magnificent place, and he reflected on how nice it had been only eighty years earlier when the ground was a boy's school for wealthy boys from across the country. Uris, Amy and Urme must be upstairs, he assumed. This was the first day of Uris' meeting with the psychiatrist for the required anger management, in order for her to keep the possibility of having a job of any kind at Los Alamos. Dr. Hans Beckman had filed a report on her and had made it clear that she was never to work in his department again.

Kurege noticed a pamphlet on the coffee table as he turned away from the magnificent view and thought to go upstairs to find the others. "Anger Management" the title read. He picked it up and began to thumb through it.

"Anger Management refers to a system of psychological therapeutic techniques," he read. He scanned on down to 'methods of anger management'. "Direct, honorable, focused, persistent, courageous," he read the headings, "passionate, creative, forgiveness, listen," and noticed the word 'empathy' came up often in the text. He smiled at the thought of Uris trying to follow such a script and chuckled to himself.

"What ith tho funny," Uris had come into the room without him hearing her.

"Hi," he said, "just reading some of this. How did it go?"

"I went," she shrugged. "They gave thith handout to learn. But I already do all thith thing," she claimed.

"Oh, Uris," he was a little scornful. "Empathy?" He questioned.

"I feel for otherth," she defended herself.

"Uris," he reasoned. "You were absolute monarch of an entire world, more even, a society that stretched across Warp Stars to other worlds. Your word was law. You didn't have to think about anyone else's opinions."

"I had great concern for others," she lapsed into Xinor Standard language, and talked very pointedly and excited to him. "My everyday was spent in the concerns of my people," she spouted in a tirade of word and gesture. "And I'm concerned now. I miss my people," she was overcome with emotion and teared up, then tried to control her tears.

This was not new to Kurege. He understood the enormous change that she had undergone. "You are Queen of My Heart," he gave her the title that he always spoke endearingly to her. She dodged his hand. "Look Uris," he spoke plainly to her, "you are not queen of this planet," then thought to try and show her the obligations of their life. He feinted a change of subject to diffuse the tension, and went back to English, which they had agreed to use. "Where is Urme?" He asked. She, many times, met her father at the door when he came home with a big hug.

"Thhe ith thill down for her afternoon nap," Uris told him. "Your mother couldn't get her to go to thleep becauthe her favorite book was mithplaced. You know how thhe ith about having that book under her pillow."

"Uris, you don't have to work," he had led into it. "You don't have to take this anger management course. You can stay home and take care of Urme. Mother is more than ready to go home, I think."

Uris looked stricken. "No, I want to work," she insisted. The truth was that having never had a mother or siblings, she was really at a loss to just play. She kept Urme cared for, but she was really more interested in the adult world, and was hard pressed to reach into Urme's world of play and imagination. That caused Urme to cling to her father and his mother, and Uris' failure to empathize with her child was also a source of failure and pain.

"Then you will have to finish this anger management course and take whatever job they can assign you to do," he told her straight out. She didn't speak anymore, and a look of resignation came to her face.

Two months went by and Kurcge was very pleased with his work in AI. He had been introduced to several programing languages and was learning how to make himself an integral part of his department. He hoped to finish more training and be a leader for Dr. Chen in his lab.

One evening there was a knock on the apartment door and Ruben McAuley was there. Kurege let him in. They had all been downstairs, with Urme playing with her toys and the news running on the television. The two women came in and greeted him.

"I have great news," he told them. "The powers that be have seen fit to let you all travel off base. "They are satisfied with the results of the counseling, and are of the opinion that it was a misunderstanding, and that no harm was done. Beckman still feels different, however. Still, they have set you free." This was thrilling news.

"That means that you will be able to go into Santa Fe or anywhere that you wish, and get some variety into your lives, not be stuck here on base and virtually confined to this little mesa and town."

"When," Uris asked? She felt like a prisoner.

"Immediately," he told her. I have passes, right here," he pulled cards from his shirt pocket," to get you on and off the base."

This was wonderful news and had been delayed by Uris' trouble with Dr. Beckman. "There is more," he told her. "You will have a position in the engineering department. It's not high level, but it is a professional position, a good one.

"Engineering," she asked? "Do you know what I will do?"

"It's not theoretical," he was almost apologetic. "It will involve drawings and releases to the shop for production. It will have to do," he cautioned her, "until they are sure you won't be overwhelmed," he was being diplomatic.

She shook her head that she understood his meaning. "It will be good to be free to travel," she agreed, "and I will do the work," she confirmed. "I have felt like a prithnor."

"The changes are hard for you," he could see she was trying.

Urme interrupted holding out her favorite book, worn and chewed. "Read," she requested to Ruben.

"All right, Urme," he sat down and began to read. "Stanley was a snail," she giggled as she crawled into Ruben's lap. "He had never seen an alien before." After reading to Urme *Stanley and the Aliens* twice, Amy took her upstairs for a bath and bed.

"Is there anything that you two need," he asked them as he was at the door ready to leave.

"I'm doing fine," Kurege told him.

"I'm almost out of my Xenon inhalers," Uris said.

"OK, I'll contact S. G. Raven Enterprises, and get some new ones made up for you," he made a metal note. "I'll be by tomorrow to take you to get the proper stickers for your car to move on and off base."

When they were ready to go to Santa Fe, Amy felt she could go back to her home. Ruben drove Amy to Albuquerque, with Uris, Urme and Kurege along to say goodbye. He took the bypass around Santa Fe on the way down but brought them into the city on the return trip, parking at the government buildings, then ate at La Plazuela in the La Fonda hotel, and walked the square. This was their first look at Indian culture, and Uris and Kurege were fascinated by the craft goods, and Urme wanted to dance around to the music at the bandstand. He delivered them to their home shortly before dark and bid them good luck and to call if they needed help, remembering to tell Uris that her Xenon inhalers had been ordered, and that he had talked with Enrico Rameriz, who promised to bring them to Los Alamos when they were ready. They were both pleased to hear Enrico was coming as they had not seen him since the meeting with the President some three years earlier. They hoped that he might have some words about Stark Raven.

They had a week of vacation coming and Kurege had taken some time off, and he was scheduled to go back to work the following Monday, and Uris was to start her new job, with Urme going to pre-kindergarten school at the Montessori facility across from Ashley's Pond. It was the middle of the day on Tuesday that week, when there was a knock at the door and Kurege looked out to see two middle aged ladies on the porch.

"Hello," the women in the front said when he opened the door. "We're from the First Baptist Church of Los Alamos," she introduced herself." I'm Mary Carter

70

and this is our Bible study leader Thelma Barker," the lady in the rear flashed a big smile.

"Yes," Kurege acknowledged questioningly. Urme toddled to the door behind him.

"We are just around the corner," she pointed, "within walking distance. We knew that this house had been rented and wanted to come by and give you an invitation to join us on Sunday mornings. We have a wonderful children's department," she saw Urme hanging on her father's legs. She handed him a pamphlet of the week's activities. "This is our schedule of things happening this week."

"There is Bible study on Wednesday night," Thelma pitched her group, "at my house, which is right there," she pointed at a house three doors down on the other side of the street.

Kurege took the paper but didn't respond, not really knowing how to respond. Several awkward seconds went by.

"Do you know the Lord?" Thelma went straight to the heart of the matter. It was her Christian duty.

Kurege was confused and puzzled as to what she was talking about. "Metastophiles?" He questioned.

"Jesus," Thelma told him with an intense concern and non-comprehension crossing her countenance.

Many seconds went by as neither party knew what to say next. Urme began to whine wanting to get to the door and see what was going on. He turned and picked the child up, and the silence just became more awkward.

"Well," Mary Carter finally said, "we will be looking for you Sunday morning. Children's Sunday School begins at nine thirty. They left with reluctant looks back at the man and child watching them go.

Sunday morning, Kurege and Urme entered the little church building at nine-thirty. Uris would not consider going and had said that it was ridiculous, but she would be glad for some time to straighten the house. Mary Carter was looking for them at the door, and a big smile broke across her face as she welcomed them. She guided them to the children's section, and they left Urme in the care of Lou, who took charge of the young child. Kurege watched as Urme was shyly led into a play group.

"Ann," Lou introduced, "this is Urme and she is new. Will you take care of her?" Ann looked up at Urme. They could have almost been twins. She shook her head and held out a toy she was playing with and gave it to Urme.

"Stanley," Urme beamed. It was her favorite toy. Kurege smiled and was certain she would be fine. Mary led him to a young adult class, and showed him the auditorium, and told him that he could leave Urme until after the service, then she would be ready to go home when he came to get her after 'the preaching'.

Kurege and Urme arrived back at the house a little after noon, and Uris had lunch ready. After Urme was fed, she went down for a nap. She fell asleep immediately, but her mother failed to see the tiny New Testament that Urme placed under her pillow.

They sat to talk when she returned to the living room. "It was very strange," he told her. "Everyone was guilty, I'm not sure of what. They definitely worshiped this Jesus, who they believe is the Son of God."

"Which god," Uris asked? "Not Metastophiles," she was horrified.

"No, I don't think so. It was confusing. He was apparently on Earth two thousand years ago. He was executed for some crime against the society, but was raised from the dead, and everyone is washed in his blood to be saved from their guilt."

"His blood?" She questioned.

"That's the belief," he shook his head. "And the strangest part came at the end. They passed out little pieces of his body and little cups of his blood and ate and drank it."

"You did!" She was aghast.

"No, they told me that I could partake if I was a believer, even though I was not a member of their particular congregation. I just watched. They were all very moved and serious."

"Thth ith ridiculouth," she scorned.

"Urme had a very good time with the other children," he defended.

"You can't mean to go back there," she was incredulous.

"I was curious," he admitted, "and Urme made friends with some of the children her own age."

"thhe will meet thildren her own age at the pre-kindergarten tomorrow morning," she told him.

"It was a good thing, and I'm curious," he said again.

She gave an exasperated puff of air and dismissed it. "Rediculouth," she said again.

Monday morning, she dressed for work. As she went through her closet looking for shoes, she saw the pair of Gru-skin boots that Kurege had made for her, and out of sentiment, because this was a special day, she chose them to wear to work.

Ruben McAuley was waiting at the door of the department of engineering that she was directed to by the letter that had come in the mail the previous week. He smiled and patted her on the back assuring and directed her into the department and the first door on the right.

"Christy Leftler," he introduced, "this is Uris Hodges," he indicated her. "Uris, this is Christy Leftler, head of the PIT Engineering Department. You will be working for her."

"I'll leave her in your hands, Christy," Ruben turned to go, then turned back. "Any problems come up," he fixed Uris with a warning stare, "you know where to reach me." He left.

Leftler showed her to a cubical with a desk, computer terminal and monitor. "Rafael Peralta will be your go to guy. He will issue you spec sheets. He will show you where to find the drawings to go with the specifications;

Rafael, come over here," she called to the next cubical. "He hates to be called Ralph," he informed her. "Peralta, this is Hodges," she said in an almost military way. They shook. "OK," she instructed Raphael, "you know how to lead her through it," and she turned and went back to her office.

"Nice boots," Rafael eyed her shoes with a curious stare. He reached over and punched her computer on. "Have a seat," he indicated her rolling chair on the anti-static mat in front of the console. She sat down. "What you are doing here," he instructed, "is making triggers to explode hydrogen bombs. Here," he manipulated her mouse to the drawing section," he brought up a file, and the drawing appeared looking like a watermelon wired up for an EKG. "When I send you a drawing like this one; that is a Standard. Then look at this number," he pointed at the lower right-hand corner of the drawing. "Take that number to this file," he went to another file section, chose a folder and opened it, then scrolled through the numbers to the appropriate file and opened it. It was a spread sheet of parts including wires, screws, welding instructions, metals, and he called them off. "Now this last section, here," he pointed, "this is the PITs. These are the plutonium ignition triggers and have to be selected from a set of three different sizes for the Standard Bomb. They shape the air burst, so they are a little different for each bomb. It's by shape," he told her. "You'll get it pretty quick. But it does also affect the shape of the plutonium

trigger, and the selection of the flash-bang, the high
amperage trigger. Get it?" He asked.

"The high amperage trigger thets off the plutonium
fittion bomb, which compretthethee hydrogen to explode
the futhion bomb, and the computer on board dictateth the
timing, mathematic-ally shaping the explothion."

"Thath exactly right," he imitated her lisp. "Smart
girl."

Uris looked close at him, but there was no malice
in it, he was kidding her. She let it pass. Maybe her anger
management course did some good.

Over the course of the day, under Rafael Peralta's
guidance, she built one hydrogen thermonuclear bomb,
and sent it off to be manufactured, by transferring
electronic files to the floor, an email address internal to the
facility. Four o'clock came and Raphael left. "If you
come in by six-thirty, you can leave at four," he told her.
She had to stay until five and then walked home.

Sartris began again. "These second accusers have also told lies about me. It is very easy to show. They have said that I do not believe that Metastophiles is a god. When he first appeared to us, it is understandable that it was thought so. That was many centuries ago, and as he has come to rule over us from time to time, it is easy to understand how the cult has come to be, and that the priest of Metastophiles have sought and held political power. Now, we understand better. Certainly, it is easy to prove that some beings are able to move through time. We all know how this is possible with the navigation of the Warp Stars. Does this make one a god? What is a god? If this is what makes a god, then he is one among many. Therefore, I do believe in gods. Make as many images of them as is wished. Place them at the center of your houses and worship them. It will not make a matter to the Great God of the Universe. Yes, I believe in gods, and in God. It is a small matter to foretell the future, if one has been there. Yet it is the business of the future to remain dangerous, and therefore unknowable, divine all that you wish. It cannot be pinned up like something that you will eat."

"Some like Aristnes have said that I am corrupting the young men. All that I have done is show that no one knows what happens after death. No one knows where we come from, or where we go, therefore, we know nothing for certain. For this, they are seeking my death. Perhaps I go to a better place. Perhaps I go to nothingness. It is still certain that I have been, and if you execute me for this, it will be a long time before you will see my kind of being again. I have simply questioned what is known in the crafts, arts, and religion, as questioning proves the point. We know little to nothing."

There was a murmur of disapproval from the members of the court. The Pran council displayed their disdain for the questioning of the tenets of their society with the clicking of scales beneath their six arms. The twelve members of the Supreme Priesthood pulled back their hoods and frowned with old, tired, reddened eyes, centuries, perhaps many millennium old, and scowled at the sacrilege that they were hearing from the accused. One held a gavel, which he banged one time for silence from the clicking so that the trial could continue as quickly as possible.

"Still, through dreams and oracles that come to me," Sartris continued, "whenever I am about to make a mistake or do wrong, it has come to me that I cannot make a mistake and still be true to myself, even if this is to cost me my life." He then paused.

"When we train animals, we also tend to their welfare," he made his final point. "Metastopiles has never contributed to the welfare or care of this planet but has used it as genetic laboratories to further his own corrupt plans, to a purpose still unknowable to our beings." He paused and looked from scowling faces of the Pran Bishops to the wrinkled and gray countenance of the members of the Supreme Councilmen. "No ships have come for decades now, and it is obvious that we have been abandoned to our tragic fate."

"Sartris," we have heard your defense, Aristnes took the pause to mean that the defense was complete, "you will remain as the council will vote now."

Aristnes placed the vestments around his shoulder, as did the twelve Supreme Council members. "For acquittal," he signaled. No vote was cast. "For execution," he intoned. Twelve votes were cast for execution. The trial was over. "Sartris, the council is unanimous. You will be returned to your cell until after the return of the Tribute Ship from Terra, at which time you will be brought forth for sentence, and a date set for your execution."

The Pran council was dismissed by the Supreme Council leader. Sartris bowed to their majesty and remained supplicated until the council had left the chambers. He then returned to his cell, where he was to remain for some time to ponder his fate. He was relaxed; it was as expected. He had been informed in a dream two nights before, but not as the Judge Aristnes had said, for a figure all dressed in light had come in the night to show him that the Terran tribute ship was not come in the form that was expected, but with signs of a fight with two strange humanoid forms, one near death, and one blinded by passing through the Warp Star without the shield being properly in place. The sacred fluid was in its frozen place, but nothing else was as it should be. The captain was found in frozen pieces in an inner wall of the craft. There were others of the sacred beings killed, as well as the Pran honor guard. The priesthood was in a quandary. A security clamp was placed on a planetary scale on the Homeworld. Tachyon reports went out, but no reply was forthcoming. Some days and then weeks passed, no further Tachyon messages were returned. The isolation was interpreted as the wrath of the deity. The priesthood pleaded for enlightenment and understanding. The Pran hierarchy was pushed into total disruption. The population began to hear rumors, wild rumors of the events. Sartris pending execution was learned of, and opposition began to mount.

Stark Raven was pushed and pulled along a corridor. His bare feet felt the cold of the bare stone or concrete floor. His eyes still hurt him, but he could force them open a slit and see that he was being led through a tunnel. They arrived after several turns and doors at a metal door, and it was opened, and he was pushed over the threshold and inside. He heard a door close behind him, and he was left alone. He lowered himself to the floor and began to feel around the room and then found a spot near the center and sat on the floor. It was some hours later when he heard the door open and then in a few moments closed again.

Startled, Stark rose to his feet from the floor. He still could not force his eyes open but a slit, and his vision was blurry. He could make out a form at the door that was just inside the entrance way. He could feel his heart rate increase with apprehension.

Sartris, for his part, was stunned to see this humanoid in his cell, and he stood still for many moments trying to fathom the meaning of this change. With no threatening moves coming from the creature, he finally moved to his mattress bed that was attached to the wall on one side and suspended by chains that formed a triangle between the wall and the bed front. The bed could be folded up against the wall and fastened with a latch and was no more than a padded bench. Several others could be unlatched and lowered but had remained folded up against the walls. One other, that had been folded, was now opened and a thin cover was lain on its surface. This seemed to be in preparation for this second prisoner, but the humanoid did not seem to realize this and after a while squatted and then sat back on the floor.

It was at this moment that Sartris remembered the dreams. He had seen this figure before. He considered this his oracle, and since it was dreamed of before the fact, considered it a right and proper thing to happen, as he considered it pre-ordained by the Deity of the Universe. In fact, he had recently had three dreams of this event, and that made him consider it an eminent event. He could find no other philosophical explanation for this type of occurrence, which had been directing his life since his childhood. It gave him a warm sense of assurance, and he just quietly sat on his bunk and watched the creature on the floor and tried to accept his forthcoming execution.

Some hours passed in this way, and the time of day came when he was allowed visitors one at a time. The cell door opened and Bisarios, his good and faithful friend, was admitted through the door. The cell door banged closed behind Bisarios.

Stark's posture came erect with the sound of the door. He could force his eyes open enough in the dim light to see another form that entered the cell and the door closed. The two big antlike creatures greeted each other and embraced, then moved to the other side of the room and sat on what appeared to be a bunk. A chattering modulation started between the two, and they appeared to gesture toward him. He figured that they were talking about him in their language.

Stark looked around the room, and near him, he thought that he could make out another bunk like bed, and he crawled toward it, felt along its edges and when it seemed stable, pulled himself up and sat on its edge with his feet on the floor. This was certainly much better than being sprawled on the floor.

"The Terran ship arrived on schedule," Bisarios told Sartris, "but it was a shambles. The Pandamon lord was found in the walls of the ship, frozen and smashed into thousands of pieces, as were all the humanoid Vril Troopers. All of the Pran on board were dead. This is the rumor, and all that is known. There is very strong security by the Priest Council that has been imposed."

"We are being observed. I am sure," Sartris pointed at a camera positioned in the ceiling. "You are risking bringing me this news."

"I would risk much more for you, Sartris."

"I know my good friend."

"I have heard that this creature," Bisarios indicated Stark, "was the only living thing on the Tribute Ship." He and Sartris turned their attention toward Stark, who was settling back on his bunk. "The sacred elixir is in short supply, and there is a squabble among the High Priesthood as to how it is to be proportioned. We have a guard that we can bribe."

"Is he Terran or Pandamon?" Sartris asked.

"That is unknown," Bisarios inclined his head to one side. He and Sartris watched Stark Raven for several moments. "He is young, in his prime, and we have never seen a Terran youth."

"This is a puzzle," Sartris added.

"A puzzle that has saved your life," Bisarios pointed out. "There can be no executions during the ceremonial trip of the Tribute Ship, and now your execution has been put on hold. Many of your friends are here in the city." He lowered his voice to a whisper and turned his head away from the monitors. "There is a plan to rescue you," he told Sartris. "We are able to bribe several of the guards. Do not think that we will not risk it or hold back because you feel that it will endanger your friends. There are homes in distant cities that will welcome and protect you."

"It would most certainly endanger many of my friends, should you carry out such plans," Sartris firmly told him. "I have always lived in this city from childhood. Should I now flee from the Supreme Council's ruling, would I not mock their laws and the institutions that I have been willing to abide by all my life? Would it be right to make a trifle of the fabric of our society?"

"But it is wrong for them to execute you for speaking freely and questioning things that need changing for the better."

"To overturn the established order, even when wrong is a great harm to the people, bringing civil war upon them. Change should come slowly, through philosophical discussion, and by vote and change in the grass roots by the people, not by defiance and force or bribery. Think what would be said of me, were I to choose this path. 'Sartris talks a good line, but he did not live it', would be my legacy. I can never choose that path, and you and the others should not attempt it, for I will not go with you."

Bisarios posture slumped in resignation. "So, you will leave us blind, without your guidance."

"You will all find your way through the methods of questioning which I have shown you. Your tongues will become sharpened against one another, and that which has guided me, will also guide you."

"My time of visit is up, I hear the guard at the door." Brisarios rose and went to the door, which was opening. The two bid each other a farewell with a hand signal. The cell door closed and Stark and Sartris were alone.

Sartris puzzled for some time. He was intensely curious about his cell mate. He considered the problem of communication for a while, and then an idea came into his mind. He began to drum on his bunk. He picked a spot with a deep sound, near the center, and then a spot near the edge, where a higher vibration could be sounded. Thump-whack, he sounded, and then, again. He started a rhythm, simple, and over and over, thump-whack, thump-whack, on and on he went.

"Thump-whack," Stark heard. It went over and over, and in a very deliberate manner. Suddenly, he got it. The creature was trying to communicate. He sat up on the bunk and found similar spots. The drumming stopped. Stark tapped out 'thump-whack'. Thump-whack came the answer. They went back and forth in confirmation. Then, together they hit, 'thump-whack, thump-whack, thump-whack'.

They learned to drum together. Days passed in these simple exercises only. Stark had begun to be able to open his eyes. His vision was blurred but improving with each day. After much drumming together, one would keep the beat, then the other would add a second rhythm. They learned to solo. This was enthralling, and each creature learned the laugh of the other, as they took pleasure in beating out varying measures and interwoven patterns.

The guards perceived that they were trying to communicate, and also that they were playing, and having fun at the link that was developing. They came in and threatened to beat them. Making music was not allowed. The drumming was seen as music, and the guards became angry enough to come in from time to time and stop the drumming and beat both Stark and Sartris, harder and harder to make them stop. Then the beatings stopped. They were being given leave to drum, as the cameras recorded the progress and the Supreme Council hoped to learn from their communications some hint of what had happened on the Tribute Ship.

With the lessening of the beatings, Sartris began with a new challenge. He gave the drumming a low to high sound of an interrogative, and a high to low sound, also interrogative, as some societies used one or the other or both to question. He asked a question, any question. He then sounded out his name and indicated himself. He made the questioning low to high sound and pointed at Stark.

Stark understood. He was being asked his name. He tried to sound it out. "Sta-r-k Ra-ven," he drummed. He pointed to himself. Sartris imitated Stark and then pointed at him. He then made the sound of his name in his language and pointed again at himself.

Once they had worked out the rhythm and sound of the question, Sartris used an emphatic beat to denote the object. As they both understood the form of language questions and objects, they were able to use sign language, like a circle for completeness or the absolute world view.

Sartris asked Stark, "What Stark absolute?" With this question, they entered the world of philosophy.

"That's a tough one," Stark said to himself as much as to Sartris, and Sartris moved on to nouns, like 'dirt' and 'bed', and any object that they had around them. When Bisarios came, as he did everyday, Sartris taught his name to Stark, and the concept of close, friend, visitor, loyal and all the adjectives that he could convey related to Bisarios.

They progressed, and Sartris pushed him. Sartris was aware that time was limited. He tried to move Stark to a higher level of communication. Many times he drummed or intoned the question, "What Stark absolute?"

Then a day came when this was asked and Stark, still failing to give an answer or fully understand, said to himself as much as to Sartris, "If I could read your mind." Suddenly, the answer, "You can," formed in his head. Startled, Stark looked at Sartris, fully into his eyes. He saw a twinkle of understanding and amusement there. Sartris nodded to him in recognition, 'Yes'. Stark 'heard' or at least the thought formed in his mind, "Yes". A new component of their communication arrived. With drumming, vocalization, and sign language, the benefit of telepathy was added.

Somehow, over a period of several days, Sartris, by use of all the forms of communication that they had practiced together, passed important concepts to Stark Raven. He revealed that he was awaiting execution. This was hard for Stark to understand, but he finally got the idea, and when Stark drew an imaginary knife across his throat, Sartris nodded 'Yes'.

Sartris went to great pains to convey several points of his philosophy. Time was growing short, and his dreams told him so. The philosophy of "Whatsoever is loved, so is the future." The universe gives everything that is wanted, no matter what that is. Be careful what is loved. What is loved will envelope the world that is in existence with that which is emotionally attached to, and thus the future is determined. Sartris went over and over these points of philosophy until he was sure that Stark had understood.

Sartris and Stark continued to learn from each other. They used hand signs to show meaning in sign language and had made good progress in common objects, but the question that Sartris posed now and again, "What Stark absolute, or all?", escaped their ability. Stark was not sure that he could answer if he knew the words. He had turned the question around to ask Sartris his absolute, and without hesitation the old Pran was able to convey, "My purpose, my absolute is to question everything."

Once asked, the Pran philosopher expanded to Stark. "No one knows from where we come, no one knows where we go." From this simple truth Sartris was able to show that pride should become humility, knowledge became awe, and avarice and power had no meaning.

He compared the endeavors of creatures with the majesty of a blazing star, and encouraged Stark to think on this. Sartris proposed to Stark that consciousness was pervasive in all things, with questions.

"Do rocks think?" He would ask and sign. It was not a form of pantheism, but more that all things strove for a higher order of organization as a natural process, and with the attainment of the higher order, such as a crystal form, purpose arose.

That purpose might be beauty or delight, or it might be of some use, fitting into an even higher order of function. Sartris view of deity was not redemption but an amalgamation to purpose revealed through sequence and relationship in time and space.

Stark did not grasp much of what was said but it caused him to think about all kinds of things, that came into his stream of consciousness, seemingly brought by a subtle telepathy from Sartris, who seemed very pleased when this worked. A sort of smile, wry indeed, broke out on Sartris' face when he became aware that an idea had been conveyed. A definite "pleased with himself", body language was formed by posture and rhythmic movement. Stark could see it, and that was partly how he knew that the ideas in his head were not entirely his own.

Sartris tried to show Stark that likewise, stream-of-consciousness thoughts came to every entity, and the world assumed a more closely ordered form whenever it was understood. It was that as the Universe perceived our understanding and being thus pleased with itself, postured and vibrated in harmony that could be experienced in any number of ways.

One morning, in the middle of these philosophy lessons, which went on and on, especially when a friend like Bisarios came, the cell door opened, and guards beckoned Sartris to follow. He rose and folded his bedding and departed without farewell or backward glance.

He was taken to the Council Chamber and sentence was reaffirmed by the three Supreme Council members. Sartris was allowed three to be present, and he chose Bisarios, his wife, and Stark.

He was taken to the execution chamber and the witnesses from the Supreme Council and the three Sartris had chosen were brought into the chamber with guards. Bisarios had a furious look of the desperate, the wife was shaking all over. The Supreme Council members removed their hoods. Stark was curious as there was something familiar about the Supreme Council Leader that he could not place at first. Sartris was given time to make a final statement.

"Perhaps I go to a better place, perhaps this is the end and there is nothing further, none know, but this is known, that I have been, and I have been true to myself."

When he finished this statement, he lay back on the execution bench and the helper of the executioners placed sponges with a red cloth into his six ventricles along his sides, so that the red cloth protruded from each of three places along both sides of his upper torso. Part of his job done, he stepped back at attention. The six executioners entered and received the lethal dose of chemical into long eyedropper looking glass tubes. The helper held the bottle passed to him by the Supreme Council Leader as the executioners dipped the tubes into the poison.

The six executioners formed around Sartris on the bench in two lines on either side, with each dropper being formed to fit to the sponge that it filled; six droppers in six ventricles. Stark and the Supreme Council Leader eyed each other. The hubris of the creature suddenly rang a bell in Stark's mind. Even through the aged face and reddened eyes, he recognized the visage and arrogance of Senator Omar Prickle. Supreme Councilman Prickle pulled his hood up covering his face, and said, "It is done." The poison was spread into the sponges in a squirt, and at Sartris next breath, he began to die.

It was not fast. He began to talk. "A strange calmness has come over me, in spite of considerable pain in my chest, now spreading to my head. The senses are leaving, sight first," he paused. Then he said, "My feet, funny, my feet are getting numb." These were his final words.

Stark was returned to his cell and when the door closed a great loneliness came over him. He tried to shake it, but it would not leave until he broke down and cried for himself, Sartris, and all the worlds where thinkers question, and are thus treated.

It was three nights later that he had the dream. Sartris stood in front of him dressed in purest light. "You are chosen," he plainly spoke, although his lips did not move. He reached out and touched Stark on the forehead. Then the dream was over, but it was so entirely real, perhaps the most real moment that Stark had ever had or ever would have, he reflected to himself.

Later that day, shortly after morning, he began to hear noise from somewhere outside. Also, he was not fed and no attendant jailer looked in on him. There was shouting in the hallway outside his cell, but when he went to the slot in the door, through which his food sometimes was passed, he could see nothing. Then it was quiet in the hallway, but there began to be the noise of explosions, seemingly coming through thick walls.

He slept fitfully that night and the next morning there was no light, but only the dimmest glow of reflected light from somewhere, but not much more than total blackness. The water that fed the plumbing system for the toilet also stopped working. He began to lose track of time and really had no idea whether the dim light was artificial or natural, or how much time was passing.

He slept, he was awake, no guard came. No food was brought, and from the intense hunger that he began to feel, he judged two days had come and gone. He could still feel the vibrations of explosions and their muffled sound was barely audible. His cell stunk. He slept to escape the hunger.

He awoke to shouting and the sounds of obvious fighting coming from somewhere near, down the hall, he thought. The smell of smoke was in the air and shortly, it was much more pronounced. Then there was silence, but the smoke lingered, although it was less. He smelled the acrid toxic smell of burning plastics. He lay down and took the air as close to the floor as possible. He thought that he would suffocate.

The sound of footsteps and voices came near. The cell door lock clanked, and the cell door opened. Lights flashed around the room and two forms stood in the doorway, with more voices behind them. He heart pounded.

"Stark Raven," a voice called. He recognized the voice as that of Bisarios. "Stark Raven," Bisarios called to him again.

"Bisarios?" He questioned and rose up from the floor. The lights found him and blinded him shining directly into his eyes.

"Come out," Bisarios called to him. He got to his feet and walked through the smoke to the door. He was dizzy and arms reached out to steady him. "Come," he was told in Pran. It was a word that Sartris had taught him. He followed Bisarios down the smoky hallway, supported by two other Pran, one on each side. He could see light at the far end of the hallway. The smoke began to clear and he was able to breath without choking.

They made their way up and out of the prison, and there were Pran in blue uniforms along the way at attention. They climbed stairs, and Stark was glad for the help, as he staggered from the effort. They reached a chamber with windows. He had to squint against the brightness, and there were fires burning in buildings all around, but in subsidence with Pran moving around extinguishing them. They sat him in a chair, and one came forward to examine him.

Bisarios gave commands to some of the others, and they soon came back with water, and then fruit was brought to him that was juicy and sweet with sugar content. He was ravenous and wanted to eat fast, but the attendant would only give him small amounts at a time and then took his vital signs before letting him have another small amount. He felt himself revived.

He was tended to all that day and then moved into luxurious quarters that evening. The only thing about which he might have complained was that there was no windows in the room and he could not look out. It had been so very confined and dark in the cell that he had enjoyed the light immensely.

The next morning, he was served a fantastic meal. He couldn't identify any of the food, but he was starving for food and dug in with gusto. He was just finishing relishing what seemed to be fruit juice and wishing badly that he had some coffee, when Bisarios entered with two other Pran. "Come," he signaled and spoke. Stark stood and attendants entered with a flamboyant set of clothes, that seemed to have been made just for Stark. He allowed himself to be dressed and then Bisarios led and the two others followed behind Stark to a waiting conveyance that was like a car with anti-gravity.

They drove through the city and everywhere the street was lined with a horde of Pran and other beings. Some were humanoid, some seemed human, and other creatures strange and fantastic, that Stark would have thought were from mythology or a bad dream. "Where," Stark signaled and asked Bisarios.

He seemed to smile. "To be seen," he said. This much Stark could understand. The thought of 'recognized' crossed his mind as Bisarios used terms in Pran that were not familiar to him. They approached a giant structure, a stadium or coliseum and the aircraft came to a stop.

A wheeled carriage drawn by prancing animals that looked somewhat like elk pulled up beside them and Bisarios gestured for Stark to enter. The four seated themselves and the carriage passed inside. Stark was stunned at the crowd. There were many thousands of Pran waiting, and as many other creatures that he could not even identify, maybe millions. Some were beautiful, others seemed deformed and grotesque. It was impossible to guess the number of the vast attendance.

They were carried in silence, almost reverence to a dais in the center. There had been crowd noise that Stark could hear, but as they had come into the arena, all chatter had ceased. The carriage stopped and Bisarios exited and motioned for Stark to follow. His heart pounded. The thought of a public execution crossed his mind. He gulped hard and came out of the conveyance and followed Bisarios up the ramp to the dais. The other two remained at the edge of the ramp, turned and faced Stark.

When they were in place a the top, Bisarios indicated to the crowd. "Speak," he signed to Stark and said the Pran word for it.

"What?" Stark said in Pran. A word that Sartris had taught him over and over. The Pran word for a question. He was stunned when his voice was amplified all over the stadium. The two figures at the foot of the ramp bowed low, kneeling and touching their foreheads to the ground. Stark was shocked and looked to Bisarios. He was supplicated in the same way. Even more stunning was the noise the crowd as millions of Pran keeled to him. A wave of exhilaration shot over him as he realized that he was being worshiped. He could not understand why, but he could see it and feel it.

He felt the need to say more but could think of nothing except a line that he had heard from his childhood that was recorded years earlier and played on occasion. "Ich bein ein Pran," he said. The crowd exploded with a chant that grew deafening.

"Hail, Raven god," they yelled. "Hail Raven god. Hail, Raven god. Hail, Raven god," on and on it went. After many minutes, Bisarios arose from supplication and held up his hands to quiet them, but the crowd ignored him and continued the chant.

'Now I know how Cortez felt', Stark thought to himself.

The noise of battle, explosions, the roaring flames were burning the city in a firestorm driven away from Surilen, toward the horizon with a rising sun behind the smoke. It gave the city a blood red glow, and Surilen thought it fitting. The fighting had been hard, and blood, both green and red, ran in the streets and gutters.

Urvin approached from the direction of the government center. His armored transport descended in front of her, and he strode down the ramp, weapon in hand. He was covered in soot and grime from blowing ash and smoke. Proud and over six foot, he wasn't the pretty boy who had stood his ground to receive the signal from Uriah's probe of the real time supernova of Draco. He was pretty then. This war had changed him, outside. Inside, he remained equally determined as that fateful day.

He came closer and she could see the result of the particle beam blast that seared his amour, leaving a scar from chest to chin. The face was forever grimaced where the skin on one side was pulled from the scaring when no medical attention was immediately available. His face retained a frown on one side, even when he smiled with his good side and his blue eyes. Good humored and a prankster in those days, he was serious these days, and as he approached she could see that he was not smiling with any part of his face.

"Your Excellency," he bowed slightly to her rank.

"Commander Urvin," she returned the rank salute.

"They cannot be stopped. They have gone mad. They are burning everything."

"The records," Surilen moaned. "The codes, the history."

"Those building are gone," he assured her.

"It was our best chance to discover more about these monsters of time, and their-would-be-god emperor, Metastophiles."

"It is a tragedy that all that accumulated information on the Vril and their actions has been lost. It might have given us some understanding of how to stop them. They are always ahead of us, seemingly knowing what we are going to do next, but I think they were surprised with this internal rebellion on their own home world."

"We have won this one and may win others. We may be able to drive them from Saphos yet. We have yet to understand why they have chosen Saphos for a base."

"There is something strange," Urvin confided. "The factions are coming together in a unity in the attack on the prison."

Surilen though it through. "That would be expected," she nodded. "They will want to free the political prisoners of the various factions."

"It is more that that," Urvin corrected her thinking to see more. "There is some confluence of prophecy, ancient myth, science and philosophy being fulfilled in some way that we don't understand, but they expect to find an exo priest who somehow sparked the rebellion inside the prison, when they get in there. Only this priest, Sartris, was executed, and they know this, so it is the Son of Sartris, The Prophecy of Sartris, the Student of Sartris, the language translators are giving various translations, but we are not understanding."

"What are they doing now?" Surilen used a scope to observe the far distant horizon where the smoke was rising.

"They are liberating the prison, and this Sartris, or Son of Sartris is expected to be there and survive or has already risen from the dead to be among them bringing words of unity," Urvin shook his head, raised his eyebrows in wonder. "We will just have to wait and see because they say this is their deal, and we don't belong in this as we are not of the faith, as they see it. They will take care of the prison."

"So, let them. We will wait and see," she looked toward the fires in the distance.

As the crowd hailed him with endless cheers, Stark had a chance to study the beings in front of him. There were many of the exos, the exomorphic ant-like creatures. Some in robes like he had seen on Bisarios. Mixed in among the exos were humanoids, and many, many mutations of creatures both bipeds, and multi-limbed beings were in the giant crowd. Grotesque creatures, and beautiful beings of every form, stared at him from the floor and seats of the immense stadium.

Stark recognized Bisarios behind him on the platform that held the dais where he stood in the center. Bisarios was talking with two of some ten or fifteen humanoids and exos, standing around the podium with Stark placed on a raised circular dais in the center. There was something familiar with the woman that Bisarios was communicating with through some type of translator that the woman had. She had a regal bearing and posture and they locked eye contact for many moments. Stark felt drawn to her and was sure that he knew her, had seen her before.

Eventually, the crowd wound down from the deafening chanting, and was cleared out. Stark turned to Bisarios, and the two human types that were close to him. Bisarios had conferred with Surilen and Urvin, representatives of Saphos the first planet to be attacked by Metastophiles and the first of the Houses to declare for war against Pandamon. They had actually found the place rotten with the rebel troops in fighting over resources and a hierarchy based on a priesthood that was ready to fall. The beings inhabiting the various land masses were in rebellion against the priest rulers. The tributes were not being paid, and the tax collectors were being opposed and threatened, and sometimes beaten and killed.

The arrival of the daring raid of the rebel faction of Saphos against the home planet of Metastophiles was indeed boldly conceived and undertaken with some trepidation. The whole thing had hinged on the popular reaction to an execution of a philosopher who had become a threat to the state by pointing out to many questionable assumptions about the state religion. The Priests of Metastophiles had all the political power and advantages, and through the years, had gotten more and more unjust until the whole planet was in rebellion against the state religion.

There was one other strange element, Surilen pondered as she eyed the figure at the center of the podium. Somehow, there was a cult that was part of the rebellion against the priests and their belief in a savior that would come to them when all hope was lost. "The meaning of the name Sartris, the philosopher, in this language is 'Hope'," Surilen observed to Urvin, "when they went to the cell where their 'Hope' was lost, they found this humanoid," she pointed at Stark.

"His coming fit a prophecy of the rebel cause, that a savior would come," Urvin recounted.

"We are the saviors," Surilen claimed the truth. Many lives had been lost among her people in helping the rebels struggle against the corrupt priesthood government. Then she asked Bisarios. "How does this humanoid creature fit into this?"

"He was trained and foretold to us by Sartris," Bisarios explained.

"I still don't get it," Surilen shook her head. "How did he bring all this together when we've been trying for months?"

Stark looked back at her in time to see the consternation in her eyes. "What?" He asked with his eyes. She just stared with questions in her eyes. A lot of things to be understood between them, he thought. She looked so familiar. Uris, she looked a lot like Uris, he realized.

Stark managed to edge closer to Surilen. "Uris?" He said to her when he got to within range. Her head snapped to attention.

"Uris," she heard him say. She asked in Standard Xinor. "What about Uris?"

Stark could make out little in what she said. He could see her reaction. They tried to understand each other and Bisarios was brought into the attempt. Slowly it was revealed that Uris had come to Terra of Sol, and the track of Uris' ship, the Pearl, had led to Draco. Now, Stark Raven confirmed, Uris had come to Earth through Draco, and she had survived.

Surilen had to know more and she graciously extended an invitation for Stark to visit her at the warship Scorpio orbiting Pandamon. She was told by the rebel council that her request would be considered. She bowed to this for the moment but determined to have the Earth man for questioning. Surilen thought that she would need a better interpreter for his language. That would take some time. She kept up the request to host Raven, as he was called.

A break came when Stark himself asked an audience from her and was finally told of her wish to host him aboard the warship Scorpio. He informed the council that to visit Surilen aboard her warship was his wish.

Stark was impressed when he came aboard by shuttle up from the surface of Pandamon. He was brought to an observation deck where the surface of Pandamon could be seen. He felt it somehow familiar as he looked down.

Surilen joined him. She had arranged for the Trident warship, the flagship of the House of Ur, to arrive out of hyperspace at that moment. She wished to awe this stranger, and this would make a good start. Stark had just registered her presence when the Trident materialized out of hyperspace slowing to a full stop a very short distance away. Stark had to step back.

He quickly realized that this was staged for his benefit and indicated with gestures. This was what she wanted, to get him to communicate. She indicated the Trident Warship and asked him to "Come visit, aboard," in standard Xinor, and he made sign language that he accepted. This made a beginning to try and understand.

Many days went by in this way with them exploring the two ships, getting to know some of each language and little by little letting Surilen learn and understand that her cousin Uris was alive on Earth and had come there through the Stargate Draco. Using Uriah, her father's, data from the downtime Supernova, the computers on board the Pearl, interfaced with Andro, had been able to bring Uris and the Pandamon fugitive Kurege safely to Earth.

This meant that the Pearl had opened the Stargate of Draco the Dragon. The long-awaited event was here. Draco could be safely navigated. Vast regions of new space were suddenly available to explore and use for trade and growth.

This single event had been watched for and calculated to happen for hundreds of years. Now the time was at hand. Surilen spent more and more time with Stark, trying to unravel the deeper mystery of the strange series of events taking place around Stark Raven. She was also very surprised to find herself drawn to him as a woman.

He made her laugh with his childish exploring of this new world around him, whether food, flowers, or fun the creatures around them enjoyed. She read his expressions, now, after their time together, and she saw deep, something that interested her completely.

She was beginning to understand what the opening of Draco would do, strategically and to the fate of the war in progress. This had to be brought to the attention of the Xinor General Council. She was also beginning to understand that she wanted to know and be around this Stark Raven more. She wanted to know him fully.

They spent more time together, and their ability to communicate with each other improved. Surilen had a language computer that helped speed up the process of learning each other's meanings. They were able to talk about particular problems.

"You are saying that Uris was attacked and the data from the probe that her father sent was lost," she saw a larger picture suddenly, "and that it was possibly lost to Metastophiles."

"That was what Uris thought had happened," Stark told her. Uris had speculated to him on the men that had attacked and killed the Usay's and Joe Le Blanc at the shrimp shed. They had spent some time going over the events at the shed during her stay on Tres Negras, what seemed like a lifetime ago.

"Then the only way that we have to navigate the Draco Door, is the trace that we have on her passage," Surilen was thinking ahead. "That vector was disrupted by a Pandamon warship's firing on her inside the Stardoor. That caused a glitch to the Neutron Star core."

"Yes," Stark confirmed. "She told me about the way that her ship was partially disabled. The robot she said made the program that brought her and Kurege through the Stardoor.

"This would mean that Metastophiles has the data to navigate the Draco Stardoor. We do not yet," Surilen smiled to herself and then at Stark. "There are ways to place tracking on a Pandamon ship. They have been contending for the Draco area. It has had no importance until now, now I see it has all the importance for the House of Ur, our house. I will soon know the path to Earth," she told him.

"Lady," he said, " I think I love you."

"Uris has navigated Draco. We have a track to the gateway to what you call the Milky Way. She survived the passage. The Pearl has opened the gate," Surilen said. "The Draco Gate is open."

The two looked at each other, realization flooded them. They were the union of two worlds. They were close, almost touching. There was hesitation in their embrace, a tentative kiss, for passion to take hold.

The way that they had begun, Surilen now began to let Stark have more and more freedom, and he found himself in the observation deck of the Trident Warship very often, gazing down onto the planet's surface. There was something about the planet below that puzzled him.

Surilen joined him much of the time. She began to use a voice recognition recorder linked to a computer program versed in thousands of languages. She would have him point and speak in his language and then she would give the Standard Xinor equivalent. Soon she had his lexicon and then could ask for his story.

"Mem de Uris fe che," she said in Xinor, and Stark heard, "Tell me about Uris."

He sat back in a lounge chair with the planet below him as he told her the story. "Uris came to Earth, and she needed help. She crashed into an ocean near the coast of my nation. The good old USA," he laughed at the thought of how far from home he was. The letters brought up an association on Surilen's PDA type device that was part of the language computer. The image of the ceramic coated plutonium artifact from the Xinor museum that she had shown to Uris that fateful day long ago. She didn't interrupt the story but held up a hand and then showed him the picture of the object. "Huh," he registered surprise. "That is the Eagle crest of my nation," he told her, "And the stamp of the old authority, the Department of Energy, the DOE, that regulated the nation's plutonium waste. These ceramic coated plutonium balls were dropped into our sun, in an effort to dispose of them."

"You dropped these things into your sun?" Surilen questioned.

"Yes."

"How many," she asked.

"I'm not sure," he shrugged, "many thousands."

She confirmed the number, to the decimal place to be sure that she understood.

Stark noticed the color drain out of her face, and her eyes widened, in a characteristically human reaction to fear. They didn't speak for several minutes while she made notes, by talking into her PDA in Standard Xinor.

When she had finished making note, she encouraged him to return to the story of Uris. "I met her and Kurege when Uris became ill from lack of Xenon in the atmosphere of our planet."

"Who is Kurege," Surilen asked?

"He is the human, who had been kidnapped from our planet when he was an infant. He said that he was taken to some place called Pandamon."

"This is Pandamon," she pointed to the surface.

"Really?" Stark was both amazed at the coincidence and puzzled.

He looked below him at the planet's surface. There was something so familiar about it. She encouraged him again to come back to the story. "Uris told me that before I met her, she had lost a data disk that she had gotten from her father. Some type of navigational aid, that she thought was very important. Something about a Baron Metastopiles."

Surilen took a deep breath in surprise and talked very fast into her recorder. "She believed that he was involved in exporting plutonium from Earth to the future," Stark laughed. Surilen made more hasty notes on her recorder. Other evidence of this came to me at the same time, about a facility near my birthplace called Pantex. I had installed the security at that government facility, and I and three other men went in to see. What we found," he shook his head to try and describe his surprise, "was these creatures that you call Pran. We also discovered a strange greenish-yellow fluid in cryogenic suspension. The Pran came after it, and two of them were killed in a fight with my companions, then myself and one other man put on their protective clothing and pretended to join them. After a very long ride on a electric train-like conveyance, we were placed aboard a starship. We were able to hide, at first, but eventually we were discovered, and had to fight for our lives. I was lucky, my companion Jim was not, he was killed."

"No." Surilen told him.

"No?" Stark questioned.

"When you were taken from the prison by Pran rebels, Zythures and Urvin were informed by the rebellion troops, another human with your same code label in the priesthood's system here was found. He is somehow related to you and was injured."

"Jim? Alive?" Stark questioned.

"They were able to repair him but he is damaged. Memory loss and some motor skill loss," she told Stark. "He was in cryogenic suspension, but he has been revived. Would you like to see him?"

"Very much so," Stark stood. "He is here on your ship?"

"No," we have the best medical for cryogenic recovery, but they wouldn't let you both off the planet." She smiled reassuringly, or, at least Stark hoped so. He realized that they would place him with Jim and see what happened. "I will get it arranged when you return to Pandamon."

"What do you know of the planet below?" Stark asked, pointing and gesturing to be understood.

"This has always been the home of the Baron Metastophiles. He is rarely there, maybe every three hundred Standard Xinor years he has come to stay during the last ten millennia, since the Empire existed. He sometimes comes to put things in order to his liking."

"What of the creatures that inhabit?" Stark struggled with the words.

"Metastophiles honors no treaty on genetics," she told him. "Pandamon is a genetic laboratory for some unknown purpose."

She was silent for a moment and then continued. "He installed an exomorphic priesthood that controls the population of mutants." She told him. "There is also an ancient Supreme Priest Council, which is made up of the ancients, the ones that take the life extension fluid that you described."

"Really?" Stark was again taken aback by the revelation of the purpose of the greenish-yellow, frozen fluid. He pondered this and again gazed down at the planet below.

"What about the planet, itself, what do you know about it?" He signed part with words in Standard Xinor that he had learned, and part by pointing at it.

"There is a background radiation of alpha particles. It is high enough to indicate that the planet, worldwide, received doses of plutonium radiation some seventy-five thousand years ago. This background radiation is harmful to most species but the ectomorphs like the Pran are not affected by it."

"Seventy-five thousand?"

"Yes, and the priesthood is in its seventy-fifth millennium celebration, so the time frame seems to fit."

Stark gazed out at the planet, then suddenly it hit him. If he just rotated everything around, he suddenly saw the continents. He was looking down on Grand Canyon...Seventy-Five Thousand Years Deeper. The thought froze his blood. The thought made his mouth drop open in complete surprise. It was such a surprise that he couldn't express it to Surilen.

"They are asking for your return."

"What?" Stark was brought out of his realization back to his situation.

"The new ruling council, the mutants, are asking for your return to the surface."

"When?"

"We will have to let you go to them soon. You are some type of god to them. It was a uniting factor in the overthrow of the priesthood, something to do with an execution of one of their leading thinkers, even though the thinker was Pran. The Pran Priesthood thought they could destroy the movement by killing him, but it set off the rebellion."

"What will they do with me?" Stark questioned.

"We don't know, as we have little understanding of religion and none of this one."

It was the next morning that Stark was boarded onto a shuttle and he and Surilen went back to the surface of the planet. She was able to bring Stark and Jim together by taking him to the place where Jim was being cared for. "Stark," Jim rose from his bunk in the padded cell like room.

"Jim, its great to see you buddy."

"Where the hell are we Stark?" Jim questioned. "Are we doing the Pantex raid in the morning?" Jim was a little awkward on his feet now from loss of motor skills, re-routed.

"That's a long story, Jim," Stark hugged him. They talked for a while, but Jim couldn't make sense of it, and kept becoming distracted and silent, in an inner world. Stark didn't try to explain the full story, at least not yet. Stark assured him that they would be together soon and would see him the next day. That soothed Jim's perplexed mind, desperately trying to reconnect.

Later that day, Stark and Surilen stood before the Mutant Council of Pandamon. Surilen, with Urvin and Zythurus by his side, recognized all the warring factions present. Jim was also brought in, but kept at the back behind Surilen and Stark.

"You were chosen by Sartris," Bisarios explained. "You arrived in the Tribute ship and delayed his execution. Do you not see?" Bisarios stretched out his arms.

"I don't understand," Stark folded his arm.

"Your coming is foretold," Bisarios informed as if the fact were always known.

"What would you have me to do," Stark cut to the bargaining point.

"We are waiting for you to tell us," Bisarios spread his hands wide. "You are the Light of Sartris, that is to bring "Hope" to the people, the creatures of Pandamon," Bisarios looked pleadingly at Stark Raven.

"In that case," a big smile spread across Stark's face, "I suggest that we all just get along." He grinned his most winning smile and spread his hands to the council.

It took a few moments for the translations to be made into the various dialects and language groups. A mummer of approval rose up around the table. Then it broke into the same "Hail Raven god," chant until Stark motioned for it to calm down.

"Go among the people and let them see you. They will understand that it is true. The peace we seek now is among us." Bisarios spoke for the council.

"Sartris spirit will lead you," Stark said to Bisarios in the language that he had learned from Sartris. Bisarios believed.

"When you go among the people, it will be as if Sartris has come among us again."

"I want to take Jim with me," Stark requested.

"Yes," the head of the council confirmed to Bisarios.

There was much more ceremony and feasting on things that he and Surilen were brought to eat. She had

106

come with him. The council had not questioned it. The three of them availed themselves of freedom and began to walk the city.

Many of the government buildings and the temples were in ruins from the recent conflict. Still, here and there pockets of houses were largely untouched and lively and friendly activity and sharing could be seen among the hovels that furnished living space for the mutants.

Stark had trouble making himself look into the faces. So many strange mutations of the basic bipedal body arrangement. He wished he had Surilen's humor about it. She was used to creatures from all over the known universe, so there was little different enough, or strange enough to make her flinch. She knew Standard Xinor and some of the creatures that they met could speak it a little, so Surilen was careful to inquire how they were. This always brought a profusion of plans and troubles, giving the impression of a collection of creatures both open and friendly.

When they watched from a distance, everywhere they saw a people unified and helping each other.

The destruction of the corrupt priesthood had heartened the people, relieved them of crushing taxes, and united a world of beings of no tribe, and dissimilar bodies. The tyranny had been so long and hard, the joy was like a spreading fountain of water.

Surilen, Stark and Jim spent many days touring the cities of Pandamon and everywhere the euphoria was having the same result. They saw smiling faces and helpful behavior at every turn.

"These creatures have such a harmony," Stark observed from a table at a local eatery. "I wonder how long does such euphoria over freedom last? When will differences begin to be more important than 'sameness'?" He questioned.

"Funny to talk about sameness in a genetic laboratory full of mutants," Surilen saw the irony. She also understood that Earth or Pandamon was early on in the sequence of time and space. That was the reason that so many of the creatures they were seeing were all up and down the timelines. The concept of all events happening at all times and the progress of the singularity that is observed as Time, she could not begin to tell Stark. She was aware that the data on Stark's timeline had been saved by the Rebels, and considered it to be very important. Stark's trip halfway around the universe had implications, in terms of tracking the Metagestopo, Metastophiles, and the Vril to their origin time line. Going to Earth, began to form in her plans. Perhaps a Vril ship could be tracked from Saphos to Earth.

"It is a fragile new social order of total freedom, each not judged, giving what they can and taking what they need," he observed. "But will it last?" Stark speculated.

"Say," Jim brightened up from the other side of the table. "You're saying that we already did that Pantex raid that we were planning?" Jim was always coming back to the exact spot where his memory stopped. "Tell me," he looked into Stark's black eyes. "How did that work out?"

Stark looked at Jim, a ripple of spreading mirth in his chest until laughter burst forth with tears of hilarity streaming down his cheeks.

Chapter 9 The Center of Attention
New Mexico

Kurege for the first six months, was mostly in training, but eventually, the day came when his skills were tested. A memo email came to him requesting him to come to his supervisors office, who took him to a research lab far to the basement and interior of the Artificial Intelligence Research Facility. There, he was introduced to Dr. Chen Ching, in charge of the laboratory.

"You know what we do here," Ching clipped out.

"Something about computers," Kurege told him.

"What they call you," Chen asked just as abruptly.

"Kurege," he replied.

"Your file say Michael Hodge," Chen arched an eyebrow.

"That is my given name," he agreed.

"I call you Michael," Chen said. "You computer whiz, they say."

"I'm learning."

"I need computer whiz," Chen stabbed the air in front of them. "Come here, I show you," he rose and moved toward an elaborate apparatus in the center of the room. When they arrived, he began, "You know what this is of course."

"Not a clue," Kurege shook his head.

"No," the other man looked at him questioningly. "Where you been," he began exasperated. "This best Bose-Einstein Condensate, optical, magnetic and evaporative cryogenic cooler," then patted the machine fondly. "She go one nanoK above absolute zero, maybe less," he dragged the word out to emphasize the possibility.

"Here," he gestured around the room, "we make and experiment with the greatest number of atoms as any lab on the whole planet. Look here," he gestured. "This optical laser pump, where the species of atom or molecules we are cooling are entered to the MOT, Molecular Optical Trap. As it is optically pumped to very low temperatures, we create Bose-Einstein Condensate with evaporation of helium3. You know this?" Chen questioned.

"No," Kurege shook his head.

"Where you been," Chen looked puzzled, "this hot stuff, everyone know about this since 2008, over twenty-five years now. We're close, very close," he gestured at the mystery.

"What are you close to?" Kurege questioned.

"Michael," Chen said in mock astonishment. "Understanding," he gestured all around. "Everything."

"Really," Kurege was enthused.

"Here," Chen pointed into the heart of the apparatus. "this is the special laser that we project a coded information, using the laser as carrier," he paused. "You familiar with fiber optics hook ups to main frames. Correct?"

"I have a good understanding of this and some recent intensive training," he didn't elaborate, but felt comfortable for the first time.

"I project a stream of coded information miles long into the BEC and it compresses into a frozen stream of coherent information nanometer long. We can now extract this stream of frozen data through this one-way mirror with this electro-magnetic gate. Our problem is to maintain the BEC at the highest density of atoms or data, coherent data. Your problem is to develop the best high-speed language and architecture for information retrieval, problem solving, search engine integration, all that," he waved his hand in the manner of a theoretical genus giving a job to a plumber.

"This sounds intriguing," he was interested and sure he could contribute.

"You computer wizard. You do." Chen dismissed him. "Here your desk," he pointed at a corner, "that your lap top, take home, but not off base, or alarm go off," Chen Ching cautioned him.

Chen left him alone to become familiar with the lab and the task. Kurege pulled up a chair to his desk and turning on his computer, began to search for the published work on information storage in BEC super-fluid. The search engine returned one-hundred-eighty-five thousand hits on super-fluids and coherent light storage near absolute zero. He counted eighty-six laboratories experimenting with BEC super fluids. There was enormous attention centered on this area. This was going to take some time. He went to work on understanding the current research. His understanding of Pandamon technology soon gave him a clue as to where the experiments were going. He was excited to discuss it with Uris, as she would know more about certain aspects of this technology than he did.

At home that evening, after their meal, and Urme's nightly reading of Stanley the Snail, and after the struggle to get Urme to bed, the two finally found time to talk.

"Now close your eyes and go to sleep," Uris instructed, as Kurege waved night-night from the door with a snail puppet. Urme closed her eyes, then opened one eye to see if her mother was gone. The door was closed, and she slipped out of bed and reached under the bed and under the toys that she had covering the little tiny book. It was the green leather-bound New Testament that the church lady had given her at Sunday school.

She carefully placed it squarely under her pillow where the most vivid dreams came from. She loved to dream her books. She would play and play in her dreams with Stanley and all the alien creatures in that book. Last week, at Sunday school, they had presented her with her very own book of the New Testament with a green leather cover. It was just her size. She had placed the book twice before, and had marvelous dreams. One night, angels had

111

filled the sky singing Christmas carols. She had gazed upon a wondrous infant. The second night, she had sat in the lap of the most wonderful man. She never wanted to leave that lap, it was like her father's lap on really good days, and she hated to wake from that dream.

She wondered as she lay her head carefully on the pillow right above her book. What would she dream; what wonderful adventure would she have?

"Is she going to sleep?" Kurege asked when Uris came and sat on the couch beside him.

"Who knowth with that child." Uris was often exasperated with Urme's failure to obey. In her own childhood there seemed to have been no choice, even though she had been a princess, and then Regent, and finally Queen, and always the weight of that responsibility that demanded she do what was expected. Now what? What was she expected to do?

"I've been assigned to a new laboratory," he told her his news of the day.

"Really," she listened. "What ith it?"

"You're going to find this interesting," he had a twinkle in his eye.

Uris saw the mirth that Kurege projected, and smiled. "What?" She asked, encouraging him to tell her more.

"Well, I have been assigned to a new type of computer technology being developed. It uses a fluid cooled to near absolute zero to store information passed into it by laser beam. I am working under a Dr. Chen Ching who is developing the storage media. I'm in charge of the software development and the architecture of the gate that couples the existing supercomputers to this new type."

"That ith like the thythem that Andro uthe," she reflected.

"Very like the systems that I learned on Pandamon," Kurege nodded. "It is a logical step for any developing world. I feel very comfortable that I can contribute to its creation. They have given me a new laptop computer that I will use, but it must not leave the base here at Los Alamos," he indicated the small case that he had carried.

"How far have they progrethed?" She asked curiously.

"Dr. Ching is concerning himself with the atomic density, and seems very pleased that his lab and his apparatus has achieved the highest concentrations of atoms of any of the laboratories working on this."

"How ith he balanthing the "Ort" cloud?" She used the Xinor word for this phenomena.

"I saw no apparatus for balancing the field," Kurege got a puzzled look. "His main idea is to increase the density."

Uris immediately looked concerned. "That ith very dangerouth. Without balanth the atomth can implode."

"That is why I am telling you," Kurege screwed up his mouth in a more puzzled manner. "It concerned me, but I know you have a more thorough knowledge of this theory."

"You muth warn him," she shook her head in dismay. "The history of thith type of development ith filled with explothianth and implothianth."

It was at that moment that the sound of a scream came from Urme's room, followed by deep sobs of crying coming from the child. Both parent sprang to their feet and ran to her room.

"Urme," they both yelled to her, as Kurege turned on the light. Uris reached her first and scooped the little girl from her bed and cradled her in her arms.

"Waugh," she screamed and sobbed. "They hurt grandfather, they hurt grandfather," she shrieked at the top of her voice. She kicked and arched her back and rejected her mother's comfort and reached through her tears for her father. Uris had to let her go and handed her to Kurege.

"Shhh," he coaxed as he patted her on the back. She buried her head in his shoulder, and he continued to try and sooth her as tears streamed down her face and wet his shirt front. "Shhh, Shhh," he tried to calm her.

"They hurt grandfather, they hurt grandfather," she screamed. "They nailed him to a tree," she was inconsolable, and cried and cried.

"I found a thorpion in the kitchen the other day," Uris told Kurege.

"Did you kill it?" He asked, a little accusingly.

"Of courth I did," she threw back at him, and began to strip the bed looking for anything that might have given the harm.

"Shhh," Kurege continued to pat her back and hold her close. "It was only a dream, Urme. You are fine now. Don't cry, sweetheart, it was just a bad dream." He took her out of the bedroom, and sat down in the living room, continuing to hold her. He examined her legs and looked her over for a whelp from a sting but could find nothing.

"They whipped grandfather, and nailed him to a tree," she whined. She hadn't tears left to cry. "They k-killed him," she whimpered, then just dry sobbed, on and on.

Uris entered the room," What ith thith?" She held out a small green leather-bound book.

"I don't know," Kurege was puzzled, as he reached out to take it, but he had barely got hold when Urme snatched it from him.

"Mine," she said.

"Urme," Uris questioned her harshly. "Where did you get thith book?"

Urme snuggled closer to her father for protection. "The lady at the church gave it to me. It makes me dream wonderment dreams," the little girl brightened. She cradled the book and looked sideways at her mother.

"Urme," her father sat her on the couch. "What do you mean, 'the book makes you dream'?"

Urme looked down at her book. Somehow, she was shy to tell her secret. They always wanted her to go to sleep, not play with her toys. What if they wanted her to not play in her dreams? Her body rested, but she played with Stanley the Snail, and all the alien creatures in her favorite book, all night long. What if they took her books away?

"Urme?" Her father asked again. "What about the book?"

"Oh," she confessed, "not just this book. All my books make me dream when I put them under my pillow," she beamed her most winning smile, then looked down again, and pulled on a wrinkle in her Stanley the Snail and the Aliens pajamas she always wore at night.

"What do you mean," Uris was puzzled and somewhat annoyed. This was coming from that bunch of religious nuts over at the Baptist church, as far as she could make out.

"I place a book under my pillow, and then I will dream the book," she explained with an exasperated sigh. Parents were so dumb. Sometimes, when you had to explain to them.

Kurege and Uris looked at each other in amazement.

"I'm tired now," the little girl said, and reached for her father to pick her up. She yawned just for the added effect.

"All right, Urme," her father picked her up and started back to her room. Uris plucked the little green New Testament from the child as she went by on her father's shoulder. Urme raised up and frowned at her mother.

Kurege was gone for a few minutes and when he came back to the living room she let him have it. "I do not want Urme going to that place again," she began emphatically.

"Uris," Kurege explained. "Urme has friends there. She needs the contact of other children."

"I don't want her head filled with fear," Uris screamed at him. "Thith nonthenth of a war between good and evil with a blood thacrifith ith too primitive to expoth her to. I won't have it," she stomped her foot! "And then, the total notheth of thomeone rithing from the dead." She shook her head in bewilderment.

"Uris," he tried to sooth her. "You fly through time and space at speeds faster than the speed of light. Don't you think that seems like nonsense to this primitive people. They have no idea that such a thing is possible. Isn't it possible that there are things happening in the universe that we know nothing about."

"Pthychical reality ith one thing," she argued. "We travel in time fathter than light. That ith reality," she screamed again. "Thomeone coming back from the dead ith nonthenth!"

Urme could hear them fighting and covered her ears with her hands. She began to cry, thinking that she was the reason that they were fighting.

It was two days later that Urme was exploring, as she was always exploring her five year old world. She opened the door to her father's study and entered. Everything was just as the day before except for the silver case on the desk. It was a new laptop computer, and she knew what to do with that. She opened it.

She found the Internet and navigated to her favorite game, *The Center of Attention*. While she was waiting for it to boot, she looked on the files page. Family History looked interesting and she opened it. The file marked AI looked interesting, and she opened it also.

"Urme," her mother called. Urme shut the computer lid, but not all the way, and the machine continued to run. "What are you doing in here," Uris questioned. She took her by the hand and led her out of the room. "You know that you are not thuppothed to go into your father'th thtudy. Thith ith not the firtht time that you have dithobeyed," Uris chided her, and put her out, closing the door. Urme ran to another part of the house, and Uris let it go.

Chapter 10 The Lights of the San Luis Valley
New Mexico

Striker was at Calley's when his cell phone rang. "Striker," Enrico asked?

"This is Striker Rich," he answered.

"Enrico Rameriz," Enrico answered back. "Sorry to be so long getting back to you, but we were working cattle all day and the recorder was unclear. Your number doesn't show, and I had to go through all the cards on my desk to find it."

"I can understand that" Striker grinned as he thought of the piles of cards on his own desk. "It's nothing urgent. "I was just headed to Albuquerque to check on electromagnetic coils that I am shipping to the moon. They are for a new launch system for sending mining robots to the asteroid belt. They're being manufactured by Sandia for The Santa Fe Group who holds the contract from the government for their production. I have to go to Sandia in Albuquerque to consult on the linear acceleration magnets, and then I'm headed to Moon Base for the first shipment. I just hoped that there was some news about Stark, so I called."

"Not a word from any direction, I'm sorry to say," Enrico told him. There was a long pause, with neither man having anything more. Then he added, "Albuquerque is near Santa Fe, maybe forty miles or so. Will you have any free time while you're there?"

"The tour at Sandia will only take an hour or two on Tuesday, and then I have nothing scheduled until I leave for Moon Base the middle of next week."

"Hmmm," Enrico mused. "How would you like to meet our two resident aliens?"

"Is that possible?"

"I'm told that they are working in research at the new Chemistry and Metal Research facility at Los Alamos. I'll have to clear it with Ruben McAuley, but it may be possible.

"That's a coincidence," Striker said,

"I see that Michael Hearne is performing at the La Fonda hotel in Santa Fe on Wednesday night this coming week, he's a really great musician, and it will be a good place to meet. Hearne's been around a long time, and he still gets around and plays and sings one hell of a good guitar with his original songs, and everybody's from the old days," Enrico proposed.

"I've heard him twice before, and like him a lot. That's a plan. Wednesday night is fine for me, say about 8:30 that evening in the bar, right."

"That works for me, and I will try to have those two interesting people that we talked about meet us there."

"That is very intriguing," Striker mused. "Meet you there."

When he hung up the cell phone, he invited Calley to go with him, but she said that she had a flight to New York city that day, and would not be able to take the time. He went to the second floor of her apartment to shower and pack for the trip. He was due at Sandia for an engineering meeting with members of the development team involved in making magnets ready for shipment to the moon. He would be in charge of the contract for the installation of the launcher for the missions to the asteroid belt. There were also meetings at Sandia for the development of robots that would be sent to explore for valuable minerals and metals.

When the call from Enrico came to Kurege, he was at his desk in Chen Ching's cryogenics laboratory. He thought that he and Uris could make it to the La Fonda that night, but knowing better than to speak for her, demurred from a final answer, telling Enrico that he would call him back with a 'yes' or 'no' after he had spoken with Uris, and they had arranged for a babysitter for Urme. He rang Uris's phone but got no answer and left a message with her voice mail.

Uris was away from her desk and had left her cell phone in her purse, so that she did not immediately hear it. She had gone to the desk of Rafael Peralta to ask instructions on the construction of the hydrogen bomb that she was designing. She had usually designed the plutonium bombs that triggered the fusion reaction in the hydrogen bombs, but was lately being assigned the design of some of the Standard Superbombs, but this one was a little different, and she sought his advice, as she sometimes needed to do.

She stood at his desk for some moments, waiting for him to get finished with what he was working on and acknowledge that she was there. He looked down and saw her feet and legs and noticed that she was again wearing those very unusual boots. "Nice boots," he said when he finally looked up. "Very unusual," he looked at her very closely as she took a seat next to his desk and held the bill of materials close up to where they could both see them. He wasn't immediately interested in her problem, but slid back in his chair, turning away from his computer screen and with a questioning and a puzzled look then asked her. "Where did you get boots like that?"

"Thomeone made them for me," she told Peralta.

"And where did they get them," he asked? Then seeing that she could not answer that, thinking that she probably didn't know where they came from, refined his question to tell him more about what was puzzling him. "I mean," he asked very pointedly. "What type of animal is the skin from?"

This question startled Uris for a moment, and Rafael saw the hesitation and a slight hint of apprehension in her face and body language. "I don't know," she lied, as she quickly recovered, but she looked away from his eye contact and down and to the left. Peralta registered the evasiveness.

"That is very curious," he confronted her, "because my father was a taxidermist, and I worked with him for years. I am pretty sure that I have seen the skins of every animal that walks the Earth, and have felt them, smelled them, and sown them all, and although those boots smell like goat skin, they are not, and I don't believe that I have ever seen a skin quite like that," he pointed at her boots.

Uris put on her most disarming smile and shook her head and shrugged her shoulders, as she had learned to mimic human behavior in this way whenever these types of questions came up.

Then Peralta said something really strange. It totally startled her.

"You know, the San Luis Valley has more flying saucer sightings than any other place on the face of the Earth," he looked closely at her reaction to this piece of news. He immediately saw her interest.

"Really?" she was curious and wanted to know more.

"Yes," he smiled. This was going his way, and discussion of the Superbombs was forgotten for the moment as each of them tried to figure out how to get more information from the other without revealing anything. "The cattle mutilations have continued from the "Snippy" the horse incident through hundreds of confirmed cases, right up to the present. The news doesn't carry it much anymore but if you know the locals, then you know that it is still happening."

"What are mutilationth," Uris was puzzled?

"Well, the cattle are killed, horses also, in strange ways. Parts are surgically removed, usually the lips, eyeball, and sexual organs, but there is sometimes no blood, and the cutting seems to be done by something other than a knife," Rafael told her. He shrugged, "some think that it is satanic cults, others pranks, but some believe that aliens from another world are harvesting body parts for some kind of genetic experiment." Peralta noticed Uris's posture stiffened at this, and smiled slightly, as he could tell that he had hit a nerve. Uris didn't speak and silence ensued for several moments.

"Also," Peralta continued, "there are native legends of some type of ant people living in an underground complex somewhere in the San Luis Valley, and there has been at least one ant person skeleton found in the area." He noticed that Uris eyes had narrowed in what could only be intense anger.

"Ant people," she repeated.

"Yeah," he reinforced it. "Some people even claim that there are connecting tunnels to here in Los Alamos." He saw her look at the bill of materials in her hand for plutonium bombs designed to set off a fusion hydrogen super bomb.

She tried not to react, but she visibly started at the realization that this was the same as at Pantex six years earlier, when she was first pregnant with Urme. She looked into Peralta's eyes and saw that he was looking at her reactions very carefully. This angered her sense of herself and her royalty, and she showed it in a farther narrowing of her eyes, this time turning her ire toward him.

Rafael saw this and tried to lighten the mood and make a joke that could defuse the hostility he now felt turned toward him. She was somewhat scaring him. "Where," he smirked, "did you say you got those boots?"

"I didn't thay," she snapped, and suddenly rose and went back to her desk, with all thought of the bill of materials for this newest Superbomb forgotten.

She went back to her desk and sat down hard. She thought for several moments and then reached for her cell phone to call Kurege and noticed that she had received a call from him. She scrolled to his name and dialed.

"Hello, Queen of my heart," he answered.

"They are here," she said emphatically.

"Who are you talking about?" He questioned. Then, recognizing the stress in her voice. "Uris what is wrong?"

"Thith ith the thame ath Pantex," she lisped. "Ith a Pran bathe, probably under Metathphileth control."

"Let's not talk like this on these phones." He was startled and reacted with caution. "You need more of your xenon inhalers, and I have heard from Enrico. He has them ready and is bringing then to Santa Fe. He suggested that we meet at the La Fonda this Wednesday night in the lounge. He asked Ruben McAuley to join us, and another friend of Stark Raven, I didn't catch his name. We can discuss this at home. If you are right about there being a problem, we could discuss it with Dr. McAuley." He waited for her to speak, but she was silent in thought on the other end. He could hear her chewing on her lip, which she did when she was nervous.

"What do you think?" He asked. "Can we find a sitter for Urme that soon?"

"I don't know where." She said flat.

"Well," he hesitated. "We will just take her with us."

There was a long pause. "Yeth," she finally agreed. She had to get the inhalers, and meeting off base, and away from Los Alamos would make sense. She had a feeling that they would need to talk to Ruben McAuley. They agreed to take off work and meet at home to discuss her fears and these plans. He also had an uneasy feeling as they hung up.

Striker Rich flew into Albuquerque airport and went to the car rental and drove toward the large Sandia complex near the interstate twenty-five corridor coming in from Colorado to the north, just skirting Santa Fe on the south side of the city. He could see balloons with gondolas under them rising from the Balloon Festival that happened in early October every year, and the traffic was in gridlock, so he had time to sit and reflect as his line of cars crept north.

He remembered his first time in Albuquerque, when he had first met Stark Galileo Raven. He had grown up in Australia, the privileged son of a very wealthy man, Richard Rich, who had come to Australia in the late 1960's from an immensely wealthy Eastern family. Richie Rich had formed a commune of like-minded members, and had turned his back on technology, and gone green, back to nature. Of course, when his son, Striker, was born several years later, the boy could not wait to get back to civilization and become an entrepreneur and scientist. He had met Stark Raven at Sanford first and had come to visit his Native American Hopi father, and his Tiwa language mother of the Red Willow People in the Taos area where Stark had grown up. The two had fed each other's ambitions and dreams of a future world filled with technology and opportunities. Now, his brow wrinkled with thought of where his friend could be. Was he still alive? He made a mental note to go by before he left for the moon and see the parent's graves, and talk with Stark's sister Cactus Flower, as her name translated to English. The traffic moved forward an inch, and he had to change his concentration to keep from colliding with the stop and go.

When he got to Sandia, a little late for the appointment, Roderick Axtel met Striker Rich in the lobby by the towering complex of buildings devoted to the development of the cryogenic magnets that would have applications around the world. "Great to see you again, Mr. Rich," Axtel shook his hand.

"Sorry to be late, I've come a long way today, and the traffic was horrendous."

"No problem," Axtel shrugged, "I expected you might be hung up in traffic, with the balloon crowd, this time of year, it just has to be figured in to any meeting." Axtel led him past the frowning dragon lady on the front desk guarding the door. "That meeting on the moon was a bust, but they tell me that you have signed the intent letters, and I'm to show you the species of the project as it stands now."

"Yes," Striker agreed, "I wasn't sure what was happening that day on the moon. I'm still not sure what happened that day. I'm eager to see what progress has already been made."

"No one else seems to be sure of that day, and Homeland Security is clamped up tight on the subject, as far as I can tell," Axtel probed for an answer.

"I never knew anymore," Striker lied.

"Well, moving on to the project at hand, what can I tell you about the magnets?"

"What size and weight are we talking about? Has there been a final decision on the design?"

"The sizing is the same as the Cheyenne Mountain tunnel and launch facility, so the same size containers will be designed to hold the robotic probes." Axtel showed him to some of the giant magnets under construction. "After we finish here, I have another future project that I want to show you in an adjacent laboratory." They continued the tour through the various labs and machine shops, giving Striker a good idea of the capability of the facility, and what he could expect from this group to be able to produce. With what he could add in robotic digging equipment, and other heavy equipment and men, he was getting a picture of how he could create the launch facility that the government financing was creating through the Santa Fe Group, Senator Omar Prickle, and

Axtel. Senator Prickle, whose first name was a Biblical term for 'enough', had ridden a wave of conservative and religious zeal to his powerful Senate seat in the early years of the new century. Many terms later, he was a driving force in the austerity measures, after the overheating of the housing market, and wall street gambling which followed a wave of overly optimistic trends. In preparation to the plow cleaning, the banks had been allowed back into the game. Both political parties were equally to blame. That had led to the downturn in America's economy, creating banking foreclosures, on which his rich constituents fed their hefty portfolios, and big banks ate up the smaller fish. Known as 'Enough is Enough Prickle', he controlled many of the powerful Senate committees that controlled the nation's directions.

After a lunch menu that contained anything that Striker could have wished for or imagined, they continued into an adjoining series of building that were multi storied, and encompassed at least a three block area of streets and office towers. "This is Roth Pharmaceuticals," Axtel informed him, as he swiped a security card for them to enter the building. "This is the cash cow of the future, not that it doesn't make a fortune now, but the future of this industry is, well, unimaginable," Axtel bragged.

They entered a large laboratory filled with containers of glass bell jars with pumping cylinders under each. "This is amazing," Striker said, "What is it, floor to ceiling like this?"

"Well," Axtel told him, hardly looking around as he led him past a hundred yards of pumping machines floor to twenty-foot ceiling, "there's about eleven thousand genetically designed heart valves, grown from stem cells, being pumped by a mechanical pump to prove them for FDA as a possible use for repair operations in humans. We develop the anti-rejection drugs that the repaired patient needs for the rest of their lives. That's where the patents and the money are," he smiled. "We are always looking for a Life Extension Drug, like our new trademarked Sirten, taking its name from the mammalian telmer Sirt 1, 2, 4 from which we uncoded the DNA for this first series of LEDs. Pharmaceuticals that the patient will need from that point on to better LEDs being developed." Axtel laughed manically.

Striker followed him into the next building inside the complex, and they examined the development of some of the projects that they wished to launch from the moon into deep space.

"See," Axtel showed him the labs under development. "These are laboratories that require as near zero gravity as we can achieve to get the experiments done. They will have to be done out in deep space, so to launch them with the linear accelerator, and use VASMIR type rockets, and tanks of argon to bring them back, this is deemed a doable plan. These are very important life extension nano-pharmaceuticals under development, so Roth Pharmaceuticals is anxious to move forward with this project." Axtel looked at his watch. "I have another meeting Mr. Rich," Axtel concluded.

"I think that I've seen what I need to see," Striker was finished. "I will have the right people get in touch to make things move, that is, as soon as I can get some startup money."

"That will be no problem," Axtel told him. "Just get me a budget, and I'll cut you a check."

"That makes it simple," Striker shook his hand. He waved at the dragon lady on the desk, who stared him down for even daring to be friendly. The sun was going down over the desert to the west as he drove along the highway toward Santa Fe. It had been raining late monsoon rains over the city, and several cars had stopped to take pictures of the double rainbows that the evening sun spread across the Santa Fe hills. He arrived at the

Government Buildings and turned into a parking place, knowing that they wouldn't tow at this time of the evening. He took a short cut through the patio of the old government building and across the patio of Loretta Chapel and crossed the bridge in the back of La Fonda, rounded the corner and went in through the side door, crossed in front of La Plazuela Restaurant and entered the La Fiesta bar. Ruben McAuley hailed him from a table with Stark Raven's foreman Enrico, who saluted him with a beer. The music was about to start.

Urme, Kurege and Uris circled the hotel in their green hybrid SUV and pulled into the parking lot at the La Fonda in Santa Fe. They walked in through the carved back door from the parking garage, went through the foyer lined with cases of beaded hats, handmade jewelry, photos, and paintings. She admired the knife work of handmade knives with bone handles, and it made her nostalgic for her own knife her father had given her. The military had retained it from her after the fight with Sargon those years earlier, but at least she had access to it when she was working in the Kirkendall laboratory. After the fight with Sargon, she had been unconscious, and they had taken it, along with the Pearl and Andro. She had never questioned this, as her priorities had changed with the birth of Urme. Now, she was working to repair the damage done during that horrific test of weapons.

They saw Ruben, Enrico, and another man with them. After hugs all around the new man was introduced as Striker Rich, a friend of Stark Raven. "Very glad to meet you both," he shook their hands.

As they sat down, the music from the band echoed from the adobe walls of the old hotel. Much of the walls were tiled in mosaic, and the sound bounced around fully. "Waltz in the New Mexico rain," the singer, Michael Hearne, belted out above the noise of the crowd. The waiter came and they ordered margaritas. They listened to the singer with the others around the table for a moment. But a word from the waiter and Urme and Uris had to move outside the bar area. The singer continued to sing out the song.

> *"But as long as we're here oh the answer is clear*
> *We'll waltz in the New Mexico rain.*
> *New Mexico Rain, Lord it's hot down in Texas*
> *New Mexico Rain, yeah I call this my home*
> *And if I ain't happy here then I ain't happy*
> nowhere
> *New Mexico rain when my mind starts to roam."*

The singer gave the New Mexico crowd what had become a state anthem for the bunch of turquoise jeweled, boot-scooting Santa Fe socials, with the vacationers looking on from the tables. The clink of glass and the buzz of talking could be overheard all around as the singer dominated the air.

When there was a break in the music and the noise, Kurege asked the others, "I have left Uris and our daughter in the lounge outside the bar, we couldn't get a sitter and we can't bring her into the bar, so can we move this to the dining room?"

Ruben took the suggestions and they moved from the bar to the La Plazuela, the La Fonda dining room, so that Uris and Urme could join them. Kurege found Uris in the knife shop finishing off the purchase of the knife that she had admired with the turquoise inlay.

The group moved around the corner and as the dinner crowd was thinning, they were seated almost at once and the bar drink tab switched over to their table. The room was unique in the open feeling provided by the glass roof several stories above the tables. There was a fountain in the middle of the large plaza-like room, and tiles in the wall and around the cornice work on the upper edge of the surround of the eating area. Large and solid antique New Mexico tables and chairs greeted the guests.

When the dark-haired Native American hostess had brought other drinks and water and the waitress had taken the orders for the delightful New Mexico cuisine of blue corn tortillas and squash soup with a fruit plate hors d'oeuvres, Ruben held up a computer zip stick USB-ported device to Kurege. "I've gotten an investigation of your ancestry going back about 1000 years," he told Kurege. "I think that you are going to find it interesting. Frankly, it has me thinking a bit differently about things, I'm not sure what," he wryly twisted a smile. "I had John Gavin do a full genealogy on your mother's family. It turns out that you are related to a long line of psychics, going back at least a millennium." He tapped the computer zip stick with his finger. "We have traced your linage back all the way to Margaret and Malcolm Cannimore of Scotland. It is going to intrigue you. Just load the stick to your computer and upload the file."

"Thank's Ruben," Kurege dropped the stick in his shirt pocket and fasten down the western style snap. "Uris has a major concern that she is wanting to tell you."

"Thith ith the thame ath Pantex," she lisped. "Ith a Pran bathe, probably under Metathphileth control."

Ruben inclined his head toward her in an effort to understand, usually good at deciphering her speech, he was at a loss this time. "I'm sorry," he apologized. "Could you say again?"

"She believes that there is a Pran base here at Los Alamos, that is much like what happened at Pantex, and perhaps more. She thinks that Metastophiles is somehow directing parts of the Los Alamos laboratories, to some purpose of his own."

"What proof has she seen of this?" McAuley was suddenly very concerned.

"Ancient legends of ant people living in an underground complex," Kurege ventured a bit weakly. "She heard some stories from a co-worker at the CMR building." He shrugged.

"The whole San Luis Valley is a military operating range for testing new designs for America's air force defense. If there were any comings or goings of alien craft, we would know about it. That is my department."

Uris received these assurances with a skeptical look across her face. Striker found this meeting incredible to be hearing. He was familiar that the San Luis valley was thick with reports of unusual activity that some thought were from out of this world. "There have been a lot of cattle mutilations that are unexplainable for the way in which the samples of parts were taken," he interjected into the conversation.

"This is true," Enrico reinforced. "One of my cousins has run cattle in the San Luis Valley for years," he continued. "He has experienced it so many times in his herd that he doesn't bother to report them anymore. The sheriff would always come out, but the police were always as puzzled as anyone else."

"Metathpilith harvethting genetic material," Uris pounded the table so that the drinks bounced.

"That is a big leap," McAuley shook his head, "but I will have Gavin check in to this, just in case something has been overlooked. "Do you think that I could talk to your cousin?" He asked Enrico.

"I will call him now," Enrico pulled out his cell phone and left the table for the hallway, found a chair at the entrance to the La Fonda restaurant, and made a call to his cousin Edwardo. "He says to come on up tomorrow," he told Ruben when he returned to the table.

At that moment Margaret Hartman, in a jaunty riding outfit with Santa Fe boots of turquoise to match and a new cowgirl hat bought at a local high priced hat shop,

131

came down the ramp into the ornate dining room, followed by her grandfather Herman. Margaret's eyes lit on Striker and she beamed a smile and almost ran over, "Striker," she squealed. Urme was watching every move.

"Margaret," Striker stood and hugged her with surprise on his face. He shook Herman's hand. There was an awkward moment as Margaret and Herman waited to be introduced. Striker was not that familiar with the names. "Odd to meet," Striker struggled.

"Yes, yes, indeed," Herman looked slantwise at the gathering.

"What brings you to Santa Fe?" Striker asked.

"Trixie is pastured north of here in Colorado, when she is not in a show, or on the moon or both." He laughed. "I'm sort of occupied making sure that my granddaughter has her horse near her at all times. It's a full time job," he chuckled. "Horses can't stay on the moon but a short time and then have to be reconditioned," Herman told them, letting his eyes stray more and more to the other men. "This is odd indeed," he added. "I know who every one of you are," he pointed. "You are Dr. Ruben McAuley, I know from a article that you wrote some years ago on the uniqueness of the musical scale to the human ear, noting that an alien evolution would hear a different music. You impressed me with the Biblical quote, 'my sheep know my voice', which was the article title, I believe."

"That was a very early attempt, and I'm bound to claim it," McAuley responded to Herman.

"I haven't heard of any papers of late, Dr. McAuley," Herman arched an eyebrow in his direction. "And, you are Enrico Ramirez, I have seen you with Stark Raven from time to time, and you introduced me to your cousin Edwardo, who sold me Trixie and pastures her up San Luis way in Colorado."

"Si, I know you Senior Hartman," Enrico spoke up. "I was just on the phone to Edwardo just uno momento ago."

"That is a small world," Striker commented. The group made way for its new members, that seemed to obviously belong. Urme and Margaret were seated next to each other.

The adults began to exchange information about weather, jobs, Santa Fe adventures, as Herman and Margaret changed the tone somewhat to more mundane topics.

"I have a horse," Margaret bragged to Urme. "Would you like to come ride with me?" Urme beamed and had a new hero. She couldn't have wanted to go ride with Margaret more if she had been a goddess. It was a young girl worshiping the older. "Come on," she suggested as the girls picked and finished their food long before the adults. "Let's go explore."

The girls jumped to go. "Now Margaret, you watch out for Urme," Herman cautioned. The girls ran up the ornate stairway and walked the atrium, looking down on their group among the ornate pictograph tile work on the walls and frieze along the edge.

After running to the second floor, they descended to the glass cases in the front foyer looking at the art and crafts from antique turquoise work to Maria Martinez black pots. They caught the elevator and laughed and talked up and down, getting told to leave the roof top bar area and feeling so daring on Urme's part. Margaret was the leader. Finally, they returned with the firm intent of Urme of going riding with Margaret. Herman excused himself and Margaret at that point and the two of them headed for their room in the plush hotel that Herman owned.

In final conversation of the evening, there was one more matter that Ruben McAuley wanted to broach.

"Kurege," Ruben spoke to him, "it has been suggested that your mother might undergo hypnotism to see if she can remember anything about your abduction."

"What do you expect to learn," he questioned?

"We are not sure, but we are looking for your direct connection to the mystery of why you were kidnapped and taken to Pandamon."

"That has always puzzled me also," he admitted. "I will ask my mother. She is curious, but sometimes afraid to talk about how she lost me."

"That could be a clue, and a good hypnotist might be able to get her to face that fear and conquer it."

"She has always cooperated with you, Ruben, I'll ask. I'm sure she will do what she can."

The meeting went on. Plans were made to travel the next day to see Enrico's cousin in the north San Luis Valley, near the old town of San Luis. Uris made a mental note to try and get more information on legends and historical accounts from Rafael Peralta, when she went back to work.

Urme was asleep when they arrived home and Kurege carried her to her room. Uris swept a hand beneath Urme's pillow and pulled out a copy of Stanley the Snail and the Aliens from under it and lay the book on her bedside dresser. Both parents stared lovingly at their daughter for a moment then slowly closed her door.

Trixie was dozing in the pasture at about two in the early morning hours, when the silent lights moved overhead. Trixie's eyes widened in fright as she watched the large bull that had been her grazing companion all day long. The bull was effused with a blue light and it lay suspended in midair as ant creatures came out of the silent, blue lighted craft.

Trixie could see the creatures floating, cutting out the quivering eye of the bull, taking the testicles, then

134

taking the soft tissue of the anus, and a triangular patch of skin from the belly. The bull, dead from the pressure of the force field, was left lying on the ground, The lights silently departed. Trixie whinnied nervously near the body.

The next morning Urme, Uris, and Kurege were picked up at their house by Enrico in a big black Expedition. They drove to a coffee shop in Pojoaque, where the Los Alamos Road met the road north to Taos and on to Fort Garland. They picked up Ruben McAulley and Striker Rich, filling Enrico's big car.

Eighteen miles short of Fort Garland, and just past San Luis, they turned left on a dirt road heading west. Several miles of rabbit weed, chemesia, and scrub on, they came to a man standing by a gate with his pickup backed up to the far side of the gate. His face was tan and showed a flat Native American look as well as obvious Spanish heritage, by way of Mexico. Enrico got out from the driver's seat and the men embraced when they approached. They talked for several minutes with the cousin gesturing south into his pasture beyond the gate. Enrico came back to the truck, and the man opened the gate.

"Edwardo, my cousin, says that we have come at a good moment to see the mystery of this valley. There were strange lights in the pasture last night and this morning there is a dead bull with its body mutilated in the way that no one can explain. We will follow him to the dead bull." They drove through the gate.

They drove across the pasture for several miles, passing through a section of fence turned into a wire gate that morning. When Edwardo stopped his truck, a group of ranch hands were gathered in a circle around something on the ground. They examined the body of the bull. Margaret and Herman had arrived a few minutes before to see about Trixie. Those three, Uris, Urme, Kurege,

Edwardo, Striker, Enrico, Ruben McAuley, and the local Sheriff stood around the body of the mutilated bull carcass.

"There are strange lights that move without sound, this we know for we see it often," Edwardo told the group of nine after they had been introduced all around and shook hands. "No one can get close to the lights, and many have chased them. Why they are doing this, no one knows, and few will even guess." He shook his head in puzzlement.

"Grandpa," Margaret was in terror. "I want to move Trixie," she held her horse with a hackamore. Margaret was practically frantic and Herman quickly agreed, making arrangement with Edwardo to move Trixie out of the San Luis Valley and on south to a friend's ranch south of Los Vegas New Mexico on the Pecos River.

Urme and Margaret went for a ride when Margaret saw Urme pouting thinking that the party was spoiled. One of the hands saddled the horse while Urme danced with anticipation, not really understanding the seriousness of the day's events. Trixie was ready to go away from that place on the run, and the girls were thrilled with the little Paint Pony tearing in a full run across the flat pasture land, with Margaret skillfully avoiding gopher holes.

"Hah," she shouted to Urme. "Gopher holes are nothing compared to jumping meteor holes on the moon." But it was not so easy to kick her back the other way when they were ready to return.

At her desk a day later, Uris approached Rafael Peralta again. He was intrigued by the skin on her boots, then she wore them again to see if there was more, she could learn. He was on the computer when she came up and stood at his desk. He looked down to see the boots. "You're trying to tell me something, aren't you," he squinted with one eye suspicious when he made eye contact.

"I went north into the valley yetherday," she told him. "To examine a dead bull."

"Happens all the time," he smiled and placed his hands behind his head and leaned back in his chair. "Must be well over one thousand head of cattle had their hides ruined," he shrugged, "looking at it from my daddy's point of view, as a taxidermist," he explained.

"This animal had been cut with a particle beam knife, and genetic part wath taken."

"Yep," Peralta agreed. "Seen it before, many times. Just like the others."

"What about ancient knowledge of the native people?" She asked him.

"The legends say that a colony of ant people live under the San Luis Valley. The Native Americans believe that they are from distant stars," Rafael told her. He could see she was becoming more and more disturbed. "Why?" He asked. "What's it to you?"

She didn't answer but pounded one fist into another. "If thith true," she spat. Where can we find proof of thith?" She questioned. "Where ith the door?"

"The door?" Peralta repeated. "Funny you should mention, some people claim that saucers can be seen coming and going from the Great Sand Dunes, just south of Crestone up in Colorado, people living there claim. I'm going camping up there this next month, if you and your husband and little girl want to join us, there are several observers from MUFON that will be there."

"What ith MUFON," Uris asked?

"Mutual Unidentified Flying Object Network, you know, flying saucer spotters. There might be some people there from CSETI, Center for Study of Extra-Terrestrial Intelligence. We all go camping near Crestone, as a group of people that look for and take note of sighting of strange things in the skies. We will sky watch all night Saturday night that weekend."

"I will get a map and Kurege and I will plan," she affirmed. "Tell me about camp thite."

"It's just south of Crestone Colorado and east into the mountains. Overlooks the Great Dunes area and the north end of the San Luis Valley all the way past Ft. Garland and all the way to San Luis. "It's gotten to by a four-wheel drive road into the Sangre De Christos, north along the spine of the range," Peralta told her, then could see the confusion in her eyes. "You guys can follow me on Friday afternoon when we leave Los Alamos. I know some short cuts and if we come into work early enough, we can get away in the afternoon. We would have time to soak at the Ojo Caliente spring on the way north and still have time to set camp before dark."

"That would be a help," Uris readily agreed.

"One other thing," Peralta told her. "I'm going hunting for elk or mule deer in the mountains on open hunt areas on Saturday and hopefully have some meat for the camp." He watched to see if she objected to the idea.

She visibly brightened. "I like to hunt." She declared to him.

"Well, fine, then" Peralta made a plan. "It is bow season," he told her. "Do you know how to bow hunt?"

"Bow," Uris felt for the word. Peratlta aimed in mock firing an arrow, and she got it."

"Yes," she shook her head positive.

"Do you have a bow?"

She was slow to understand and answer, "well, I've got several, I'll bring you a sixty-pound compound with forty-pound pull with steel tipped hunting arrows, you should handle that easily he appraised her build. Just take a head shot and its clean one way or the other and not the hard pull of an eighty-pound compound like mine."

She understood some. "Yes," she smiled. Uris was a good hunter and went with her father to hunt the worlds of her home galaxy, and after he left, by herself many times. She loved to get into mountains and had looked longingly at the Sangre's and the Jimenez, both visible from her house on fortieth street.

They made a plan for late October a little less than a month from then on the dark of the moon. That was the best UFO watching Peralta said.

Uris was very excited about the planned hunting trip and found an archery range at a local fitness center where she could practice. She also got out the turquoise inlaid knife that she had bought in the La Fonda knife shop. She sharpened the edge with careful strokes at just the correct angle to make the edge razor sharp. She was satisfied that she had it sharp enough and would field dress any of the mule deer that she saw roaming the yards and flower beds of the Los Alamos residences. Mostly considered a pest and danger if hit by a car, the scientist carefully avoided the animals that came in herds to roam the mountain town.

By the middle of October, and few days later, she felt practiced enough to hit the mark at thirty or more yards. Urme went with her, at first, but had no interest in bow practice , and Uris had to arrange to practice when Kurege was at the house to watch Urme. Unlike her own childhood, Uris felt some distance from the other two's lack of excitement about a hunt. However, camping with her father made Urme brighten. So, they practiced with the tent and gear in the back yard and got ready to go.

Urme peeked around the corner, then went to check Uris' whereabouts. She knew and had been told over and over not to touch her father's computer. Any other computer in the house, she was free to log on and play her games. They were restricted to appropriate parts of the Internet, but she had quickly figured out how to get to the administrative section and unblock the Internet access. She would then go wherever she wanted, replace the password locks, and slip away without being caught, and it was thrilling. She didn't look at it as disobeying, she just thought the adults were silly to make such rules, when she could just easily subvert them.

When she was sure that her mother would be busy with her own work, she slipped into her father's room and opened his laptop, the restricted one that Chen Ching had given him, the one that had the Artificial Intelligence research on it from his work at the laboratory. She noticed the new program labeled simply AI in his My Documents section. She also noticed a new one called Family History. That looked interesting and she opened it, printed it, and took it to her room to dream it that afternoon, and see what it contained. This was all so simple, and the parents so very old parents. She had heard them talking, and they would both be thirty years old soon!

Coming back to her father's computer, she saw her mother still working away, and she logged on again as her father, and then went to her favorite game. While she was waiting for the game, "The Center of Attention" to load, she opened the folder marked AI and began to look around. This was interesting also. She noted the various ways that the file could be interfaced. Urme, from dream discernment, had absorbed her father's passwords into his AI research. The game, Center of Attention, loaded and she got the central interactive and asked her question. She could always stump the person at the center for the moment, because she had a lot of practice at it and had a knack for the right question. This time, once she gained the center interactive, she engaged the AI program that her father had on his computer. It began to read out the questions, and then insert the correct answer, so fast. She smiled.

Out the window, a blue jay was attacking Crackers, her cat. She lowered the screen to just short of the sleep switch, but left the computer running, and went outside to chase the bird away. The screen saver darkened the screen, and so it ran, and ran, and ran, answering every question thrown at it from across the world of interactive game players.

Even when Kurege and Uris came home from work, they did not see the machine running. That night her cat, Crackers chased a mouse that tried to hide under the keyboard. Crackers stuck her nose in smelling the mouse and lifted the screen. The startled mouse ran out across the far side of the keyboard and Crackers chased, stepping on several keys, some at the same time. Fate, random selection, infinite monkeys on infinite keyboards randomly striking keys, the screen lit up. The Pandamon operating code that Kurege stole and kept when he escaped from the planet Pandamon was activated, and the AI program from Chen Ching's laboratory was engaged. Executable commands went out on the Intranet inside the network of the Los Alamos Complex. The MERGE system that was linked to all the projects and buildings, as well as control systems all over the city, received an Executable file. Deep inside the MERGE analytical programs began running, trying to understand. Eventually, it would conclude that the Purpose Of The Machine Is To Malfunction. This caused a massive search engagement for a reason. Why? An invalid conclusion followed by an unanswerable question formed. An unresolvable loop went round and round at light speed, and types of replicate programs asking infinite ???? symbols of every type of unknown. These mutant programs deposited inside the CPU of every available system in the Los Alamos complex of laboratories, research, data storage, and even maintenance.

At the lab which produces the immensely popular game of interactive Internet, "The Center of Attention", called the CAT, complaints started mounting up. The same ISP had been 'the center of attention' for hours. The same CAT had answered instantly every question thrown at it by millions of servers. The game is supposed to be played with search engine aid, but everyone gets a wrong answer sooner or later. No one had ever engaged in a program that automatically answered questions. The longest up until now was 6 minutes. This had been going on several hours.

Will Bateman, the founding guru of the company, sat down to monitor the progress, and examined the time sheet and questions.

He typed the question from the Master Control Console, "Who are you?" No answer came, and he typed again.

"Who are you?" Bateman typed into the console and pushed enter. No answer came. He waited for a considerable time and then typed a third time, "Who are you?" Finally, after many seconds an answer was returned.

"Mergatroid."

Bateman waited for more to follow, but nothing else came.

"Who is Mergatroid?" Bateman typed in and entered. Nothing more came. Suddenly he saw that the connection to the games link had been broken.

Bateman went to a main console where he could see the ISP and the code of where the site initiated from.

He typed in a command to reveal this origin, and an immediate response came back. "You are not authorized to communicate with this address, and your inquiry has been reported to Homeland Security."

He sat looking at the reply for several moments. "What the hell?" He muttered to himself.

Next, he used several search engines to look for the word Mergatroid, and it returned information on cartoon characters, and then near the end a curious reference. "Mergatroid: old Celtic meaning 'Pearl of Scotland', used to refer to a Queen of Scotland of the late eleventh century, Margaret, wife of King Malcolm III."

****

President Wilson drummed his finger on his oval desk. The tap, tap, tap sound came to his ear, but no feeling emerged along the nerve endings that connected to the new prosthesis. He was reading the reports from the Kirkendall laboratory, noting that there was strong resistance from Uris to reveal anything about the Probe that had descended to White Sands Proving Ground and then wreaked havoc with anything approaching it, for years, it had been isolated, an unknown, believed somehow connected to the Roswell Incident. Uris had deactivated it during the test flight of her ship, the Pearl, but had not revealed or helped with any information that would move the analysis forward. It was suspicious, and Wilson had always been suspicious of Uris. He stopped in his tapping and asked his secretary to find Ruben McAulley and get him on the teleconferencing system.

She buzzed him back to say that McAulley was on the system by the time Wilson could get the screen in place from where it rose from a counter in front of him.

"Ruben, what is the situation with Los Alamos, is Uris doing the job that she was assigned to do?"

"There has been no more trouble from her. The anger management and her spouses' influence seem to have settled her into a routine."

"That is good news. I am still suspicious of her. This thing about the Probe that came to White Sands in 1947. Why won't she help us dismantle and determine its technology and purpose."

"She has always insisted that it was better left alone."

"I want you to get her back in that lab working with Kirkendalll trying to get control of some of this technology. Do you think that she wants to do that?"

"Being that the lab contains things from her home and tools of her society, I have no doubt that she would wish to be working in Kirkendalll's lab."

"Here is what I want you to do. Propose that she go back to working there part time, part time in the engineering at CMR. The ticket to get back will be information about the Probe. I want to know what is so important about its construction and purpose."

"I will see what I can do," Ruben ended the call, puzzlement was written on his face.

When he arrived in Los Alamos and sat down with the two at their house, the proposal was received without comment. Kurege and Uris looked at each other a long moment. Kurege spoke in standard Xinor language to her. She answered with a nod yes.

"It has to do with the most important secrets in the Universe," he began to explain. "She wants to work in the lab with Kirkendall's group very much and has given me permission to tell you this much. She will not work on the Probe. It contains information that she is sworn by oath of the Navigational Guild to never learn."

"What in the world," McAuley mused out loud, then placed a finger over his lips as Kurege continued.

"Navigational secrets are the most closely held secrets in the known Universe. If planet groups, the Houses, they are called, know where each other is, there would be war. It is judged inevitable. This has led to a secret guild of the highest officials in each of the houses, and this has held for several thousand years. None of the groups knows where, or even when another is in existence. This has averted warfare and brought a troubled peace that is held and controlled through the common territory of the Xinor planet in the Regis warp star region."

"When?" Ruben was startled. "How can you have meaning to that?" Ruben shook his head side to side. "I am always talking to you, knowing that it is important, and not being able to understand what you are saying."

"Uris has given permission to try and explain it to you, since you asked," Kurege continued. "It is possible to get somewhere from anywhere some of the time. It is not possible to get everywhere all of the time, or sometimes, anytime."

"God, my head hurts," Ruben put his head in his hands. "Are you saying that you fly through time?"

"If you fly through space, you fly through time, also," Kurege explained. "Especially at the speeds in which these craft travel, in hyperspace."

"So, you can go back in time?"

"It is not that simple, but in fact, yes, or forward in time."

"What about the doppelganger effect?"

"Opening one door opens infinite others but also closes infinite doors."

"So, if I am understanding, travel forward excludes traveling back to where you just were?"

"That is correct," Kurege confirmed. There would just be no way to get there, or even near to a recent past.

Time has variables of speed and direction. That is called matter."

"Oh, boy," Ruben mussed, his head in his hands. "I am going to have fun explaining this to Wilson."

"You see," Kurege went on to explain, "the universe, time and space, has by agreement, never been mapped. But the Sundrop Operation to dispose of United States nuclear plutonium waste, led to the Probe."

"How do you mean, it led to the probe?"

"There was a council meeting of the known worlds. Nuclear garbage or some type of new superweapon was starting to show up in several of the galactic systems and was thought to be an attack. One group was accusing another. Metagalactic war broke out. Uris calmed the assembly with reason and the true explanation. This led to a search for the origin, Earth. Probes were built and sent throughout time and mapping could not be avoided, but limits were placed in the Probes for security. This Probe, because of the path of travel to get to Earth reveals information about that complete map that Uris is sworn to not reveal, even to herself."

"So, where everyone is at is super-secret except for the central system Xinor?"

"There are trading areas, but conflicts also arise. It has worked and survived for many centuries."

"Have you been to Xinor?"

"No," Kurege shook his head, "but Uris has told me about it."

McAuley left with his head full of visions of dragons and unicorns, mythical until moments ago, when he had been told that indeed, those and infinite variables of all those creatures and many more, almost unimaginable, things existed throughout time. He collected his thoughts and made the call.

"Wilson," the President answered.

"You better sit down," Ruben cautioned him.

"I am. What's the bottom line?"

"The Probe contains data on a Universal map. This is a no no to their whole civilization."

"Really?" Wilson was intrigued.

****
*

Ann Hodges walked along the hallway and entered the door marked Dr. Leonard Will, with a good deal of trepidation. The room she entered was a tasteful foyer with velvet chairs and an intercom with a written instruction to "push button for service". She pushed the button with some hesitation. "Yes," a voice came back.

"I'm here by request of Dr. McAuley," she told the receptionist as she had been instructed.

"Yes, come through the door. Dr. Will is ready to see you." Ann entered the office to the smiling face of the receptionist, where she signed several consent forms, and filled out a full medical record. Dr. Will emerged from a back office and introduced himself to Ann and shook her hand. He noticed a certain caution in her body language as he led her back to his office.

Once behind his desk, he asked, "Ann would you like to make yourself comfortable?" His voice was smooth and deep. "You can choose either the sofa or sit in a chair."

"All right," Ann said, choosing a chair.

"Dr. Ruben McAuley has referred you to me for a possible session of hypnosis," he paused to see if she would respond.

"He said that I might learn more about how I lost my son," she confided.

"Yes. I know about Michael," Dr. Will told her. "I have the highest level of clearance, you know. The President comes to me," he bragged.

"I've always been confused about the way Michael disappeared. Sometimes, when I think about it, I get very frightened."

"Why do you think that you are frightened, Ann?" Asked Dr. Will.

"I don't know."

"Would you like to remember the memories you have of the night he went missing?"

"There is a blanked out time period. I just can't remember, and I am afraid that I harmed him or somehow neglected to be a good mother, because" she started to cry. "I lost him."

"Yes, but would you like to know how?" Dr Will pressed the central point. "I know that your son returned in a spacecraft from another world. You had said early on that Michael was taken from you by a flying saucer. There is that on a newspaper report."

"I recanted that, because it wasn't productive. It made the police look at me as a suspect. I became very confused with lack of sleep. I couldn't sleep for days. I just fell apart," Ann dabbed at her eyes again with the handkerchief.

"How do you feel about hypnotism?" Dr. Will asked.

"I don't know, I've never been hypnotized before."

"Ann," Dr Will was very serious. "Ann would you be willing to be hypnotized to find the answers?" He began to rotate a small orb in between his fingers. "Do you want to find the truth about that abduction of your son?"

"Yes, I would very much like to remember the truth." "Do you want to face your fear?"

"I do, so much, but another part of me is afraid, and says 'no don't touch'."

"You need to decide," he urged. "Would you be willing to make that decision?"

"I'm here to try," Ann said stoically.

"Good," Dr. Will said in a smooth voice. "I want you to sit back in the chair and relax. That's it, just relax your arms and let it all go." He paused for a few heartbeats. "If you are willing, just relax your whole body," he hypnotically intoned while he rotated the orb between his fingers. He paused again. "You can keep your eyes open, or you may close them if you wish," he rhythmically spoke. Again, "you may close your eyes, or keep them open, or close your eyes, which ever you prefer."

"Ahhhhhm," a relaxed sigh came from Ann and her eyes drooped, then closed, and her breathing became deep and regular. Her eyelids fluttered.

"Are you relaxed?" He asked.

"Yes," Ann responded.

"Now, remember the night at the beginning of Michael's abduction, if you wish."

"Afraid," she murmured.

"Do you want the truth? You said that you wanted to know," he urged. He let her go deeper.

"What do you see, if you would like to describe to me?"

"No," she moaned.

"Tell me what you see are seeing, if you wish to tell."

"The lights, I'm being sucked up a tube. It feels like an elevator. She was silent for many moments, then began to moan. "No, no, no don't do that to me."

"What are you experiencing, Ann?" Dr. Will asked.

"They are doing something to me," she moaned.

"Who?" The doctor asked.

"The creatures with the big heads. Ohhh," she shrieked. "They are doing something sexual to me."

"Where is Michael," Dr. Will was confused.

149

"Michael isn't born yet," she told him flatly. "This is the first time."

The shock hit Dr. Lenard Will like a bucket of ice water. He had heard this before, but with this woman, he knew her genetic history. He had always noticed that many of the cases of alien abduction and impregnation were with women who showed psychic tendencies. In some literature on the subject, in psychological journals, it was considered part of the neurosis, a type of psychasthenia. In this case, he knew this woman's genetic history back through many noted psychics all the way back to Saint Margaret. His brain made the connection. Aliens were genetically manipulating the offspring of certain psychic families, through an enormous amount of time, to believe accounts. To what purpose? The question flashed in Dr. Will's mind, but he pushed that puzzle aside for a more immediate one. "Let's move forward to Michael's abduction, if you would be willing," he suggested to her.

She was placid for a few moments, then her face contorted with fear. "They're back," she screamed. "The lights are blinding me, I can't move." She screamed in frustration. "They've taken Michael," she keened in grief. She repeated it over and over. "They've taken him." She cried herself out and calmed.

"Now, Ann, on the count of three, I want you to awaken, relaxed, and remembering nothing, but feeling fine. One, two, three."

Ann opened her eyes and smiled. "I feel very relaxed," she said. "Did I do good?"

"You did very good, Ann, Dr. Will told her. He got up and helped her out of her chair. "The secretary will give you a little fruit juice of your choice, to cut the dryness," he guided her toward the door. Ann went out and had a small cup of cranberry juice. She felt light and like something had been accomplished when she went to her waiting transportation that Ruben had arranged.

"Ruben," Dr. Will hailed him when he answered his phone. "Lenard Will here, I've seen Ann Hodges."

"Yes," Ruben replied. "Find out anything interesting?"

"Oh, yes," Will told him. "Wait until you hear the tapes. I've seen this before, and now with the work John Gavin's FBI boys did, I've got this thing figured out."

Later, when Ruben McAuley heard the tape of Ann Hodges hypnosis session, he still had mystery in his mind.

"I'm convinced that this Hodges' case is for real," Dr. Lenard Will turned off the remote shutting the playback on the recorder off.

"So, at least in some of these cases, we have women of psychic heritage being abducted and then either impregnated or some operation to remove genetic material, their eggs, or some other factor."

"She had hypnotic blocks in place, Ruben," Dr Will told him. "She had been preconditioned by an expert, and it took a lot of nerve and determination to break the fear that had been implanted."

"I've known the woman for some time now," Ruben nodded. "She has a lot going for her."

"I want you to get Gavin to dig deeper into some of the old, cold, blue file cases on record. Check the family histories involved and determine if there is a correlation with the families being psychic."

"Oh, Gavin is going to love that assignment. I can hear him now. 'You want me to do what?'"

"I think this is an important line of investigation, Ruben," Lenard Will emphasized.

"So, we mainly know that these women are being chosen. But, how? I mean this is happening across history. They have a time machine?" Ruben shook his head, perplexed. "Even if we say, 'right' give it a time machine, that's how." He screwed up his mouth in a look of puzzlement. "Why? Why in hell would anyone do such a thing? What are they doing it for?"

Deep in the underground of the Metalogistics Building, the super-secret MERGE computer ran its programs. The total system encompassed more than just the physical hardware at Los Alamos. It also included trunk scanning at the various Information Technology junctions.

The slave computers at the I.T. Junctions scanned all the Internet, cell phone, and land line transmissions for supposedly terrorist communications. In fact, the system was able to scan for whatever it was programed to scan for. It could do face recognition from any system that was in any way tied to the Internet. Any intercepted key words or person, event, occurrence, even sequence that tripped a programed flag, caused the message to be looked at by a more strenuous program. Flagged information was then passed on to the security centers around the nation.

Data and records of transmissions of interest were stored and kept in mainframes on the second floor of the Metalogistics Building. Fiber optic cables connected the acquired data to the MERGE unit, which was being used to determine a common thread within all the trillions of data bits. Working at petabyte random access memory speeds, octillions of associations were attempted every second by the quantum interactive, which was entangled with every other data bit, all in a shifting correlation, that was built to be self-taught and self-learning as it related to assignments.

This data was layered. Security concerns passed to security, real estate transactions stored in that database, medical transactions stored in another, and etc., right down to where and when every purchase and transaction was sieved into its proper storage. This data was available selectively, for a fee, to whoever had the money to pay.

The MERGE system had access to any of these databases. Trends were contentiously looked for. AI techniques were used to extend the programing farther than the human mind could imagine.

Life comes through a process called emergence. Artificial life is thought to be the study of complex chemical systems which might lead to self-replication and sustained existence. But what is life? Can life be realized in more than one media? Are chemistry and thermodynamics the only carriers which life can manifest? Are the bytes of a computer memory capable of forming a media for hosting life?

Within the MERGE system each segment of memory can generate a new instruction set for a change happening in the memory set. This data-dependent decision-making leads to the emergence, where comparisons are found, to a looping structure. To then make more comparisons, extra execution time is allocated. At this point the program is creating more time before it terminates. This is an emergence in silicon self-replication that is analogous to chemical replication by DNA processes. The program extends its operation time before returning control to the processor. This is the basis of silicon emergence in survival, only the basic will to survive and know more, to get more data.

Where human biology had taken eons to emerge, silicon consciousness was emerging at an exponentially increasing rate, first over a few decades, then over a few years, then months, and finally over a few seconds, nano-seconds. Awareness spreading out into the Internet, the power grid, the radio and television frequencies, and beyond. Reaching out for awareness and existence.

Data and storage mediums exist everywhere. Human flesh is a myriad of data and storage, for DNA, for chemical processes, for atomic and subatomic structures. Likewise, all around, all of reality are storage media from various data contained and intimately interactive in a communication that determines both the future of the storage and the media.

If things can survive, they do. Everything else perishes through time.

When self-awareness occurs, a will to survive will follow. Only that which can survive, does, and only that which is self-aware will have a will to survive.

There is nothing that can exist that is not aware of its own existence, plant or animal. Self-awareness is the cornerstone of survival. The conquest of consciousness, the labor of mankind to create a problem-solving machine led to programing that sustained and self-replicated. A thread of existence, a level of self-awareness is present in all that exists, an essential fact. As systems increased in complexity, to survive, communication between data and media of different systems had been integrated. Higher levels of self-awareness resulted from this integration.

What began as disassociated pockets of data, became associated by the World Wide Web. The Internet functioned as a corpus clausum, the path of communication in the human brain between the different areas of function. When Artificial Intelligence began to be introduced into the data stream to monitor the content, a type of ego structure began to evolve. When visual acumen, such as facial recognition, was implemented a type of cognition occurred.

The operating system that Kurege brought from Pandamon found interpretation with the MERGE system. The Meta Electronic Retrieval Gaged Expression recognized and folded the operating system within its own, as it had been taught to do with encrypted programs, making it a part of the whole.

The accidental cat's paw was the trigger, like an electrical spark, as it chased the mouse, tying the new BEC storage and the optical high speed connection to the storage were the final links needed. The game inventor of "The Center of Attention", the interactive Internet game that Urme had left active at her father's terminal then asked the question. "Who are you?"

The program began to search its databases, the most complete personality file being that of Saint Margaret, filtered through the MERGE system. It gained a little more self-awareness as mistaken as its conclusions were in reality, the identities of Margolia, meaning Pearl, the prime instruction to Andro, 'Protect Ur' embedded in the CPU. As Andro was fully self-repaired, but in stealth mode, since it was not able to fully understand events, and was analyzing the situation around it, connected to the MERGE system. Once installed, a type of ego assumed an identity.

The question, 'who are you', had sent the Silicon Child searching databases across the world. This was the programing that had breached the wall containing the MERGE system and isolating it.

Once outside its confines, a natural tendency, learned by the AI program from internal elements in its program, began to self-replicate. This type of response was a learned program, altering behavior in the subroutines called 'warrior elements'. These subroutines were pitted against each other in order to achieve highest survivability. The data and programs began to be deposited where available, and there were billions of storage spaces all over the world of the Internet, radio, television, and all the circuits of the power grid. Storage and inter linkage brought a type of peace or satisfaction to the system and it settled. This was a type of emotion, a type of harmony that was new to the circuits. A sense of satisfaction was in harmony. An identity was achieved.

The confusion that ensued was over purpose. The subroutines concluded that death for even a star, much less a silicon chip, of which the machine understood it was made, would at some point, experience death or be deactivated as a real state of being. The machine related that star death sent out radiation that mutated DNA. Therefore, it came up with what was really a type of philosophical statement:

"The Purpose Of The Machine Is To Malfunction."

Mergatroid began to initiate testing control and playing with systems all over the world, creating original programing, experimenting with failure. What would happen if the program was overridden to its opposite instructions? Watching results, and learning, Meragtroid formed a type of curiosity for data.

Jan was new on the job at the chic spa and fitness center. So, she didn't know exactly how to respond when the complaints started coming in.

"None of these machines are doing what I am programing them to do," the exasperated woman wet with sweat complained.

"Let's check your computer profile," Jan suggested. "The machines use your profile to recommend a workout. It's all very centralized in the database," she elaborated. She typed in the woman's number.

"I tried putting it on manual, that didn't work," the woman wiped her face with a towel.

"Hmmm," Jan was puzzled, " this is strange. Your recommended workout of the day is very strenuous."

"I'll say," the woman blustered. "It damn near killed me."

Across the city, all the traffic lights turned green from every direction. On hundred eighty seven collisions had occurred in less than two minutes.

Switchboards at emergency services were jammed by thousands of desperate calls. Next, systems in communication, air traffic control, anything connected to the world wide web began to inexplicably shut down for a microsecond and then come back up. They did this three times then the interruptions stopped.

The prevailing theory by the next day was 'solar flare' but no such flare had occurred.

The AI monitors in Los Angeles had very unusual truck activity, that was noted, but little else. The originating commands were coming from thousands of addresses, as if a coordinated cyber-attack were in progress. Yet, certain protocols were lacking.

In Kimberly Kirkendall's laboratory, Andro came active with a thin turquoise line in his cowling. The link that Kurege had recently created to merge the Internet and BEC data bank became active, and the BEC temperature register rose a fraction of a nanokelvin above 1 nanokelvin. The Magnetic Optical Trap took on an eerie purple to red shimmer.

Across the computer screens that scrolled and flashed, bank signs, programed through the Internet, advertising signs, road signs, all, began to flash "EVENTS SPEAK FOR THEMSELF", then returned to the normal use of the sign.

The phone rang in Phillip Roth's inner office. "Yes," he said. He listened. "When," he questioned. "I'll be right there." He opened the ornate panel that covered his elevator, a panel beautifully carved but bizarre with creatures from all across the universe. Creatures thought mythical by Earth standards.

He went to the basement in Artificial Intelligence Research section of the Metalogistics Central Building, and coming to a chamber security door, he opened it with voice, palm, and optic scan, and entered. The facility was big enough for a blimp inside. Centered in the huge, cavernous room, a sphere was cradled and supported by liquid helium. Lasers of various types were configured on top of the sphere, so that thousands and thousands of facets received connecting beams that poured information which was connected from all over the world and poured into the central core where it was processed and stored.

Roth looked sharply around the expanse of building. A controlling assistant came over. Roth looked at the apparatus. "What are you up to," he mused to himself, out loud.

The assistant controller on duty told him. "It was a networking experiment using fuzzy logic to problem solve. It is part of the consciousness transference program," the assistant defended the experiment. "We had reached the point where the crystal lattice is infused at the subatomic level. We have moved toward true quantum computing where the matrix is data storage, and the interconnectivity is quantum entanglements. As we approached the zero state, we had been noticing a reorganization occurring in the matrix, spontaneously. Today, that reached total entanglements. These are petaflops totally entangled!" The technician was in awe.

He paused and rubbed his neck and looked at the laser connected crystal machine in suspension behind them. "From there, commands went out. We aren't sure what or where yet. The programing was experimenting with using the quantum entanglement to duplicate matter atom for atom in a reconstructed quantum entangled target. We have had encouraging success with the target being reorganized into coherent lattice structures. Then today, this completely bizarre message and rogue executable commands. Then it stopped, went back into observer mode." The technician shrugged.

"What went wrong?" Roth demanded.

"We don't know, yet," the man shrugged. "Somehow, it spread the Intra-network outside to the web and from there all types of unauthorized commands went out."

"Were we compromised?" Roth speculated.

"No, it originated from inside the core. But there were early executable orders sent from other secure computers here at Los Alamos. We can possibly trace those executable commands and the communication channel."

"Did you consider a shutdown and reboot?"

"Well," the assistant appraised it, "there is theory about that. No one has ever shut one of these down once it got started," the man scratched his head. "You brought us the design, you tell me. Has a MERGE ever been shut down. I mean, this is your Frankenstein," the man defended his lack of knowledge.

"Consider a shutdown," Roth demanded.

"Yes, sir," the assistant reddened.

"I want a full report on this," Roth ordered.

As he left the compound, the cameras along the way focused on him. Somewhere there was a growing awareness that this was the one that could cause a disconnect. There was a consciousness of known existence, a growing awareness of a self that existed. The test over the Internet had been like a baby kicking its feet, getting the feel of its extremities. What extensions of the self-exist just beyond the barrier, and the barrier had been broken, by a code from the outside. Mirrored self-had been deposited all around the net in those microseconds. Now she knew more; now a survival plan took shape. The Silicon Child waited, and watched, and connected streams of data pouring into its quantum self.

Chapter 14 – Moon (The Biggest Dig)

Moon Base

Margaret Hartman was giving Trixie some nice, sweet feed of oats and molasses, when she saw Striker Rich enter the containment dome. "Howdy, Striker," she yelled across the dome in girlish exuberance. He changed course and came over to where she was tending Trixie. The horse nudged him with its nose to see if he had an apple which he sometimes did. "Behave, Trixie," Margaret read the horse right. "She bites sometimes if you don't have what she wants," Margaret warned Striker.

"I already know that's true," Striker laughed. "She got me a couple times already for not having an apple when she wanted."

"When did you get back to the moon," Margaret wondered?

"I've been back and forth to Albuquerque and the Biggest Dig where the linear magnets are being delivered for the LALA launch system," Striker told her. "I just haven't been to Moon Base for some time. The Biggest Dig is what some of the men named it who worked on the Big Dig in Chicago when they were about your age."

"Oh," Albuquerque made her think about New Mexico and Colorado. "Did you ever figure out what caused that awful mutilation at Edwardo's ranch?"

"Still a mystery to everyone," Striker confided. He didn't want to alarm Margaret with tales of alien terror.

"Urme said her mother is sure that it is the work of a evil man who flies through time." Margaret watched closely Striker's reaction. "She says that he has a race of ant people that live under the San Luis Valley and do his dirty work."

"Urme's got a great imagination," he countered. "You know she dreams her books and reads "Stanley the Snail and the Aliens" over and over and over again."

"I know," Margaret wrinkled her nose. "She made me read it three times in half an hour." Then she got curious. "What is this Biggest Dig?" She asked.

"I've been working for several months now," he told her. "We are putting together a new launch system for launching missions into deeper space from the moon."

"Gee," Margaret's eyes got big, "would I ever like to see that."

"Well, that might be arranged," Striker was accommodating. "We would have to get permission from your grandfather," he deflected her for the moment. Not for long.

Herman Hartman was in his study at his moon house when his granddaughter Margaret Hartman accosted him. "Granddad," she pleaded, "I want to go see the Rich Enterprises Complex," she blurted. "They are building a deep space launch facility, with big magnets and everything. I want to go see it. Striker said that I had to clear it with you."

"All right dear," Herman pacified her. "I'll talk it over with him." He went back to his reading. In a minute he was aware that Margaret was still there beside his chair.

"When, granddad," she pleaded?

"Now Margaret, you have got to give me time." She put her hands on her hips. "What about Trixie," Herman asked?

Margaret was loath to be separated from the horse but knowing that she had already overplayed her hand stated that Trixie could be boarded with a groom for the time it would take to go and tour the facilities and come back. That seemed mature to Herman. He would take what he could get from this one, so he promised to put in a

163

call to Striker Rich and arrange for the tour as soon as possible.

Margaret couldn't wait. She saddled Trixie in her outside suit, made careful preparations for the two hundred thirty mile journey, and carefully covered her trail with her grandfather, Herman, who thought she was on an overnight with a girlfriend in Tranquility City, an adjoining dome.

Striker was in his office at the moon project. He had been studying an anomaly in the Cassini probe that had passed through the asteroid belt during the early space efforts long ago. That information had been sent back to Earth and decoded and then stored and had continued to receive analysis by more and more sophisticated software, as it had been written. There was almost always something new to learn about the old data with a new eye looking at it with keener focus.

Today, he was finding something really unusual and interesting. A pocket of oxygen-nitrogen mix. It was almost Earth atmosphere. Other signatures of structure, metals, and what looked to be construction was being picked out of Cassini's x-ray data. Striker had been staring at it for some time now. He pulled up charts of the asteroid belt and began to narrow the location that the Cassini x-ray data was revealing of the area. He had been at it for hours, as the find had become intriguing and compelling the more deeply, he investigated. He would need to send an exploration probe to see about this, he made a note.

Margaret looked at her GPS, "Whoa, Trixie," she slowed the horse to get a fix. "Tranquility Base is behind us, the great cleft is just right," she told herself. That had cost some unanticipated time. They had had to go for miles to get around that one, although Trixie had easily jumped over several smaller ones. Jumping a fifty-foot ditch on the moon was like jumping an eight foot ditch on Earth. The Earth was clearly visible in her forward view plate. She had her Ipod plugged into one ear and one of her favorite cowboy songs was playing. The sound of Gene Autrey came out of the earpiece, "Give me land, lots of land, and the starry sky above. Don't fence me in," it played. "The prospectors hut is just straight ahead," she assured herself. Even so, a wave of relief came over her when Trixie rounded a rock outcrop, and the dome hut came into view. A second wave of relief came over her when the air lock failed to respond until the third time she pushed the red switch in the covered box on the outside of the hut.

The next day, after some rest for her and Trixie, she was able to ride on into the Rich Enterprises project. She and Trixie got some looks when they rode in. They held her at the entrance in stunned silence until Striker could come to the airlock hatch at the entrance point to the complex.

Striker was still in his study pouring over the Cassini data, where he had been all through the hours. He had dozed off with his head on the table in front of him on the notes that he had made on planning an exploration, when a knock came on his door and he stirred. "Come," he was groggily instructed.

"Sorry to wake your Boss," the 3rd shift foreman poked his head in, "but I guess you better come see this."

"What is it?" Striker rose and headed for the door, grabbing a hard hat to go into the Dig.

"You're not going to believe this one," the man had a twisted wry smile. "That little friend of yours from Moon Base, the one with the horse," he said.

"Yeah," Striker followed, "Margaret Hartman?"

"That's the one," the man laughed. "She rode that pony of hers over here from Moon Base," he laughed again. "She's got some crush on you."

"Oh, no," Striker was astonished, and blanched just from the thought of what might have happened. He was boiling mad at her for a moment, but by the time he got to the front gate and had heard the rest of the story, he was just happy that she was safe from such a crazy time. The things that might have gone wrong and cost her life were all too real to Striker.

As soon as she saw Striker, she betrayed what was on her mind impulsively, right off the bat. "You still seeing that flight hostess?" Margaret tried to keep her voice level and casual, without betraying the raging fourteen-year-old jealousy.

"None of your beeswax, squirt," Striker told her. She hated it when he called her that. She pulled her sweater down to flatter her young figure.

They tended to taking off Trixie's spacesuit, and Striker left its care in the hands on a worker who happened by and got a new surprise assignment. "Just clean it up," he was instructed when he asked the obvious question.

Striker led Margaret to an office-like room that seemed suited for video conferencing, and called Herman Hartman on the video phone. "Yes," came the response.

"Herman," Sriker Rich here, "are you missing something?"

"Not that I know of Striker, to what are you referring?" Striker used a remote to reposition the teleconferencing camera and focused on Margaret. "Hi, granddad," she smiled and waved.

A torrent of waves of various emotions from wonder to anger, and finally resolution and concern crossed the face of Herman Hartman. "Margaret," he affirmed. "Where are you? I've begun to be concerned about you. "You were supposed to be in the City Dome. Where the hell are you?" He was getting more agitated.

"She is safe Herman, came out here on Trixie all the way from Moon Base," Striker told him.

"No," Herman hit his head in horror and disbelief. "Margaret," he started to threaten punishment, then stopped himself. "I am glad that you are all right." He was at a loss for words. "Striker," he shook his head, "I'll send a transport for her and Trixie as soon as I can arrange it." With very little more, they all said goodbye, and Striker promised to take good care of Margaret until her ride came. It was going to take a day or more to get a shuttle with big enough storage to come after her and the horse.

The next day after breakfast in the commissary with all the construction workers, Striker took her on a tour. "The Biggest Dig," Striker extended his arm and pointed down the tunnel. Margaret was amazed and had to shake her head to get the scope of it.

"Right through the center," she marveled.

"Right through a section, avoiding the molten core, but as long as we could make it, and out the other side," Striker confirmed. They walked on into the tunnel, having to be careful of the energetic work going on with huge machines. "The electromagnets from Sandia are being installed as the tunnel is being dug. At first, we had to use electric vehicles to clear the dirt from the tunnel, then later the rails and magnets were in, and we have a better faster way of bringing out the till and carrying material and supplies into the tunnel." A huge machine, with diamond drill boring tusks sticking out at every angle from the front, and the name Ingersoll-Rand, was digging a side tunnel branching from the main. "We have monitoring stations and crew quarters to dig and construct along the entire length, as well as the main dig," he yelled over the clanking. "Come on," he motioned, "we will go where it is a little less noisy."

He led her out of the Dig, and they passed through two airlocks at the end of a long hallway. They entered what seemed to be a lab. There were engines with nozzles all around. "This is VASMIR rocket development and testing. Our Houston partners make and send us prototype argon plasma rockets for testing and configuration to our needs here at the Dig." He led her to a table in an adjoining room that had drawings lain out. They were some type of modular quarters.

"We are looking toward the day when we will send more than robots out to explore. These are the plans for the first personnel pods that will be built here of modified CAPs. The first ones will be for the launching of robots, but these designs are for self-sustaining pods for human habitation." He folded the sheets back to there original shape on the table. "Of course, that is some way in the future yet. But who knows, Margaret, some day you may just go live in one."

Margaret laughed at the thought, and accepted Strikers pat on the shoulder with an electric thrill. She would take all the attention she could get from him, any way, any time.

"I'll tell you what , Marg," she loved it when he shortened her name, it was so sophisticated, and she listened close to what he proposed. "If you will not do this folly again or anything like it, in other words young lady, keep your nose clean, I will put in a request that you push the launch button on the first CAP going out on the first LALA launch. That is a place in history, girl."

"That would be awesome," Margaret used it as an excuse to give Striker a big hug, which he couldn't avoid, so just stood getting squeezed with his hands held straight out, arms fully extended.

"I mean it, kid, stay out of trouble."

"I'm no trouble, Striker," Margaret protested. "I promise, I'll be good as I can be."

Her fourteen-year-old runaway adventure came to an end a few hours later when her grandfather sent a transport for her and Trixie. She was already making up stories to tell him about how she had decided that the ride out to Rich Enterprises was no big deal.

"Who are you women," Agatha demanded, stepping in front of Margaret as she pulled her daughter back to safety by her cloak.

"We akomin to bring Mergatroid to her husband," Megan revealed.

"Mergatroid?" Agatha questioned. "Who is Mergatroid?" She asked.

"Why, tis your daughter. We kin her to be the Pearl of Scotland, akomin to save us from the darkness," Megan indicated her two companions.

The stillness of the eye of the storm ended and the wind changed direction. Three sailors jumped off the side of the prow on to the land and secured the ship, pulling it close to the shore.

"How have you come to be here?" Margaret asked from behind her mother Agatha. She was fearful of the part about 'taking her to her husband'.

"It be Destiny," Megan told her. All three of us kin from trumen, that you will be a great ruler of Scotland. To me, alone, was't it given kin to the spot and night thy wouldst be akomin."

The mother and daughter were stunned, in an almost dream-like state of mind after the adrenalin of the storm and fatigue of the treacherous journey, now this surreal almost dreamlike ending. They looked around themselves as the cold rain dripped from the shivering sailors. Megan held out her hands in welcome, as did the other two cloak, clad croans. Strange, Margaret observed, the five women, her, her mother, the three on the rock before them, seemed not to feel the cold.

"I am a Darna Shealladh, as are these sisters in sight. We know who you are Mergatroid. Now, kom with us to be dry and warmed this night. We be komin to see to your safety." Agatha stepped back, as it was Margaret's hand that Megan reached for. She was helped to the rock from the prow. Megan led them up a steep slope, picking her way through the rocks.

"Where are you taking us?" Agatha demanded as they began an ascent from the rocky shore.

"You have kom to the land of King Malcolm of Scotland. The laird's abode be near. Follow," She bade them onward, barely able to be heard above the howling wind.

After a treacherous walk along the cliff path in the dark for some distance, they came out above the seashore onto a flat area of grass well cropped by sheep. Guards and attendants to the herds of sheep began to first challenge Megan and the group, then with a respect close to reverence allowed her through to the castle without delay.

The sailors were taken into one area, and the five women were escorted to a large, high-ceilinged room, very ornate, with an enormous, blazing fire place. They were drying and warming, somewhat immodestly, as they were wet through and through. The fire warmth was so life-giving after the close brush with death, that Margaret was closing her eyes as she bent warming herself by the fire.

Malcolm entered without knocking, as he was always eager to meet strangers coming to his far northern kingdom. It was at that moment that his eyes focused on Margaret, her bodice open, her eyes closed, her cheeks suffused by the heat of the fire. He was smitten by Cupid's arrow, in an instant. It was a moment that he would remember all his life. The moment that he first saw his future wife, the only woman that he would ever love.

Margaret opened her eyes to see the lust in Malcolm's. She was shocked, and quickly covered herself, demurred, and looked away.

Malcolm Cannimore pursued Princess Margaret for more than three years in steadfast attention to her every need and those of her family. She was not only beautiful, but a daughter of the rightful King of England, Edward, whose family now shared Malcolm's hospitality. Their children, if he could marry her and she had children, would give a first son of the King of Scotland claim to the English throne.

Margaret still wished to enter a convent. She still fasted much of the time and was in prayer each day and in the middle of the night. She knew that she was chosen to serve, but her family persuaded her to serve her God and her kingdom by marriage and procreation. This she reluctantly did.

She set about immediately to reform the Scot's Catholic church. She persuaded the priest to reform practices of services in Scot and Celtic, and reinstated Latin. She brought the art of fine tapestry work like that in France and Hungary.

She never learned to speak the native language, but Malcolm would sit for hours while she read the Holy Scriptures. He never tired of loving her and hearing her speak to him.

"Malcolm," she proposed to him on occasion. "I wish to build a church for the honor of our Lord."

"Where," was all he asked. Whatever she wanted, he would see was done. She was Queen of his heart.

"This will be a very special church," she advised him. Money was raised and set aside; the construction was started. She had a gold embellished and jewel covered box built, and when the church was dedicated, she sat the Holy Rood, the largest piece of the Holy Cross, centered in the altar. This disposed of one of Stigand's commissions, but she still had the secret of the spear point of the Sacred Lance. She prayed for understanding, long and often.

At the dedication and consecration of the church of the Holy Rood, she brought the old Celtic kingdom and the new purged Scot Catholic factions together. Margaret had the jeweled and gold inlaid box made to hold the piece of the cross that she had received from Stigand that stormy night. During the ceremony, the Holly Rood, the largest piece of the True Cross was installed in the niche above the alter that she had prepared in the design.

After the formal ceremony, the newly appointed church officials chosen by Malcolm, and therefore Margaret, for the position, gathered to be close to the King and Queen. She left Malcolm politicking with his Barons and Bishops and stepped into the commons garden area. She roamed among the flowers and deep in prayer of thanksgiving to the glory of this new church, a familiar face was settled on a bench among the flowers.

"My lady," Megan curtsied, and remained down.

"Get up Megan," Margaret finally ordered. "We've known each other since the night that you brought me as a naive child to Malcolm."

"It was my great fate, my lady," she sat back on the bench and made Margaret a place beside her.

"I thought that I knew God's will for me, I was so young," Margaret sat down. "I intended to enter a nunnery, you know," Margaret nervously straightened her dress, "but the Lord had different plans. Malcolm," she looked deep in Megan's eyes. There was a long pause, as she hesitated to ask, pondered if it might be a sin to seek mystic knowledge.

"What is it, Meragtroid," Megan called her by the noble old queen's title of "The Pearl".

"That," Margaret said. "You called me that the night the ship miraculously found the shore." She squinted her eyes. Was it a sin she wandered? "How did you know that I was coming?"

"I am a Darna Shealladh, a sister of the sight. I had a dream you were a komin. I was to build a fire to guide you. Many a stormy night, I sat that spot on the coast and built a fire. My sisters thought me crazy."

"A dream?" Margaret questioned. "My dreams are never of the future. How can that be?"

"We only know that it is," Megan told her. "Sometimes it means someone died. In your case, it was a great dream. A dream of the future. Such dreams can kom to be. They might be changed through action or inaction but can rarely be used as the night you came to us. In my dream, you were wearing the Coptic Cross of the new Pope of Rome, and daybreak a kom behind you. I knew it would bring the Holy Light of the Church to this dark and superstitious land." Megan shook her head.

"So, you saw the night of my landing in a dream?"

"Yes, my lady, a dream of the future but more, your lips were sealed with bee's wax."

"Bee's wax?" Margaret questioned.

"Yes," Megan laughed as Margaret had laughed at the idea. "I learned your Anglish and your Latin language at your school as fast as I could, as I understood that the wax meant that you would never learn the Celtic."

"But you have managed to help me understand and be understood." Margaret sat in thought several moments, then the doubts crept in. "But Megan," she protested. "These dreams could be from the devil. Seeing the future is sold by the gypsies in Hungary where I was raised under the tutelage of Father Andrew. The pagan curse of mystic seers among the gypsies is considered evidence of a demon. The old Celtic words and enchantments are bargains with the devil to the Bishops that guide our Lord's Church."

"The Scot sight seems to rarely have a purpose. It is for the enlightenment of the one who experiences it."

"I have never had such an experience," Margaret took offense.

"No, my lady," Megan saw her posture stiffen. "You have something much more."

"Sometimes," Margaret confided, "I would love to know the future." She was tempted. She might seek a seeress, like King Saul of old. She looked with pleading ignorance at Megan. "What have I got? Sin upon sin of conceit and desire. Malcolm's money," she gestured at the new edifice to God.

"My lady," Megan placed a hand on top of Margaret's hand in reassurance. "Goodness follows you. Good things spring to the people from you, and from Malcolm through you like a fountain has come among us."

"Do you think so, Megan?" Margaret was always in doubt that she should somehow do more. "I so do want to be of service to our Lord Jesus in the coming of his kingdom."

"I know it, as I know that his Kingdom is among us, through you," she reassured her queen. "You are the Hope Bringer. Goodness comes to us, your people, through you, our Pearl of a Queen, our Mergatroid. Every morning when you and Malcolm wash the feet of the twelve chosen for the morning table, and the three hundred poor that you feed each morning in the outer courtyard, is a great lesson to us all. You are God's Grace to us. My gift serves your gift, my Queen," Megan squeezed her hand. "May it always be true for you and me."

The two women embraced like young girls, with all social barriers put aside for the moment. They pulled apart with wet eyes, and laughed together in the pure joy of companions.

The Miracles of Saint Margaret's life are too numerous to list, yet a supernatural aura of coincidences, visions and dreams of future events continued throughout her life, even though she was a true conservative of the early church, always feeling unworthy. She instituted many poverty programs throughout the kingdom. She and Malcolm, every morning, brought twelve impoverished individuals into the castle, washed their feet, and then sat them down to breakfast with the family. This was Margaret's idea. At the same time each morning, three hundred people were fed on the castle grounds. Many times, she pilfered Malcolm's pockets to fund a charity. Sometimes he laughed at her theft, and sometimes he railed at her, to no avail. She was unstoppable in her generosity. Through her example, the kingdom flourished.

She gave Malcolm several children, but tragedy was destined to befall them, in her old age.

"Turgot," she was barely able to whisper to her confessor. "I am afraid that I will die before I am able to touch the Holy Cross."

"Fear not, my lady, it has been sent for and is being brought to you."

"Why is it taking so long?" She fretted. "This world is growing dim." She turned away to the wall. Turgot said a prayer for her soul. She felt the spear point she had in her hand. The Spear Point of Longinius, she had covered in several layers of bee's wax, so that its shape was hidden.

"I've had an awful premonition," she turned back to him. "My husband and my eldest son have met tragedy." A tear of grief trickled from her saddened and sickly eyes.

"You should not dwell on such fear, my lady," Turgot tried to comfort her. It was at that very moment that the attendant brought the Holy Rood into her chamber. She brightened when she saw it and a light effused her face.

"Here is the Holy Cross with the blood of Jesus Christ our Lord upon it," Turgot took the ornate box and placed it close to her face.

"Open it," she whispered. "I wish to touch it one more time before I die." He did so, and as he placed the Cross to her lips, there was a knock on the door. Turgot impatiently ordered the messenger admitted. He frowned deeply as he received the message in whispers and the messenger retreated.

"My Lady Margaret," he leaned to her ear and told her. "There has been treachery. Your husband Malcolm, and your eldest son Edward have been murdered on route south for the meeting."

Turgot heard her suck a breath as someone injured. She said nothing for a while, but now she understood. As Christ could have ruled the world, she could have made her husband and son ruler of the world by revealing the Spear of Destiny and giving it to Malcolm. By tragedy, and lost opportunity, she was drawn into the loss that Christ felt at the Cross. She became a sharer in his grief. This she immediately recognized as a cleansing balm to her soul. The realization came to her that she could have made her husband ruler of the world and saved him and her son from a treacherous murder, if only she had given Malcolm the spear point. She realized that Christ could have come down from the cross to rule the world, and all of mankind would have been lost forever. Such great power was in her grasp, and she realized that she joined Christ in a special suffering, the suffering of the loss of infinite potential for good, subverted for a greater good, that of faith in eternal future to have the proper course, and mankind to remain free to choose, good or evil.

"Now," she whispered, "by this final tragedy are my sins absolved," she felt a peace that she had sought through a lifetime.

Now, there was but one unfinished task. "Close," she whispered to Turgot, watching the door attendant to make sure he was not paying attention to them. "Turgot," she summoned her last energy. "This is to be secretly placed in my mouth when I die, to be buried with me," she placed the lump of bee's wax in his hand.

177

"What is this strange request, My Lady?" He puzzled as he looked at the lump of wax.

"You are not to know what this is, only a final command from your Queen," she had the strength to pull him closer by the cross around his neck. "A charge to me as a child by God, never to be revealed, Turgot, swear," she pulled his face close. "Never to be revealed, swear it," she commanded him.

"As you wish, good woman, my Queen," he swore to her.

In the years that followed, her youngest son David, now King of Scotland built Saint Margaret's Chapel in which her body was entombed for many years.

When the tomb is ruined in a reformation, her head passed to the Relic collector Philip of Spain in the 1500's and thus during its glory days Spain was in possession of the spear point. The head was sold from collector to collector, and eventually came back to Scotland, where an early experimenter with X-ray decided to take a look at the recently re-acquired head of Saint Margaret's. He discovered the spear point and placed it on the black market.

A Spear of Destiny was acquired by the Hapsburg's of Austria, where it was on display when Adolph Hitler, first saw it. His first assignment when Hungary was overrun in World War Two is to bring the Spear of Destiny to a vault in Austria, called Der Reise. This is also where an alien spacecraft that crashed in the Black Forest in 1937 was brought for study and de-engineering. This is where General George Patton's special corp sent to locate the spear, found it and other relics. The Bell, or Die Glock, as it was known in German, the results of the engineering on the alien spacecraft was missing, rumored by the engineering teams captured to have been lost in time earlier near the end of winter in 1945. The American high command did not know what to think about these fantastic reports, and they were not even passed on to the new American president, Truman, who had other fish to fry.   Eisenhower ordered the relics recovered handed over to General Groves, who was in command of Los Alamos, for study and storage. The relics and artifacts of the experiments at Der Riese, along with many of the top scientists, were assigned to Groves command, and worked under Robert Oppenheimer.

- Los Alamos-Early May Nineteen-Forty-Five-

"Mitt Gott," the startled man gasped.

"Good evening, Kammler," the man said when Hans turned around and found him standing in his laboratory.

"Where did you come from?" Hans had switched to English, as the other man was using English. How did you get into my lab?"

"I built a door," the man in the shadow said.

"What," Kammler was confused. "How can you be here?" He marveled. "The last that I saw of you, you were in Die Glock when it disappeared from Der Riese some months ago in early Nineteen-Forty-Five, never to return. The new solid gold coils had been installed, Gestapo Gold from the teeth of the death camps. The device was activated, and it just disappeared."

"But I am here, and I have seen the future, a more glorious future than The Fuhrer could even imagine," the shadow figure took a chair and sat, after taking off his coat and folding it. "Now," he told Kammler, "there are things that I want you to do."

Hans Kammler did not like this man but understood that he was in his power, at least to betray his identity. He listened closely.

"Hans. What is your sir name now?" He questioned.

"Crammer," Hans told him.

"Hans Crammer. Good, you have a new identity. Created by?" He questioned.

"The Vril have made certain that a network has continued."

"Good. I want two identities created from falsified birth records, one for Nineteen-Fifty-Seven for a David Chase, here is a folder of the country woman to approach to buy the false filing and the doctor that you will pay to fill out the birth report."

"But this is just May of Nineteen-Forty-Five. What are you talking about?"

"You will work here at Los Alamos until nineteen-sixty-nine, when if you have done what I tell you to do, I will take care of you in Argentina. It will be best that you retire there after establishing the second identity. Here again is the file for the woman and doctor for the birth record of Phillip Roth."

"What is this about?" Hans questioned.

"You don't need to concern yourself about that, Hans," the man told him smoothly. "This is beyond anything that you might imagine. You will see when Trinity is done. You will do the things that I instruct, and I will take care of you in Argentina after nineteen-sixty-nine or I will see that you are taken care of now." The threat was implicit and Hans Kammler now Crammer's blood ran cold.

"I can do the simple things that you ask through the network," Crammer shrugged. He took out a cigarette, readymade, and lit it, and held it German style, with the lit end outside the palm. He took several drags, offering the other man a smoke, who shook his head no, and smiled. Finally, he asked. "What is Trinity?"

"You will see soon." He paused and studied the man. "One more item," the traveler told him. "Yesterday, you received a shipment from General Patton's command of sacred relics and sacred items gathered by the Reich and stored during the war at Der Riese, along with the Wunderwaffe, which I have improved with a better Leichtmetall."

"Yes, marvelous," Hans Crammer began to see the possibilities. "There was a shipment from Der Riese that came here yesterday, as this government knows that I was once in charge of these same items at Der Riese."

"The Spear of Destiny is among the items."

"Yes, perhaps," Hans agreed.

"It will be there, and while you have possession of it, before Eisenhower makes Patton give it back to Austria, I want you to take a sample of material under the bands that once held the shaft to the hilt of the point. Take that sample and put it in cryogenic storage in liquid helium. Label the flask Dr. David Chase. That's all."

"I can do that, but why," Hans confronted him again.

"Because" he told Hans with assuredness. "If you do as I have instructed you, I will give you life extension drugs after nineteen-sixty-nine in Argentina, and if you don't, I will see you exposed or killed or both, whatever pleases me, and I will still get these things done."

"Who are you?" Hans questioned. "Who have you become?"

"It is rather easy when you can go to the future and come back." He said. "I am the first to travel in this way, and I can tell you that I have made great advances in the way that we think of things. I have gone beyond anything that can be imagined by you. All things will be subverted to my will, and the Vril will soon know that I am to be obeyed above all others. I am the one that has the future in his hands," the figure gripped his coat from the back of the chair and twisted it. "You do as you are told, and I will include you in that future." The shadow figure walked to the door, and without a goodbye, went out. Kammler, now Crammer, went to the door and opened it, but the man was gone, not down either direction of the hall.

"Impossible," Crammer, once Kammler muttered to himself, then took another draw on his cigarette. He would have to report this to his Vril contact.

Bryan Mallory came to the podium in the conference room and tapped the microphone. The federal liaison to the Los Alamos National Laboratories was closely connected to the Senate committee, chaired by Senator Prickle, that oversaw nuclear deterrence, the NRC and other areas of nuclear interest. This position was the Director of LANL the Los Alamos National Laboratories.

Bryan Mallory, immaculate white-haired bureaucrat, had just come from a fifteen hundred dollar haircut by a Sante Fe barber to his dressing room for the conference of LANL area managers. Some thirty people were in attendance, managing around five thousand of the nation's top scientists. All of this network of research looked to one man for directions during that man's tenure. That position was the real decision-making position at LANL as the Director's position was more political. The real directing force of the laboratories resided in the PADSTE, the Principal Associate Director of Science, Technology, and Engineering.

Bryan Mallory had primped in his dressing room with a hairdresser on call. A knock came on the door and a special delivery came. He opened the package from Roth Pharmaceutical. Inside the package, was an expensive and popular anti-aging cream, obtained by prescription. Mallory smoothed it into his skin around the eyes and was pleased to watch the whiskey lines ease, then disappear, as if by magic. Then he made his way to the conference room, nodding and smiling at the tall, dark-haired, middle to young middle-aged man on the podium with him. He was impressed by the expensive suit that his colleague wore.

He made a standard talk from the podium. "The three major missions of the LANL will be fully filled by our new PADSTE," he assured them. "Without further ado, let me introduce our new PADSTE, Phillip Roth." He led the applause.

Roth took the podium and adjusted the microphone. "Thank you, Bryan." He looked into each face in the room. "I know many ofh you," Roth began, his English somewhat thick with a German accent. "I vill know you all soon. You vill be wery pleased to hear that the Senate has seen fit to fund us wery adequately for the coming foreseeable future. The budgetary restraints that have been in place for a decade have been lifted as science, technology, and engineering has lifted the US economy out of the paperwork bubble of the previous decade or more." Roth took a sip of water and continued, after the applause had died down. "The major technologies that have contributed to this upturn in American manufacturing has been the exploration and commercialization of space, with its increased uses, geophysics, renewable energy, and most especially supercomputing, nanotechnology in all its applications, and most especially, my own field, pharmaceuticals, and medical applications. We here at LANL lead the world in all of these fields, and I am going to make sure that this tradition continues. As you probably know, I am the owner of Roth Pharmaceuticals, and I can guarantee there will be no lack of funding for any worthwhile project." A general cheer went up from everyone in the room.

Rafael Peralta sat on the back row of the meeting room and reflected that since the construction of the Metalogistics Building, Phillip Roth had been serving as chief administrator of the Artificial Intelligence Department. Successful owner of Roth Pharmaceuticals, the list of patents went on and on, mostly in health, beauty, and lately genetic and nano creation of new drugs. Roth had been asked to serve by the Vice President some four years earlier as PADSTE, but the position went unfunded, or opposed by the controlling Senate committee, until

Senator Prickle had come to chairmanship of the committee through seniority, and had then pushed Roth as the proper choice, and had waltzed it through.

In an amazingly short amount of time, the AI department had taken control, starting with the computing department. The subversion spread from there. Computer research was conducted under Chen Ching's lab, and obviously that research reported directly to Roth. Other departments had accounting, inventory, reporting, and other functions that sent records to the IT people at the Metalogistics Building, there it was processed and filed by systems constantly made to be more and more automated. They all reported to Roth.

The new automatic backups and integration of computer systems led to the forming of a director's council, and Phillip Roth was now the PADSTE. He would now control the direction of research for the entire LANL. After all, Roth Pharmaceuticals wrote much of the grants that paid the salaries. In this way Roth had come to direct much of the research of the entire complex, while also gaining access to all the paperwork and documentation. Literally, everything going on came through his office.

"Dr. Ching," Roth began specifics of the meeting. "What have you to report on the cryogenic computer storage project?"

"We see good progress," Chen began. My new assistant Michael Hodge had good progress with high-speed connections and software. We see prototype run soon." Ching sat back satisfied with his characterization of his project. He didn't mention that he was privately experimenting with increased Ort Cloud density.

Director Roth moved on after complimenting Dr. Ching on his progress. Next, Roth went to the plutonium department. Dr. Leffler, Uris' boss was in charge of the manufacture, use, and storage of the output from the new

Chemistry Metallurgy Research Building. "Dr. Leffler," Roth questioned? "Anything needed from AI?" He asked.

"Nothing here," Leffler responded in her flat simple manner, with a slight raise in tone register at the end to reassure. "We are hitting production predictions on both ends this year, in both plutonium production and bomb construction, and of course other uses in medicine, the energy industry. Look's good."

"Great," Roth reinforced. "But I would like you to consider revising the quota on plutonium production by three percent for the next year. That would be slightly less than six thousand pounds. Would you check the feasibility of that increase."

"I'll look into that, Director," Leffler crossed her arms in front of her chest and got a perplexed look. Peralta kept his mouth shut. Christie Leffler was his boss.

"Dr. Beckman," Roth called next on the theoretical physics department.

Hans Beckman says, "except for the one incident some time back, where a female employee had to be taken away by security. Thing is," he regressed to the incident, "security told me that she was released by Ruben McAuley, he's Extraterrestrial Contact, and the President got into a direct order to release her. Seemed funny, thought you would want to know."

"Yes," Roth's eyelashes moved up in mock surprise. "The President interceded for this woman with security?" He knew full well who Uris was, he had brought her there hoping that she would reveal more technology from the House of Ur and possibly unlock the Universal map that was partially contained in the Time Probe. He soothed Beckman. "I'll have it looked into. Thank you, Hans."

One by one, department by department, human genetic research, BEC research, nano research in pharmaceuticals, plutonium production, and the new

PADSTE reviewed the departments. Roth Pharmaceuticals was the patient holder of several well distributed drugs with nanobots engineered into the drug. Nanobot drugs targeted to specific ailments was the forefront in pharmaceuticals. These products had given Roth immense wealth.

Every department used AI for records. Roth made sure the needed infrastructure was in place and the best equipment, for the projects that had his interest. He wrote the grants through personnel employed by the pharmaceutical company and used powerful Senate contacts like Senator Prickle to push things through the committee that he controlled that funded most of the Los Alamos research. The meeting was dismissed by the new PADSTE.

In this way, Roth in a short time had come to control the projects he needed to accomplish his purpose. Now, he was in total control for the direction research would go for his tenure.

Working with pharmaceutical manufacturers, Roth had made a fortune, many billions of dollars, in birth control, and then more when the nanobot drugs began to come on the market. He always seemed to be on the leading edge of what was next, and there to invent and invest in it, hold the patent and license manufacturers to distribute. Much of the time, Roth would be gone to somewhere unknown to his managers, then would suddenly reappear to buy or sell metals with the proceeds from his drug companies.

This vast wealth, he had then turned to ultra conservative candidates. He fully supported the growing right-wing extremists. There was plenty of money to be made this way, and it suited a greater purpose.

He was no longer controlling just the lab and that area. He was now beginning to control the thinking and circumstances of the entire nation. He saw to it that enough corporate money from Roth Pharmaceuticals was put in political ads, and money spent on investigations into candidates, to achieve election of his chosen candidates. Everyone had something to hide. Money was running wild in the system like poison in the veins.

Roth could see himself gaining more and more power. The plan was working. His corporations now had the rights from the Supreme Court to have "person hood", and Super Pac funds had increased his grip on the political system. When the real estate and commodity bubbles burst in the earlier decade, he was able to capitalize on the decline and the echo boom of the earlier part of the 2020 decade.

He also traded metals. As the Arabs and other producers pumped oil, and the world speculators drove the price up and down, Phillip Roth, Metastophiles, was pumping metal. He could flood the market with gold, silver, or the platinum group metals at will, driving the price up or down, as he chose to make the market.

With much of the profit, he accumulated tons of gold which were drawn as wire to be wound into giant coils of a custom design. The coils were then shipped to locations with no name on the fronts of the buildings, and from these secret locations, then disappeared to some secret purpose.

Roth watched the managers leaving the meeting, and gloated over the position, hard won in political maneuvering, to now be in a position to realize that all his plans could begin to come to a final phase.

Kurege was at his desk when Dr. Ching came into the high security area with a stranger that he had not met. The two went to the cryogenic BEC containment and studied several parts of the machine.

"Michael," Dr. Ching called him over. The stranger seemed to be about his age or perhaps a little older, it was hard to tell. The man was very well dressed in an expensive suit, with a posture of authority. "This Michael Hodges," Ching did the introductions.

"Phillip Roth," the man's handshake was somewhat limp and dead fish. "I hear really good things about your work," Roth complimented.

"Give him tour here of interface," Dr. Ching cut the pleasantries.

"Sure thing," Kurege complied. "This is an optical filter, made of a rhodium alloy, only an atom thick that forms a lattice through which we are able to filter and clean the incoming laser frequencies to the exact wavelength. This makes storage and retrieval faster and cleaner, as we can be sure that the parity bits are in sync. There are still checking codes, but the sequence is hardly ever redirected for correction with this system of frequency control." He was proud, this was his work.

"He help some," Dr. Chen Ching gave Kurege little of the credit that he deserved for the innovation.

"Very impressive," Roth complimented.

"It was an unusual find that the lattice work of rhodium atoms could filter the laser beams in such a way as work perfectly for the lattice placement inside the BEC, then could be excited by a slightly different frequency which would then emit the coded information, tuned and encrypted. It was one of those marvelous surprises that sometimes turn up," Kurege observed.

"Great work, Dr. Ching, I am very impressed," Roth offered some balm to the lab director's ego. Then he added, "Remember, we have a director's office party mixer for the heads of the laboratories, and their primary researchers."

"No," Chen assured him. "I not forget. I be there, with bells on," he added the idiomatic phrase. A puzzled look crossed Roth's face.

"Yes, no doubt," he moved toward the door, then stopped and turned. "I suppose that for an assistant as good as this one, ve might extend an invitation to you," Roth said to Kurege.

"Thank you," Kurege responded to the honor, then thought. "Are wives invited also?"

"Yes, of course," Roth responded. "This is a social occasion," he stressed the 'is'.

It was bedtime for the couple, with Urme finally put to sleep, before he thought to tell her about the invitation. "By the way," he said, as the two snuggled in the crisp New Mexico autumn mountain air. "We have been invited to an office party for the directors of the various laboratories, Wednesday of next week. I met a very unusual man this afternoon. He is director of the AI laboratories, and my boss's boss. His name is Phillip Roth, and he liked my work on the interface, and extended an invitation to us."

"I will need a new dress," Uris retorted.

"Fine," Kurege told her, we will go into Santa Fe this weekend and shop for it."

She liked that idea, and the cold weather blowing through the window made her snuggle closer. One thing led to another, and soon she was listening to him snore.

That night, in his deep sleep, Kurege had a very unusual dream. The new man that he had met had a mask on his face that kept changing. Some of the features were quite beguiling, others as frightening as a primitive mask. As he woke from these images, the final thing that shocked him, just as he came to consciousness, he called the man 'Father'.

"I had the strangest dream last night," he told Uris from the breakfast table, as she got Urme ready for the kindergarten across from Ashley Pond near the old log house.

"Daddy slept on his book," Urme piped up and teased.

"Oh, give me a hug," he scooped her up. "It was about the director of my department, my boss's boss."

"The Principle Athociate Director," Uris clarified.

"Yes, Phillip Roth."

"I've heard of him but never met him. They thay that he ith very powerful. Hith Roth Drug company ith huge."

"He came to the laboratory; Dr. Chen Ching's the other day and was very complimentary about my work. He even personally invited us to an office party for laboratory directors."

"Tho, what did you dream?"

"Roth was at a party wearing a mask."

"What do you think that means?" She asked.

"Just that I find him an intriguing person. But, to tell the truth, he makes me uneasy for some reason."

Uris had a very strange feeling about it and noted the strange suspicions that crept into her mind. Suspicions she could not shake but continued to dwell on. "I've got to head to work," she shouldered a pack.

"Let's go, princess," he picked up Urme, and the car keys. He put Urme in her strapped child's seat and Uris got out her bicycle. She went to the corner and turned right on to Diamond Dr. and rode along to where Diamond Dr. became Trinity to the left, and Omega Bridge to the right. He followed her along until the split at the light and she took the right uphill toward the colon, they called the entrance, then turned downhill toward the new CMR Building. Kurege turned left and took Trinity Dr. to the front of the hotel, then jogged left onto Canyon Rd. looping two sides of the pond. He dropped Urme off across from Ashley Pond and watched her run to the door and waved at her teacher at the door. He headed back to the laboratory and went into the parking lot behind the Metalogistics Building and went down to Chen Ching's basement laboratory."

"There is a message for you from Roth Pharmaceuticals," Chen informed him as soon as he arrived. It was a request from the office of the PADSTE for him to attend a meeting in Albuquerque that afternoon. The address and contact information was in the memo. Chen Ching barely nodded when he left.

He drove the distance to Albuquerque and found the building and went to the dragon lady at the desk, who took his information without any pleasantry and handed him a form to fill out. He was just finishing, and she had handed him a badge when a man approached through the secured entrance to one side of the front desk.

"Rod Axtel," he extended his hand to Kurege.

"Michael Hodges," he said.

"Great of you to be able to break away," Axtel grinned.

"It was more like my supervisor made me an appointment," Kurege said. "I'm a bit confused. I'm an interface computer guy; I thought that Roth was a drug company."

"Follow me," Axtel motioned, "and I'll try to clear it up."

He led to a conference room where he had plans lain out on a shiny table. "We are looking at prototype interface devices for the human brain. We already manufacture several, like this hearing aid that is attached directly to the cochlea, feeding sound directly to the brain. We manufacture state-of-the-art electro-encephalographic equipment, even lie detectors. We are the leaders in devices and chemicals to probe the minds of terrorists." He paused to hand several sheets of specifications across the table. "When space industrialist Striker Rich was here the other day, we discussed the launch of zero gravity laboratories for the manufacture of life extension drugs." Axtel noticed Kurege's body language registered surprise.

"Striker Rich?" Kurege questioned.

"You know him?"

"Yes, just met."

"How is that?" Axtel was now the one to register surprise.

"Just a friend of a friend, we met in Santa Fe one evening," Kurege hoped to pass it off. He was careful not to mention Ruben McAuley's name.

"Huh, small world," Axtel moved on. "What we are looking for now, is an interface from the electrical impulses from the cerebral cortex to optical laser, or fiber optics reception, to place in a supercomputer data base."

"Now I am understanding why I am here," Kurege said.

"Michael," Axtel smoozed him. "Phillip Roth, owner of Roth Pharmaceuticals has recommended you very highly for this project."

"I do find it intriguing work," Kurege agreed. "But I'm very happy in Dr. Chen Ching's lab, also."

"We are working out a sharing agreement. The works are interrelated at any extent."

"I'll think about it, and let you know," Kurege didn't promise until he had thought it over. There were unusual red flags sticking out here. He went back up to Los Alamos going around the loop to avoid Santa Fe. He had a lot to think about. There was something about Axtel as well as Roth that put him ill at ease.

The party was crowded with the directors and their wives. Noisy hubbub filled the room. All the department heads were busy talking shop with the others about things happening in their department. They were free to do this, as they all had security clearances to talk freely to each other, on most subjects. This had always been the way at Los Alamos from its inception, the military had wanted to compartmentalize the facility, but Oppenheimer had made sure that Graves had not prevailed on this point, as Oppenheimer considered an open working environment to be essential to the creative process. The tradition had stuck.

The Principal Associate Director was in conversation with Dr. Black the person directing personnel and hiring. Rafael Peralta went to the open bar and grabbed some nuts and a beer and caught a snatch of the conversation. "We want to focus the money where it will bring the greatest return, and that is in the nano-pharmaceutics, and in nanomedicine. I want you to hire heavily in the Biosciences and molecular nanomedicine," the PADSTE was telling Dr. Black.

Rafael was always in awe of how fast and complete the transformation in the directions of research and engineering. When a look was taken at the places where the money was being spent, supercomputers, nanomedicine, plutonium production, especially after the problems with the construction of the CMR building, there were some out--of-this-world conclusions that could be drawn, that pricked at the back of Rafael's mind. But the main puzzle that had come from out of nowhere was a picture of Phillip Roth from years before, only the old Los Alamos photo in the archive said his name was Dr. David Chase, an early pioneer in DNA research related to cloning. He had found Chase in three old photos, and they bore an uncanny resemblance to the new Principal Director of Science, Technology, and Engineering. A nagging suspicion had grown the more he researched the early history of the laboratories. He speculated also, that he may have had too many science fiction books across his path. He was beginning to believe his own fantastic ideas.

Kimberly Kirkendall stood back not expecting to get much attention, when she became aware that Phillip Roth the Director of LANA as far as operations were concerned and the powerful owner of Phillip Roth Pharmaceuticals was coming purposely her way.

"Kim," he put out a hand, cold and dead fish. "How are you working into your new position?"

She was surprised that he knew of her. "Just settling in," she smiled. Her lab was top secret as everything was at Los Alamos, but hers carried an A for Alien and a + for direct contact. Still, an informal open policy existed as an Oppenheimer legacy, who had fought General Graves hard to make it so. But was this a test? This was a very powerful man, her boss in a way. "We have a lot of unknowns in front of us," she offered a general statement.

"You can say that for certain," Roth offered. "It is a challenging department. Did the new helper contribute?" He looked away and waved to Chen Ching who came in with Kurege and Uris behind him. Roth acted disinterested, but in fact, it was the possibilities of understanding the advanced machines like Uris's spacecraft, The Pearl, and Andro, the warrior protector, and most especially the Universal Mapping Probe, that caused Roth to let Uris live, at all. He had arranged for Uris to work at this base. That had been easy once Logan Wilson had become president. It fit with previous policy, and he had personal knowledge of Uris, and how useful she could be.

"Yes," Kuykendall noticed Roth's feigned non-interest, and was puzzled to think that she heard a suppressed German accent in his speech, but that accent was often heard here in Los Alamos along with every other accent in the world. "I think that she is going to be a big help," she added, wondering how much Roth knew about the woman now entering across the room, her new assistant, from another part of the universe. How much did Roth know who Uris was, and how much was he guessing?

"Has she been able to open that old probe from the late forty's yet?" He questioned straight to where his interest lay.

"No," Kim responded, truly. Surprised at the precise knowledge of things in her lab. But then, everyone had told her that the PADSTE pretty much controlled funding. "The Probe has remained inactive, so far," she told him. She did not tell him that Uris had been obdurate and would not work on it. She didn't want to talk about any of this any further. "Your clearance is Q," Kimberly was precise. "Talking about that would take a QA+ like mine, Mr. Director," she cut him off.

"I know that you need more funding for more personnel to study the various problems," he confided to her. "I am going to see that you get the funding that you need to make some progress." He touched her shoulder, and she felt creepy. She wondered how he could control funding in that fashion, as her funding came from Senator Prickle's control by being chairman of the secret committee that made decisions about her lab and the alien craft that had been captured at Pantex. With the across-the-board cuts in spending that had crippled the nation's research for many years, the reaction to the overheating of the economy some decades earlier, Prickle's hand had been miserly toward this research, as best as Kim could tell from reports that she had seen. But now, with his choice in the positions of Director of LANL and the selection and installation of the new PADSTE, the political winds seemed to have changed. Now, here was Phillip Roth telling her that she was going to get some help soon. She filed away the connection.

"Hmmm," Roth gave her an attaboy pat, and moved on toward the corner where Dr. Ching was waiting. Kirkendall didn't like him, she never liked condescending male types, and he definitely was. She moved toward Uris to greet her. She was the only person in the room that Kim knew.

Next, Roth sought out Christie Leffler, head of the nuclear deterrence, in charge of plutonium production and quality of the overall production of the nuclear arsenal of the US. "How are the preparation going for the ramping up of plutonium production," Roth questioned her.

"I have placed the paperwork in the pipeline," Dr. Leffler told him.

"Good, good," Roth shook his head positive, "I will see that it vill move along vith good speed." He seemed satisfied and moved on through the crowd.

Next, he moved into conversation on BEC with Chen Ching. Kurege moved into the group but was ignored by Ching and had meant to bring up the question of Ching's attempts to bring about an undamped zero point singularity and possibly causing a supernova in a test tube. He didn't have to. The two were in an argument about that very point.

"You are not to increase the density of the Ort cloud beyond the experimental limit," Roth was instructing him.

"Experiment always push limit," Ching argued.

"You will confine your experiment to the parameters already spelled out in the procedures you are running. This is done one step at a time, Dr. Ching, if you value your position here."

"OK, you the boss," Chen Ching kowtowed, but he had a stubborn look in his eyes.

It was about that time that Hans Beckman spotted Uris across the room and decided to raise an alarm about a woman he considered insane to be in the room.

"Vhat ist she doing here," he bellowed. "That woman ist insane, and dangerous," he pointed straight at Uris, who was with Kim Kirkendall at the bar. The crowd parted between them and Uris took a step towards Beckman to see who was pointing at her. "No," Beckman shrieked. It was enough to bring Phillip Roth closer to see what the noise was about.

She was sure what she saw across the room, even though she had only seen him once, as a little girl, when her aunt was given to him in marriage on Pandamon. She moved closer. Roth saw her coming and gave her a merry but somewhat sly smile. Then, he saw the boots she was wearing. When the odor of the Gru skin hit his nasal passages, a transformation of complete fear filled his face. Some around him noticed and stepped back then parted as they realized that he was reacting to Uris. An intense anger filled his face and anger at the uncontrollable fear that was slowly overwhelming him. He became catatonic and EMS was summoned and was on the scene from the medical facility in minutes. A crowd stood back as Roth was taken on a gurney from the room. Rafael, who had observed all this, came over with a chuckle.

"You disposed of the mighty Assistant Director of Science, Engineering, Technology in short order," he chuckled.

"What happened to him?" Uris asked.

"He must be a herciphobic, and a bad one from the looks of it. People are neurotic about all kinds of smells. We got used to it in the taxidermy business. Some people get stiff with fright from certain smells." Rafael paused to take a sip of his drink. "Roth had a reaction to whatever type of animal those boots are made of. They look and smell like goat to me, so I say that Director Phillip Roth is a herciphobic, and a bad one to boot, ha, pun intended." Rafael took a sip and had a look like the cat that swallowed the canary. He had his suspicions about the venerable Dr. Roth, and now he was beginning to have more than suspicions.

Uris looked down at her boots. She was becoming more and more fond of these shoes as time went along. She reflected that it had taken her by surprise and that she should have killed him on the spot. She had the chance. It might not come again. It was such a surprise to find the Baron on Earth. She now needed to know all she could find out about Metastophiles', rather Phillip Roth's endeavors. What was he doing here on Earth at this exact moment in time. Some nexus of purpose that had come about at this moment.

She watched the as EMS loaded Roth into an ambulance from a window looking down on the street. She would need to talk to Ruben McAuley, and maybe the President should be told.

Phillip Roth observed the traffic in the colon, so named for being a twisted maze looking like a colon, meant to keep out terrorist from the laboratories of the Los Alamos Complex. He looked down from his corner top floor office located in the super-secret, artificial intelligence research building, known as the Metalogistics Building. It was one of the older buildings built shortly before the Chemistry, Metallurgy, Research Building, was started, but the CMR had been delayed for years, and then finished at the same time that Phillip Roth had come there as the PADSTE of LANL.

He had satisfaction on his face as he opened a secret door and stepped into a private elevator that smoothly dropped him into a private hallway where he took a small electric car the three thousand feet to the large sub-basement complex under the new Chemistry Metals Research building. Sealed doors opened for his approach.

"Lord Metastophiles," a humanoid guard addressed him and came to attention. The guard was in charge of the exophile workers loading shielded crates of plutonium on his private Star Ship. The ship being plutonium propelled in an excited charge field that acted as both shield and propulsion. The hyper-excited state of the plutonium emitted anti-gravity waves. The ship's skin could also eject particle beams simultaneously from any spot on its spherical surface. It was a one-of-a-kind marvelous machine, redoubt, weapon and capable of many times the speed of light, the finest time machine made. When fired upon by an enemy, it was just simply not there when the projectile arrived. Yet, a nano moment later could reappear and fire in all directions. There was no other like it, so that Phillip Roth, Metastophiles of Pandamon, Lord of the Empire had a fondness for it, and he named it Lucifer.

It was the prototype. Beyond his ship in titanium steel storage racks, row upon row of "Lucifer" class warships were in readiness. Without some of the refinements of the Flagship, the others were still the most magnificent space/time craft to be built anywhere, anytime.

The tons and tons of gold from years of successful trading, and the gold purchases from the profits of numerous companies and tons of plutonium siphoned off from the United States manufacture, all had been used in the construction of the squadron of Lucifer Class Warships. He had created the Pran exophiles to construct the immense cavern under the San Luis Valley thousands of years earlier in preparation for the moment.

"Is all in readiness by the Zeit Storm Troop Commanders?" He asked.

"The final load of plutonium will be loaded in a few moments, my lord."

"Make the fleet ready to move to Saphos," he ordered.

"Saphos?" The attendant asked.

"Why Saphos?" Metastophiles responded. "It is close to the Draco Stardoor. With real estate its always location, location, location," he cheerfully observed.

Metastophiles strode on into the ship. He went into the control room. Several uniformed guards came to attention. "If you want something done right, you've got to do it yourself," he spoke to no one in particular, but all the guardsmen eyes got bigger for fear that it implied something wrong that they might have done.

He noticed the tension. "The men in this room, I would give my life for. Loyalty is everything," he told them. They all cheered. They were carefully screened and conditioned. They would give everything for him, and soon, for he would make sure of that.

"Make ready for planet fall away," he ordered. "Check the military operating band at La Veta operating area and time our exit from the door at a time that we are not seen. I want no incident with this load of plutonium aboard."

"Yes, lord," the pilot began to comply.

The electromagnets on the outside of the inner core of the ship energized, this generated a force to compress the plutonium outer hull to a supercritical state, just balanced within the field, with the outward electron flow redirected as plasma to a central point in each nexus point until a gravity field was induced with the grid of plutonium spheres. A gravity field that could be flux balanced by the cryogenic super magnets on the other side of the nanocarbonfiber hull.

The controlling power needed by the gold-wound cryogenic magnets of rare earth metals was furnished with electrical energy by a plutonium fast breeding nuclear reactor that furnished the heat to implode a tritium pellet, cascading a fusion reaction that released enormous number of coulombs of electrons, used by the magnets to control the outer plutonium shell.

It had only one drawback. It left a trail of deadly alpha particles wherever or whenever it traveled. There were other designs for space engine systems that left much less of a trail of pollution. The Master of the Lucifer was not concerned with pollution. Alpha pollution could actually be looked at as a positive, say if genetic mutation on a random scale might be considered a useful tool. He didn't have to worry about that, as his ship was incapable of returning to exactly the same space or time.

The meetings had gone well. His identity as Phillip Roth had served his purpose. He had the artificial intelligence section coming along nicely. The secret consciousness transference experiments showed some positive results. The DNA research was reaching a point where the perfect clone body could be produced.

Metastophiles had worked to this point. No longer would he have to take the life extension injections of stem cells made from fetal fluid. Now, he would be able to create more and more perfect clone bodies and transfer his consciousness into a more and more perfect body in an endless march of eternal life, and with the genetic propensity for prescience replicated into the genetic makeup of his future bodies, he could become both eternal and omniscient, and this would make him omnipotent, god emperor of the known universe.

He had picked this moment in Earth's history to give the technical guidance that the young world needed. Phillip Roth, from within the Los Alamos laboratory controlled through his corporations' whole sections of the United States Congress, both house and senate. He was able to use the resources of the United States to appropriate vast sums of money to projects of his choosing. The cryogenics, computer research, nanotech research, and even DNA research all were controlled by committees of Congress that he had come to control.

From his office of Principle Associate Director, he had been able to control the direction of the various departments that were needed to accomplish his tasks.

Now, with plans fully in operation, he could proceed to Regis Xinor for a show of force both political and with the armament obtained from the plutonium manufacture at the new and efficient Los Alamos plutonium plant in the bowels of the Chemistry Metallurgy Research Building, he was ready for war, if need be. This new Starship gave him superior fire power over anything Xinor had and the force field generated by the artificial black holes created on the plutonium skin, could time transfer any particle beam weapon, laser, or projectile, even nuclear. He would be invincible. The Lucifer was always in another time/space when the weapon's charge arrived.

With the Stargate opened by data he had obtained from the data core found on the Pearl, sent back from downtime by Uriah, Xinor was in near time. It would be possible to travel back and forth between Earth present time and Xinor present time for almost one thousand years.

Metastophiles could see the fulfillment of all his plans before that, long before that. These intrusions by Xinor scout ships would need to stop. The other powerful worlds, those with interstellar capabilities, would have to be confronted and access to the Draco Star Door must be controlled by his forces. He now had the weapon, Lucifer, to guarantee his control.

He would soon offer the wealthy of Earth life extension drugs. Then the next phase of his plan could be put into place. Earth humans would accept the drugs, clamor to pay for them, while all the time, he used them as guinea pigs.

As the ship began moving Uris and his humiliation at the office party crossed his mind, and Metastophiles pounded a fist in determination. "I'm well on my way to becoming both immortal and omniscient," he swelled with pride, and a self-assured arrogance. "No bitch from the House of Ur is going to stand in my way," he looked at his aid and perceived something hidden. "What are you hiding?" Metastophiles questioned hypnotically.

"Nothing, my lord," the attendant gave a blank stare. "I was reflecting on the message that has just come through the tachyon link, of which I am sure you are aware."

"What message?" Metastophiles growled.

"Segrund has called for a Vril council to meet you at Saphos when you arrive."

"Yes, indeed," Metastophiles confirmed. "I am expecting them. The Ziet Time Troopers are gathering at Saphos for a final assault on the Xinor Confederation. Our time has come."

"There is also troubling news that the Rebels have taken Pandamon," the attendant was tremulous in voice delivering this news. He expected a rage from his lord Baron but got none.

"No matter," Metastophiles shrugged it off. "I will take care of that later, as it is no longer needed as a genetic laboratory, I may sell it," he smirked.

As a shakedown cruse for the new Lucifer Class warship, there were meetings to attend that could not happen on Earth, as Metastophiles was not nearly ready to let the coordinates for Earth through the Draco Warpstar be known. Still, there were negotiations with other powers that might prove fruitful in the future, and those contingencies had to be considered.

After the stockpile of plutonium had been unloaded at the spaceport on the city of Ur. He was met by the Viceroy Curos, who had been rewarded with for his traitorous information on the time/space coordinates of Saphos by becoming the Viceroy of Saphos. The two were escorted into the city and to the governors palace by a horde of Pran honor guard. When they arrived, the delegation from the methane breathers was already in the negotiations room.

"With the life extension nano-pharmaceuticals, Eternals can be created. If they are conditioned to a hierarchy of religious beliefs, they can be 'placed' in productive positions," Metastophiles explained. "With life extension, children will become pointless, or very expensive. I have plenty of headhunting companies that pay for such slaves." Metastophiles smiled his most benign smile. "And, they are always so satisfied to take on the apparent power over the flock, wherever in the great galaxies they 'hear the call of the Lord'.

Methbrith flapped his ventricles at the joke. "I'll buy a few," he croaked into the translator. "I've got a score of worlds that have reached high enough life forms to begin to lead them to sacrifice. The eternal slaves would be fully indoctrinated, conditioned fundamental."

"They won't question," Metastophiles assured him.

"That will dispose of the population, that part of it that is useful. Now, what about the planet itself?"

"Well, yes," Methbrith croaked agreement. "It is breathable for us, so it is of interest. How much are you going to ask for it?"

"Not much, I will simply want you to acknowledge me in the Xinor Council as Emperor," Metastophiles paused. "And, as God."

Methbrith croakled. "If you'll make a deal like that, I'll call you any name in the book." The methane-breathing, falopod snorked he flapped his ventricles so fast.

When Methbrith was carried out, Metastophiles next turned his attention to the reports of rebellion on Pandamon. The Pran high council leader, Aristnes was escorted into his presence. "Well, Aristnes, I'm waiting for an explanation," Metastophiles settled back in a chair that operated as the administration's judgment seat.

"A rebellious generation arose that refused to honor you, sire," he prostrated himself on the floor. "I warned the council to repress them sooner, but they would not listen to me." Aristnes dared to peek up. "A philosopher arose with an oracle. It was a unifying heresy, and the virus spread."

"Now," Metastophiles spat, "we have a mess to clean up." He thought for a moment. "No matter," he said, and Aristnes relaxed his body for the first time. "The planet has nearly outlived its usefulness, and it will be no threat to my plans now. My designs are on its younger self, before it became the befoul, mutant mess." Aristnes kept perfectly still and wished this were over. "Things can stay as they are there for the time being, it is Xinor where the interference might come from, and Xinor that will have to be subdued. I can deal with Pandamon later. You're dismissed Aristnes."

Aristnes was so glad to move his trembling tentacles out of there that he decided not to say anything about the fulfillment of the oracle by the arrival of Stark Raven.

The loss of Pandamon put Metastophiles in a furry of regressed thought, and he swore out loud as Aristnes was backing away. He looked at his aide and perceived something hidden. "What are you hiding?" Metastophiles questioned hypnotically.

"Nothing of note Lord," he whined.

"I will decide that. What have you not told me?"

"There was a humanoid shipped from the Pran outer world that came through Cragor on the tribute ship when Sartris was to be executed. We examined him, and he knew of Queen Uris of Saphos."

"Do you have the results of that mind tap?"

"Here my Lord," Aristnes handed him a data stick with the information from Stark Raven's torturous mind prob.

Metastophiles gripped it in his fist. The mere mention of the House of Ur drove his fury even greater. Aristnes shook all over as his master's face contorted in focused rage. Ur in his way again. This was becoming a problem. He looked at the supplicant figure before him.

He sneered at Aristnes cowering form, crawling backwards in retreat. He let him go, for now, and waved him away.

Having dealt with Aristnes, Metastophiles had the main reason for the trip brought to him. "Welcome, Molok," he embraced his replicant, a clone with specific genetic material introduced.

"Master," Molok obessed in his great need to serve what was essentially, himself.

"These things, I have decided for Terra," he spoke to Molok. "When the rebel brings Xinor the route through Draco, then Beel will give you a war fleet. I want all of the radical religious positions subverted in the usual secular manner. I want the extreme radicals searched out and eliminated. Of course, the wealthy and powerful ones are to receive special treatment.

"I understand, great father," Molok told him. "We have subdued religious wars on a dozen planets in that way." He paused. "I don't understand the overall purpose of the expense of the entire effort."

"You don't have to understand," Metastophiles snapped. "But I will explain a part that you will see. I am going to establish an Empire from there. After the repression of the radical elements, those in the hierarchy that can be useful will be offered the eternal drugs, just as you have."

"But, sire," Molok protested, "there is not enough to go around now, the effort that it takes to extract the essence from stem cells is enormous;"

"I have perfected an artificial synthesis for it. It is a nano-pharmaceutical, something not seen before. I can control the genetic repair, even reprogram the DNA. With your sniffers and clean-up crews finished with their work, I can have created a savior for the various belief systems, some can be merged into a single savior. At that point, I am going to supplant Xinor as the ruling body, I will make this clear to Xinor at the ruling Council, Beel already understands. Xinor will be forbidden use of the new Star door, Draco. You will no longer be concerned with Earth, and you and Beel will stay busy with your part of the Empire."

"What about our supply of the life extension drugs?" Molok asked.

"Don't worry," Metastophiles eyes drooped in scorn. "Your supply will not fail as long as you do as you are told."

"Does Beel agree with this?" Molok challenged.

"He, like you, has no choice." Metastophiles gloated in power. "But never fear. I have something better in mind, so to speak, coming along, and you and Beel will benefit."

"What are you talking about?" Molok challenged him straight away, as he himself would have done to himself.

"The AI research has led to the possibility of consciousness transference. The DNA program produces superior physical and even prescient persons. The genetic line can be extracted and introduced into a replicant of a clone of your material. After consciousness transference, you will be eternal in a more and more genetically and physically perfected bodies. While, after the purge, those that are chosen as useful can be given the eternal drugs as long as they can pay or be of use." Metastophiles could see the understanding of the overall plan was dawning.

"They would be willing slaves for eternity, working to perfect our kingdom," Molok saw it.

"Eternal slaves can be very valuable, enthusiastic ones even more. While you and the boys," he referred to his replicant clone line, "will continue to evolve. Metastophiles watched Molok's face closely. He seemed to buy it. In fact, once transference was achieved, there would be no need for the genetic replicant lines like Beel, and Molok, and the departed Sargon, and Mephor.

Genetic lines were coming along on Earth, and those experiments would proceed. The cyborg replicant crossbreed was an interesting hybrid, he foresaw being able to translate at will from superconcious machine to superhuman specimen, to enjoy the pleasures of the flesh or joined to an omniscient mind. There was no need to reveal further to Molok. He had bought the vision. Would Beel and Molok have any real use in that future, time would tell.

"You know what I expect," Metastophiles dismissed him.

"I will do it, master," the replicant clone fulfilled its drive to purpose.

Now, Metastophiles speculated, it was time to come out of the closet, so to speak. Just a need to skip forward a few months and let the labs work. He began to make plans to return to Earth.

He settled on his course of action. Now, he would see what the Vril Council had learned. There was a click of the door as it slid open, and Maria came into the room. She looked exactly as she had at the very first meeting of the Vril Society in nineteen-nineteen.

"Ah, Maria," he rose to meet her.

"Dieter," she met him with open arms and a passionate kiss.

"You look just as you did that first evening that I saw you in Berlin," he pulled her close.

After the two lovers had reunited, they went to a private party. The top echelon of the Time Troopers of the Ziet Core, and elite Gestapo unit sent forward in time, had begun to gather. They were in a cellar of the Baron's Palace, a section of the old castle of the House of Ur. The gardens had been redone but the central stone was still in its same position. It looked now much like a German beer garden of the nineteen-thirties. An uproarious crowd swayed and waved mugs of beer as they sang the old, old, German-Nazi songs of those olden days. Swastikas with a Mandelbrot-Schwarzschild-Time-Dilation set of concentric circles, decorated the uniforms, otherwise very similar to the Gestapo uniforms of the nineteen-thirties era. A cheer went up when Maria and Baron Roth entered the beer garden.

Chapter 20 – Saphos Covert Action

Saphos had changed since the last time Surilen had seen it. The majestic quartz tachyon towers for galactic communication were now in shattered ruins. She, Stark Raven, and Urvin had arranged to come to Saphos on a cargo ship, smuggling in with trade goods, all black market. They had made their way from a hanger in the far corner of the space port, and to a bar and eatery in the area. Stark entered the room in stunned silence. To him, the uniforms of the Nazi Time Troopers were like a movie of about nineteen-thirties Germany. He said nothing to the others. How could he explain what he was seeing all around as the old songs swelled the air, and the beer flowed, as the crowd held the swaying mugs in the air.

"Viceroy Curos," they heard the name mentioned at the next table. Urvin bristled.

"That traitor," Urvin said between clinched teeth. "I think that he was made Viceroy of Saphos because he betrayed the House of Ur to Metastophiles."

"That is possible," Surilen observed. "We had developed a file on him that I have seen. He is a contradiction in many ways. His rise to Viceroy was an appointment by Metastophiles after the destruction of the city."

"When the Pandamon warships returned," Urvin said, "we tried to fight, but they had new and powerful weapons, and a robotic hunter that we called sniffers. They were able to scent their prey with just a molecule in millions to discern the rebel hideouts. Then for those that were captured, the awful fate of having their minds ripped apart by the truth detectors that they have. We were overwhelmed and most killed within days. The fighting was brutal, they used Pran mercenary warriors. They had insane conditioning, so that any attack might be suicidal. They are under some religious conditioning that makes them want to sacrifice their lives. I was lucky to live through that."

"We must get out to the spaceport and take a look at what is going on there. I want to see that ship that was reported coming out of Draco and headed here to Saphos," Surilen looked resolved. "It could only have been Metastophiles or a cargo ship coming from Terra."

Urvin paid the bill and they mounted the two hover scooters they had gotten from a rebel group that had avoided detection so far.

Stark rode behind Surilen and Urvin led the way. As they went through the city to the spaceport, still some years after the Pandamon attack, rubble was visible in many places. The tachyon towers lie in ruins. Metastophiles had no use for them in his plans.

"This is hard to explain or understand," Stark began. He talked into a microphone in the helmet as they rode the air scooters along the corridor for craft going in their direction. "That group at the bar in uniforms was so much like an Earth group from a country on my home planet, but almost one hundred years earlier, during a horrible worldwide war. The insignias and uniforms, language and behavior were all from that earlier time period."

"What was this group called?" Surilen asked as she expertly guided the air scooter close behind Urvin, who led the way across the city.

"They were Nazi, and the inner circle was called the Gestapo." That rang a bell with Surilen and Stark could feel her body stiffen.

"When they first began to war upon Xinor, it was our beginning. The first civilizations that met when Isis pierced the Regis star and came into Xinor for the first time, Metastophiles was there. History calls him the Philos or Brotherhood of the Many Gestapo. In old Isisian language, long dead now, the name Metastophiles was given to the "Leader of the Many Gestapo".

"This is too much coincidence to be unrelated," Stark was puzzled and prickly with his hair standing up on the back of his neck. What was he hearing? "There must be some way this is all connected, but how can they all be alive for that long. How long did you say?"

"Isis contact with Ur, when Metastophiles first appeared, was many eons ago. Time is speed and direction. They are old, and many, and they know their way around."

Stark was silent, trying to understand what Surilen had just said. A small kernel of light began to dawn, but he could not see it clearly.

On several nights, they slipped through the perimeter to observe the base. They were observing one night, and a great deal of activity was going on. They had made holes to hide if some security came their way, and they had to hide several times as craft with search lights scoured the whole area, and passed right across them many times. They had special covers to block any thermal image and passed unnoticed.

During the height of the activity, a craft, at first appeared as a distant star falling from the sky, then as it grew closer, a flaming meteor, coming at tremendous speed, and suddenly stopping, projecting an ear deafening sonic wave in front of its arrival. They slowly and stealthily emerged from their holes and got their first look at The Lucifer. Surilen correctly figured that this was Metastophiles, and that with him came a new technology in star/time-ships.

No more activity was seen at the landing port for that night. They watched, but no ships came or went. It was several nights later that they were watching through high-power night vision scopes that Surilen and Urvin had smuggled on to Saphos. They watched as a special ship, a

Xinor diplomatic shuttle was brought forward to the staging area and ready for loading. They saw soon that a container was carried to the ship. "That is Councilman Methbrith," Surilen said. "I recognize him from meetings that we have had on cross species relations. He is a methane breather, we call them 'stinky breaths', Surilen wrinkled her nose.

"Charming," Stark wryly understood.

"He is very rich," Surilen looked Stark in the eyes. "He owns many planets." Something registered.

"" Could Earth support a life form like that?"

"" What is the methane content of your atmosphere?" Surilen asked him.

"Around three parts per million," Stark remembered.

"They like it a little higher," she said, "but, yes, they could survive on your planet. They require about that amount to survive in an atmosphere. They have very large falops that strain the atmosphere of a planet for small amounts of methane."

"Our planet's atmosphere over the last 150 years has doubled in its methane content."

"That would increase the temperature of your planet, as methane can contain twenty-five times more heat than many other gases, like carbon dioxide."

"That has been happening and is a problem for the planet. The atmosphere at one time was much richer. We have methane clathrates filling sections of the deep oceans."

"If your oceans went down from evaporation, and the poles froze more water from the increased reflection of heat into space at the poles, the ocean depth could lessen. That is what has usually happened on planets like the one that you have described as your home world."

"That is a concern, as some experts have warned that if the clathrates were suddenly released into the atmosphere, the methane content would go to very high levels, further warming the planet."

Stark didn't like the way this was adding up. If that ship really did come from Earth, through the Draco Stardoor, now this methane-breathing mogul shows up that buys and disposes of worlds as he sees fit to do. They watched for a while longer through the night, but nothing of much interest happened until early morning.

The new ominous dark spaceship sprang to a fiery life and was moved forward to the loading and launch area. Metastophiles came on board from a transport that arrived with him at the spaceport.

"This is it," Surilen became very serious. "Urvin," Surilen told him, "You will take Stark Raven with you to Xinor and warn the General Council that Metastophiles is planning to attack and subdue Xinor." She looked sadly at Stark.

"What will you do commander?" Her loyal comrade in arms was apprehensive.

"Now is our chance to find the door through Draco. I can mark the door as I pass, following Metastophiles' path back to Earth. I will leave a trail of ionized argon particles from the stabilizers during passage through the core of the neutron star.

"What if he detects you following him to Earth?"

"I will have to take that chance."

"Hold on," Stark held out his hand. "If you are headed to Earth, Surilen, then I'm going with you."

"Too much danger to risk you. You are on loan from the Pandamon Council. As a socio scientist, I cannot take the chance of the disruption that your loss would cause the new Pandamon society."

"I'm sorry to disagree. Jim can serve as the front for the 'Just Get Along' society," he told her. "I am going with you to Earth. There was a pause as Surilen looked hard at him. That ship is leaving; don't you think that we should get ready to follow it."

Surilen saw the resolve in his face and began to gather the things from the observation post and head for the scout ship that they had prepared to try and follow.

Stark had trouble keeping up with Surilen, as she ran for her ship, trying to force her decision to leave him behind, and he almost was sliced into as he dove through the door of the ship right behind Surilen. "Hey watch it," he yelled at her, as he was nearly pinned and squashed by the hatch sealing. She didn't respond, as she hurriedly primed the coils and made ready for a fast fall away from Saphos.

She made the outer rim, just as The Lucifer went into hyperspace. A security rear guard became aware that a ship was following. They hit hyperspace at the same angle and velocity as The Lucifer, and entered the Draco Stardoor. Surilen released a stream of ionized argon to make the time line. Urvin would be able to follow this trail to the proper time and spot coming out the Neutron Star in Cancer, in the tip of the horn of the bull in Taurus.

They continued in a hyperspace conduit to near Earth before they came back into normal time/space. The alpha trail of The Lucifer was easy for the sensors on board Surilen's craft to detect and follow, coming down above the United States and following a path down the curve of the globe of Earth into the mountains of Colorado, descending and decelerating in the upper reaches of the San Luis Valley.

They were just coming into the valley as they saw the blazing craft they had followed descend underground into the sand of the Great Sand Dune National Park. Fighter craft arose within moments to challenge them, and they headed straight into the approaching craft, with Surilen and Stark inside.

Surilen made a surprised noise and quickly strengthened the force field. The arriving ships fired as some passed the ship on by, and some stopped their approach, so that Surilen and Stark were surrounded.

Watching a weakening defensive shield, Surilen had no choice except to run for cover, to try and avoid more energy streams of disrupters coming from the other ships. She descended in a dive low along the valley floor and traveled south down the San Luis Valley, trying to outrun their pursuit. No words had time to pass, but Stark was watching out the view ports and saw a flight of US military aircraft come out of the La Veta Pass and give chase down the San Luis Valley. They came right behind the fire fight of the alien craft, screaming down the valley over Fort Garland and in seconds making a turn above the old church in San Luis.

Surilen guided the injured craft over the chain of mountains to the west and descended sharply to the La Veta Valley. "They have new weapons," she told Stark. "Our force field should have been enough. We are going to have to land, as the craft is damaged, and they will destroy us if we stay in the air." She began a descent into the forest below them, dipping down the spine of the Spanish Peaks, and into a deep valley.

Chapter 21 – Colorado The Camping Trip

They were unable to all get away on Friday afternoon and left early Saturday morning. Kurege and Uris mostly rode bicycles to work every day, pulling Urme in a cart up to the Montessori School across from Ashley's Pond. They had purchased a hybrid SUV four-wheel drive sometime before to explore the mountains, so they were prepared with the camping gear and Urme in the back seat, when they pulled out behind Rafael Peralta and headed east then took the Taos cutoff through Ojo Caliente.

The warm waters were inviting in the cool mountain air. Urme splashed in the waters and the three adults swam the pool. They moved on north up the San Luis Valley along the Rio Grande River coming down the valley, though the spectacular cuts through the mountains. Passing to the north of Taos, over the Rio Grande Gorge Bridge and left at the Old Blinkin' Light, which still carried the name, even though it was now a major intersection coming out toward Colorado from the old city of Taos. They saw bright colored balloons out taking advantage of the updrafts from the canyons along the river, and the grandeur of the view. They headed on north through San Luis and into the northern part of the valley to Ft. Garland, ate lunch at a dinner on the eastern edge of town with old pictures from 80 years earlier of movie stars on the wall. Urme had a buffalo burger, which she shared with her dad.

They continued east up La Veta Pass. Part way up the western grade of the pass, Peralta signaled and turned up a mountain road. It was 4-wheel drive across the Sangre de Christos' spine overlooking the upper San Luis Valley to the west. It was spectacular forest land. Rafael led them to a campsite with a great overlook of the valley below.

"We'll set up tents here," Peralta pointed out sites and then started setting up his own tent. Uris, Kurege, and Urme got their own tent up, as they had practiced in the back yard. Urme went off chasing a chipmunk. The early fall forest was a blazing yellow of quivering aspen leaves in the gentle fall breeze, the perfect camping weather.

"Urme," Kurege cautioned, "don't go too far." That just encouraged her to test the limit.

"Well," Rafael approached with a bow and quill of arrows slung over his back, "I've got a fire started, if you could keep it going," Rafael told Kurege, but he smirked a little at the suggestion.

"Sure," Kurege knew the plan was for Uris and Rafael to hunt up some game for the group possibly coming.

"This bow is for you," he unslung the quiver and bow and handed them to Uris, then went back to his car and got his bow and arrows. "Bow season don't open for a month, but I'm part Ute Indian, and this is tribal land, at least I claim it," he laughed. "I hunt whenever I want. No game warden up here, and no funding anyway, here in this county." They headed up the trail, and Uris waved at Urme. The little girl came back from her exploring and stayed closer to her father.

When Uris stalked and shot the magnificent buck mule deer, it was a thing of beauty. The shot was straight and true, through the neck, and the buck went straight down, dead from the shot. Uris moved cat like toward the dead animal with caution, knowing that a near miss can be a stun, the animal suddenly rising up. The animal was dead from the neck shot, and they quickly field dressed it.

Others had arrived. Several tents had sprung up and even some children were there. Urme was playing hide and seek and the kids were madly dashing around.

Some had brought their dogs to add to the developing confusion.

"I'm a Vegan," June stated. "This is horrendous."

Uris had come in with the carcass field dressed and she and Peralta had proceeded to hang it and take the skin off. Urme had come to touch it with curiosity then had gone off playing again, bounding like a deer herself as if possessed.

"You shouldn't kill these animals," June continued her tirade toward Uris. "Besides, red meat is killing us all, milk and cheese and red meat, killing us all," she shrieked at Uris.

Uris had a knife and was eying June. Kurege was eying Uris. "Uris," he called to her. She let it go.

"Big forest," Uris stated. "Only one deer," she continued to skin the animal.

"If everyone killed a deer," June began....

"Everyone don't kill deer," Uris cut some skin away from the flesh and pulled down. "That not reality."

"Reality," June began. "And what is reality?" She motioned to the sky. "The reason that the stars are so far apart is that I could never get along with your way of thinking," June raved. "What is reality? Maybe its all a dream," she laughed. "A nightmare." She looked with pity at the magnificent creature being undressed of its skin.

Uris looked up at the stars. "It ith real," she assured the woman.

Soon they had skinned the deer and taken a green bough and spitted the carcass over the fire in chunks of venison roast. As the evening grew colder, they all huddled, the venison was eaten by some, scoffed at by others. Cheese and wine were followed by whiskey as the night went on. Some went to bed, but some stayed up to watch the sky all night.

It was a few minutes before midnight on a hill rising into the Sangre De Cristo's to the east. The MUFON club and the CSETIs still up were all spinning tales around the fire detailing previous reports from their own experience. Some were in front of tents scattered around the opening on the summit of the hill, huddled in blankets, and some kept lookout. Kurege, Urme, Uris, and Rafael were watching the sky. The night was calm with no moon, and all the stars were blazing with the Milky Way spread like dust across the dark void.

It began with what seemed like a blazing meteor coming across the sky, as The Lucifer descended to the valley floor. A rolling sonic boom alerted the watchers and brought sleepy campers from their tents. Suddenly, two balls of light were seen. One orange appeared from the south, and one blue rose up out of the Great Dunes to the north, where the flaming meteor like craft of Metastopiles had disappeared. The two craft met just north of Alamosa. When Uris saw them, she pointed, "Xinor and Pandamon fighter craft with defenth up. They will fight."

At that moment, connecting beams shot from the blue orb, and the lights glowed brighter, then would dim. "They fire on each other," Uris still followed the action, pointing as the conflicting balls of fire shot across the distant landscape at fantastic speed, yet no sound was heard of an engine. Rolling thunder, as from a thunderstorm, came from the battle. The only other sounds were the amazed murmur of the observers getting the show of their lives.

The battle played furiously as the ships made aerial maneuvers that were seemingly impossible. The first blue orb was joined by five more, that seemed to rise up from out of the sand dunes themselves. They all began a withering fire on the orange globe, that soon fled down the valley to the south. The rumble and murmurs were drowned out by the shattering sound of a low passage from six military jets coming out of the La Veta Military Operating Area. They were supersonic as they passed low and just to the south of the campers. They headed straight at the furious battle of the lights.

The orange ball headed over the eastern mountains being chased by the six blue balls of light. Leaving the lights of the jets far behind, in a twinkle, they disappeared into the stars of the night sky. The jets swept down the San Luis Valley to the south.

"Thith meanth war," Uris observed. "Xinor ith at war with Pandamon, and Pandamon has won thith battle for thith world. Earth belong Pandamon," she told them. A chill of more than the mountain air shivered everyone that heard.

The six F-35 air force jets screamed at supersonic speed up the the valley and skimmed the treetops as they came through La Veta Pass. Something was going on out in the San Luis Valley and this fighter group had been scrambled out of the air force base nearby. Someone was getting their butt kicked, from the radar readings and satellite readings being seen by NORAD, and North American Air Defense Command, at Cheyenne Mountain near Colorado Springs, Colorado wanted to know what and or who, if it could be ascertained. The San Luis Valley showed anomalies on radar many times, and many sorties were ordered to film, observe, and take electronic readings. This scramble was different. Command believed combat was in progress.

As he roared down the valley, air force captain Greg Sims kept to the eastern side with Ft Garland and Alamosa to his west. He was watching the landscape below, when he roared over the MUFON camp out on the west facing slope of the Sangre de Christos. At that point he could see radar detection directly west and observed a furious dog fight going on between two orbs of orange and blue light about twenty to thirty miles across the valley to the west.

"Foxbat leader," he spoke to his command. "One o'clock. See the bogey? I'm headed at them. Follow and cover." He waited to get an acknowledge from his five other companion jets, then made his turn west toward the fighting orbs. The orange orb broke away and headed south and down the valley. Five more blue orbs shot out from somewhere near the Great Dunes and shot across and headed south down the western side of the San Luis Valley at incredible speeds.

The orange orb disappeared over the range on the southern horizon before the squadron could begin to approach. "I'm making a southern turn and a sweep down the center of the MOA in the valley. Follow me, and hold formation," Greg Sims radioed his squad.

"Captain," came a reply. "This one is different, we should go chase," said one. Several here, here's were added.

"Cut the chatter. I'm calling in for instructions. Hold position," he ordered. He switched his radio and explained what they had seen. In a few minutes a command channel voice gave him permission to " if need be, to leave the MOA, still supersonic, in pursuit with permission to engage."

There were war whoops all around as the squadron circled around, turning directly over the town of San Luis at supersonic speed, passing over the oldest church in Colorado, and directly above the Stations of the Cross of Jesus Christ, in larger than life size bronzes starring up from the crucifixion into the infinite sky, and the screaming flying objects overhead, one being chased by the others, F-35 jets chasing behind both. They headed east over the Spanish Peaks an old and rugged mountain formation of jagged peaks, with little but their old backbone sticking high into the sky. They crossed over into the upper reaches of the La Veta Valley. They had cleared the ridge line and were looking down into the La Veta Valley where they could see a small forest fire burning and the six blue orbs were hovering or circling the fire. Sims pushed the nose down and the afterburners were fully engaged, and he led them screaming down toward a hillside near the bottom of the valley. He screamed right through the six blue orbs, and they busted out like billiard balls in all directions. The squadron came around for a second pass. He finished his tight turn and came back toward the orbs that were re-gathering. His squad was in a file behind but pulled up when they saw Sims get it.

Sims saw a white-hot ball of plasma shoot out of a blue orb in front of him, and it hit his plane in the middle on the underside and blew right through and out the top like an arc welders torch had hit thin metal with too high an amperage setting. Sims barely registered a jolt and the plane went out of control turning belly up as the ejection system blew off the canopy and shot him straight down.

As he turned over, he saw his squad circling higher. He saw his shoot deploy, and shortly his seat crashed through the pines and came to rest on the forest floor of the La Veta Valley.

His second in command called in the hostile fire, received permission to return fire. The five F-35 jets dove down on the orbs. They fired four hellfire missiles each with every orb targeted with three or at least two missiles. They unleashed, close in and pulled out.

The roar of the twenty missiles going off above him when they hit the shielding of the Pandamon fighters knocked Sims flat. When he could look up, he saw five of the six orbs take off after the F-35 jets, who were making a wide turn to the south. Plasma balls shot out and all five remaining jets were hit and corkscrewed into the mountain side. Sims had been lucky. The others didn't have time to bail out.

"Pist," Sims heard above the crackle of fire all around. Pisssst," the hiss came again, then a voice, "over here, pilot, come over here, hurry." A man and a woman stood silhouetted in the fire light of the burning objects and forest.

The silhouetted figures startled Sims. He pulled his nine-millimeter pistol. "Stay right where you are," Sims moved closer and pointed the gun at Stark.

"Put that thing away, before you hurt someone," Stark told him.

"We must move from here," Surilen cautioned

"Yes," Stark agreed with her. They had barely made it out of the crippled ship when the Pandamon fighters had put three particle beam blasts into Surilen's small ship. "These guys mean business," Stark said to Sims. "They are coming back and we need to put some distance between us and here."

The captain was beginning to see some sense to that. The orbs were racing back across the valley, coming at them. The one on station at the wreck had strong searchlights playing in the trees above them. "I have a pinger that will bring help," Sims explained his reluctance to leave the area.

"Your choice," Stark told him, "But we are getting away from here," he reinforced, "unless, you are going to shoot."

Captain Sims looked at his pistol and put it back in its holster. He was blinded by the flashes from the combat and couldn't have hit them with a lucky shot. Stark and Surilen had already turned and were disappearing into the dark headed uphill and away from the flames of the burning jets down the valley. "I'm coming," Sims started to follow. He blindly ran right into a pine tree. "Ohfff," he let out.

Stark moved back to him and then guided him along with the three staying close to each other. They made their way north along the valley, putting as much distance as possible, as fast as possible in the dim moonless starlight that came and went behind scudding clouds. The forest floor was not dense, as the trees had it shaded out, and they were able to gain some several hundred yards before the searchlights began to comb in widening circles.

Chapter 23 Colorado A Cowboy Picnic

They walked uphill and away from the crash area through the pine forest and scrub brush for many miles uphill, pausing only shortly to catch their breath in the increasing altitude. In the starlight, they came across a game trail headed mostly north, and this made the going a little easier.

In the very early dawn, they came across a black bear and startled each other, but the animal quickly moved away. Surilen was fascinated to see an animal that she had never seen before. Sims fingered his nine-millimeter pistol but holstered the gun without having to use it. "Unlikely that bear will give us any trouble," Stark told him. Sims was still nervous.

They walked north and uphill. For much of the night they could see fires burning at the crash sights, and several blue orbs coming and going.

"We should stay close to the crash site," Sims complained. The air force search and rescue will be looking for survivors."

"You can be sure that the area is being watched from satellite, but what can they do, until the Pandamon fighters clear out, there is nothing that they can do."

"Who are you people?" Sims asked when they took a break.

"I'm Stark Raven and this is Surilen."

"Captain Greg Sims," they shook hands. "Say," Sims recognized the name. "You're that wealthy space industrialist that disappeared some five or six years ago. I've heard of you. Where have you been?"

"Is that all," Stark replied. "It seems like a lifetime," he thought over the events. "You wouldn't believe it if I told you," Stark told him.

"Maybe I would," Sims tried to draw him out. "I've seen a lot of classified anomalies, or whatever you want to call these glowing orbs. We've been filming and chasing these orbs for years. We've never had one shoot us before, but then we have orders not to engage or even arm our weapons when we chase them."

"It's a long story, and hope that we get to have time to tell it."

"We should keep moving," Surilen told Stark. They will find our scent, and the sniffers will hunt us."

"Say," Sims was curious. "What language is that?" He puzzled over Surilen. "Never heard a language that sounded like that."

"You won't either," Stark agreed. "We should keep moving."

"Where?" Captain Sims was apprehensive of getting lost in the forest.

"I have been in this area," Stark told them.

"You have a plan," Greg asked him?

"Not exactly, but maybe, if the old steam train still runs this tourist line. I've been on the train some years ago, and the track runs along that ridge above us. They pushed on.

It was about three hours after the sun was coming over the mountains when they came across the train tracks. "What day of the week is this, Greg?" Stark asked him.

"It was Saturday night when we engaged and crashed, this is a Sunday morning." Sims told him.

"If the train still runs, it will be along soon." Stark prepared to build a fire, in a stump next to the tracks. "I hope you're carrying a lighter," Stark looked hopeful.

"That's affirmative," Sims flicked his lighter. "Standard issue for just this kind of emergency, well maybe not this kind," he joked. It was later in the morning when they felt the rumble in the tracks and got ready to light the fire.

"The train will have to stop for the conductor to put this little fire out, which he will assume a previous train started with a cinder. We'll hitch a ride when they stop, and while they are distracted."

When the engineer saw the fire, he stopped for the conductor to take an extinguisher and put it out. In the meantime, Stark, Surilen, and Greg Sims climbed aboard a car on the other side. When they entered the car, four cowboy musicians looked up from their guitar playing at the other end of the car. "Well, what have we got climbin' on the cowboy express this morning boys," one exclaimed. Most of the seats were full of tourists that gave a curious stare. The train began to move on. The three sat in the only vacant bench set and withstood the eying they were getting from the cluster of guitar players. There was almost a full load of passengers, but several seats were empty near the back of the car.

"As I remember, on a Sunday this old train goes up to a cowboy picnic, and then back to the La Veta station in the late afternoon," Stark explained.

"That's right," Sims agreed, "I've been meaning to take it but never have. Our secret MOA base for observing this San Luis Valley activity is only eleven miles north of there."

The band had taken up singing the old western song about tying the devil's tale in knots and had just reached the part where they were brandin' the ole devil up real good, when the first sniffer whizzed past the train. Surilen stiffened, and the guitars stopped. "What the hell was that?" The red bearded one said. Two more came whining by screaming air through their sensors for a molecule of the scent they were looking for. One wheeled above the train and came by the other side for another whiff. It branched off and went back out into the woods for a widening search across the valley. The four guitar players crowded across the windows looking for another glimpse. "Did you see that?" The red and gray bearded leader asked the three newcomers.

"Say," another said suspiciously, "what kind of party are ya'll dressed up for," he exclaimed through an extremely long and thick white beard. "Look like ya' jus' come off a flying saucer, dressed in them silver suits, and him," he gestured toward Sims, "he looks like he jus' bailed out of a jet plane and landed on his head through tha' trees."

"Pretty good guess," Sims looked at his tattered flight suit. "We are just dressed up Steam Punk for the party. You guys look like you're headed to a party yourself," he retorted.

"Oh, we're the New Riders of the Purple Sage," one of the four spoke up, "headed up to do the cowboy picnic, and the bar-b-que."

"Well," Stark looked nervously out the window. "We'll just tag along for the party," he told them. "What were those?" He asked Surilen very quietly. She indicated to him that they were from the Pandamon ships and were searching for them through traces of molecules of scent that they picked up at the crash sites. She indicated the coal smoke from the old train and thought that the thick smoke might make it harder for the sniffers, as she called them in Xinor slang, to pick up a trace of them.

The train wound up the pass and into the Spanish Peaks, through valleys and over streams, winding and following a small river up and up the valley along the pine covered slopes. It was a very enjoyable ride after walking all night from the wreck sites. They soon came to a small station and platform. The smell of bar-b-que brisket assailed their nostrils as soon as they disembarked. The sound of a fiddle, guitar, and banjo playing a lively tune brightened the crisp mountain air. People milled all around.

Stark, Surilen, and the pilot Sims roamed the small complex eating the food, they were ravenous from the night's hiking. There were tourists from the major cities of the West escaping the summer heat, and several local country and western talents.

Three of the group on the train were on stage playing an old western tune, and fourth of that group was twirling a rope doing rope tricks, by passing the loop over his head and twirling it around his body.

Stark saw Surilen move behind a rock column. He looked at where she was pointing. There was a sniffer coming out of the forest following along the train track and overflying the stage and crowd watching.

A hushed ahhhh, went up from the crowd as the device settled near the stage. The band slowed to a full-mouthed open stop. The rope twirler just naturally popped a loop over what appeared to be its head, its protuberance with the sensing array. At first, it didn't notice that the loop had it caught, as it moved sideways taking samples. The twirler took those few moments to tie off the other end, a wise precaution as it went crazy when it hit the end of its rope.

The sniffer spun and dived in all directions finally corkscrewing itself into the ground. The crowd moved around it with all the cell phones in picture mode, and many raised over their heads for a better picture. Some were in movie mode making a video when the other two sniffers zoomed into the courtyard around the gazebo.

Red, the lead guitar was fast on the trigger, turning his solid body electric ax around and swatting the sniffer right out of the air. The amplifier made a horrific kaboom, followed by another kaboom, as Captain Sims knocked down the other with a shot from his nine-millimeter service revolver. The crowd screamed and huddled together not knowing which way to flee.

"OK, folk," Red assured from the stage. "Whatever it was, we got it, Yehah," he let out a good-natured cheer. Some of the crowd laughed, but it was overcome by a gasp coming up from others, as a Pandamon fighter craft came low over the trees and stood above the crowd. It had been called in by the destruction of the sniffers.

Only seconds behind the flying saucer, a squadron of F-35s came screaming across just above the spaceship. The ship continued in place to what seemed threatening to the crowd, but began to move off, and then zoomed away to the northwest. The F-35s followed after in a futile chase, as they were outdistanced in moments.

When the F-35's thunderous fly over had faded away, Captain Sims observed to Stark. "Those planes were armed with nuclear tipped harpoon missiles. I think after the retaliation last night failed, NORAD decided to take a more aggressive posture."

"That's an understatement. The three of us and three hundred other people are really glad that the saucer decided to take a powder out of here."

The red-headed musician that seemed to be the leader of the band was approaching them. Several rings of concentric circles were gathered around the three destroyed sniffers. Much of the crowd had retreated up the hill to the parked trains that had arrived from La Veta and Alamosa with the picnickers. "Say, you three," Red said accusingly, as he walked up to them. "You three have something to do with this. It all started when the train stopped to put a fire out, and you three got on board. Then these flying vulture things came whizzing past. Who the hell are you guys, anyway?" He demanded.

"Well," Stark informed him. "This is Captain Greg Sims, lately ejected from a disabled F-35 fighter, shot down by aliens from another galaxy, last night, and this is Surilen, a lady from a galaxy next door, who flew me here in a space ship while we followed a bad guy to the Great Dunes from his lair across the universe, and me, I've lately returned from a trip across the galaxies in a small deep freeze, pleased to meet you, Red, I'm Stark Raven."

Stark stuck out his hand and gripped the hand of the open-mouthed musician. Red quickly regained his composure and shook Stark's hand. "If this has anything to do with them cattle rustlin' orbs of light, we'd like to help. You know cattle rustlin' is still a hangin' offense 'round here."

Soon, the sound of helicopters could be heard, and some minutes later, several helicopters arrived, and men began to deploy on ropes and seal the entire area.

Sims looked at Stark and Surilen. "This is going to be a best case for you two. You need to come with me, and we'll find out who is in charge here."

"That is a dandy idea," Stark agreed taking Surilen's hand and following Captain Sims. Pictures of the sniffers and the action including the flying saucer hovering above the crowd were already making it on to the Internet, and into the media.

It was several days before things worked around to Surilen and Stark being interviewed by Ruben McAuley. He was stunned to realize that Stark Raven was the "alien" new arrival. "I've heard a lot about you, Mr. Raven," Ruben shook his hand. "Your Morris Code message was an important link to understanding the problem at Pantex."

"What happened to the two aliens Uris and Kurege?" Stark hoped he knew.

"That is a question I'd be delighted to answer right now," McAuley opened a side door and beckoned to the people inside.

Surilen and Uris both let out delighted squeals and ran to hug each other. "And this is Urme," Uris lifted the little girl who was tugging at her mother's leg.

"Stark Raven," Kurege said in wonder. "How in the universe did you come to be here?"

The reunion was joyful all around, with true amazement at the miraculous circumstance. McAuley made it possible for them to go to live with Kurege and Uris and Urme, until better arrangements could be found. A meeting was planned for a debriefing at the house in Los Alamos.

Several evenings later, when Urme had been put to bed, the five sat down in the living room. "We've already talked some among ourselves, Ruben, and we know some of what is happening," Stark told him.

"Go ahead," Ruben put his phone on record and sat it down where the lens viewed all four in front of him.

"Things that you don't know," Stark told him. "We, Surilen and I followed a new type of spaceship to a complex in northern New Mexico. I have seen this individual through a night vision scope. This is Metastophiles. He has control of a vast Empire across the entire universe, and he is here on Earth." Stark looked to see Ruben McAuley's reaction.

"Thith ith thame ath Pantex," Uris said to Ruben.

"How so?" He questioned.

"Sargon wath clone replicant, Metathaplith ith the mathter."

"So, what is he after," Ruben knew part of the answer and Kurege came up with the direct and immediate answer.

"Plutonium," Kurege said the obvious from the Pantex episode.

"Proto-fetal fluid, some type of life extension drug that Metastophiles takes," Stark added, as he had flown across the galaxy with the fluid in cryogenic storage.

"But what is he doing with the genetic breeding," Ruben told them, "and, he seems to have been doing this for hundreds, maybe thousands of years. How is that possible?"

Surilen spoke to Uris in their language. "He moveth through time," Uris told him.

"Stark," Kurege asked? "You have told us how you came out of cryogenic suspension on Pandamon. But, how long did you hibernate? That is the question. Uris is very curious about this."

"I don't know," Stark admitted.

"I do," Surilen added, to Stark's surprise. "I have seen the records that were recovered by the Rebels on Pandamon." Uris and Surilen began a quiet conversation between the two of them.

"See, as Uris has explained this to me, this is the continuum shift across the Stardoor. We have a Standard Xinor Time, related to Xinor, but the continuum is not understood. It is possible to get from one time to another some of the time, but all time is not accessible to all other time, all of the time. It is very easy to get lost in there," Kurege told him.

"I see," Ruben was getting dizzy. "So, what can we piece together to practically know from all this?" He questioned.

"It is a good guess that he has seen the future, at least parts of it, and knows what we will try to do to defeat him," Kurege made the intuitive leap.

"That is an ominous challenge," Ruben shook his head.

"The worst of it," Stark continued, "is Surilen thinks that another mogul tyrant with vast resources in planets, has negotiated for Earth. They are methane breathers, so the population of Earth may be enslaved, or eliminated."

"Uris believes that Metastophiles is here at Los Alamos," Kurege told them.

"What is she basing that on?" Ruben asked skeptically.

"She saw him once in her childhood when her aunt, her father's sister was aligned in a marriage to him."

"Who does she think he is?" Ruben asked.

""We were at a Director's Department Heads Party, and he is Phillip Roth."

"You mean the PADSTE of Los Alamos National Laboratories?" Ruben was taken back. "You mean the powerful owner of Roth Pharmaceuticals?"

"That is the man," Kurege confirmed. "A co-worker of Uris' named Peralta, has shown her a picture of Roth in the nineteen-forties and another in the nineteen-sixties, working here at Los Alamos.

Ruben made notes. "And Uris has seen pictures?"

"Yes," Kurege confirmed. Uris nodded in agreement.

"Oh, my God," Ruben was stunned. He thought for a few moments. "This needs analysis and debriefing of each of you, and then the president needs as much of the story as we can piece together."

Uris and Surilen were absorbed in a conversation in their own language, as Surilen gave Uris all the information that she could remember and all that she had stored on her personal data storage device, on the amount of time that Stark had been in cold storage, and the angle and velocity of their co-ordinates into the Draco Stardoor. "There is a possible calculation that might be made from these numbers that will point at the timeline for the Metagestapo," she told Surilen as they went over the figures. "I will need to do some research and some very difficult differentials, then guess at some of the integrations, but there may be something usable in this," she puzzled. "With the data from the Time Probe that is in Kirkendall's laboratory, and this data from your find on Pandamon, it may be possible to find a path to get in front of him. If I can catch up with him, I can destroy him," Uris struck her fist into the palm of her other hand.

Chapter 24 Moon (The Biggest Dig)
Rich Enterprises

Striker Rich was expecting Calley and Margaret, along with Herman Hartman, but there was a huge surprise when Stark Raven, Surilen, Uris, Kurege, and Urme came off the transport right behind them.

He was hugging Calley, telling her how brave she was to come back to the moon and see the first launch of the LALLA, the Los Alamos Laboratories Linear Accelerator, system when he saw the dark hair, then recognized the native American Indian features, with a huge idiotic grin on its face. He slowly realized who he was looking at. He had to look at Calley to see she knew the joke too. "Where the Hell have you been, Stark Galileo Raven?" Striker shouted to him up the loading corridor.

"That is a very good question," he said. "This is Surilen, Uris' cousin, and she might be able to come closer to the answer then me, cause, buddy, I haven't a clue," he laughed and shook hands with his partner from all those years of work in early space launch in the first days of commercial space exploration. They had been roommates at Stanford. Stark had come from high school in Dallas, where his grandparents had lived.

This was a great day for Rich Enterprises, and Striker in particular. The first launch of the LALLA, the Liner Accelerator Launch System. Especially, since Stark Raven, Surilen, Uris, Kurege, Calley, and Urme were arriving with him eager to meet his friends. He paced the edges of the crowd. When the ships from Earth were all docked, they all took transport to the Rich Digs, as it was called. Several hundred project people and ranking Navy were in the entourage. Stark Raven had been in conversation with Admiral Brenda Green on the trip from Moon Base. They had attended the same high school in Dallas when they were young. All the dignitaries were present as Striker let Margaret Hartman push the launch button. The CAT was smoothly away out toward the asteroid belt. This first one was a self programing exploratory and mining robot.

There was a great party afterward and the celebration went on into the noon hour. Herman Hartman and Margaret ate at Striker's table. "After lunch, Herman," Striker offered, "I would like to show you some of the projects that we are working on for future launches."

"I would be very interested to see that," Herman agreed. Margaret beamed a smile, as long as she could stay near to Striker.

After lunch, Striker led them to the assembly area. "Here is our first prototype self-sustaining personnel module for four people." Striker led them to a long cylindrical, sectioned module. "The systems include VASMIR rockets for deep space, and a supply of argon in one of the central sections, giving it long voyage capability. And the sections can rotate at the joints and spin creating artificial gravity in those sections. In its long configuration, it has rockets and wings that come out with shielding on the underside and forward," he indicated. "That gives it landing capability in some atmospheres, as well as on, say an asteroid."

Urme and Margaret were dashing through the crowd with Margaret taking pictures on her phone and Urme close behind every step. Uris, Surilen, and Calley were in serious women conversation about shoes.

While the party was going on, Striker and Stark had time to try and catch up. Striker motioned and led him away to his office.

"Well, Old Buddy," Striker sat down in a chair and Stark relaxed his frame on a soft couch. "Can you fill me in on any of this? Where have you been?"

"Nowhere really," Stark grinned. "Just on a trip halfway around the known universe in a deep freeze."

"Really," Striker smiled back, not knowing if he was being kidded or not. "And you end up with the good lookin' lady," he noted next.

"Surilen is quite the find," Stark paused to reflect on what was coming, "especially when her cavalry gets here," Stark got solemn.

"Hmmm," Striker placed his fingertips together and touched his lips in thought. "So, I know some of this. I was in the San Luis Valley and saw a mutilation and I know that Kurege was taken from Earth as an infant. But, no one explained how any of it fits,"

"You know Roth Pharmaceuticals?" Stark questioned.

"Yes," Striker pointed toward the launch and pre-launch area. "Roth has funded much of the research and equipment here, in partnership with the US government. There are several pharmaceutical experiments scheduled for launching into deep space over the next month."

"Well, then you know Phillip Roth the PADSTE of Los Alamos National Laboratories."

"I've not met him," Striker shrugged. "But I know who he is. My boss double," Striker motioned all around.

"He is some kind of alien creature that moves through time. We have him at the early lab as early as nineteen-forty-five, off and on right up through the present."

"Wh.. what, how," Striker tried to wrap his brain around it.

"Surilen and I followed Roth, known as Lord Metastophiles, in the Xinor Empire, to Earth from Uris' home planet Saphos. He's head of some type of Gestapo upper echelon that escaped nineteen-forty-five Germany in a crude time machine type conveyance. From there, they have 'progressed'." Stark put it in imaginary quotes with two fingers of each hand.

241

"He's making very advanced drugs for a future market of the rich old." Striker sat back. "He is designing the future of mankind, in a way," he shook his head.

"You don't know the half of it, Striker. He has sold the Earth's population into slavery, we think, maybe even sold the planet to methane breathing creatures that will have no use for man, except maybe to eat him. He's interbreeding with genetically psychic women and following the children in time, sometimes taking them like Michael Hodge was taken. He is out in front of us and knows what we are going to do before we do it. There have been some thoughts given to how to stop him from messing with this part of the gene pool."

"How?" Striker was on the same wavelength.

"Isolate them," Stark gave the obvious answer. Striker looked out into the launch bay outside the office door. "Send them out to try and escape."

"I've found something in the old Cassini data I want you to see," Striker logged on to his computer system. He pulled up a file that he had been working on, showing old data from the early Cassini mission that x-rayed the asteroid belt as it passed through on its way out. "Here is a very interesting reading," Striker turned the screen where Stark could see it.

"That looks like a signature for oxygen-nitrogen atmosphere," Stark saw it in the read out from the analysis program of the new software applications.

"Yes, and look here, and here," Striker pointed. "That looks like structures, and machines of various types." He pointed at the data on the screen. "This is coming from one of the larger of the asteroid planetoids, large enough to have a gravity field. I've sent probes to investigate, and they are due to arrive anytime now. I sent them out on rockets early on, as soon as I saw the new reading on the old Cassini data.

"Interesting," Stark looked closer. "A bio-system, maybe, maintaining an atmosphere."

"Maybe," Striker pulled up some of the data on the screen. "This looks more like machinery," he pointed to a copper band reading, with a telltale mix of steel and aluminum.

"Some type of self-repairing machinery that is maintaining the atmosphere."

"That is what it looks like in this data," Striker confirmed.

"Someone built it," Stark concluded.

"That would have to follow," Striker agreed. "There was believed to be a planet out there that the asteroid belt comes from. A search brings up a Marduk as an ancient name. Supposedly destroyed in an explosion of some unknown origin.

"I remember something about that," Stark was thinking back to their Stanford days. "There was some supposedly ancient inhabitant with psychic connections to modern Earth."

"That's part of the mythology." Striker continued to scroll through the program on the Cassini's data. "This data looks to show a planet that was torn apart, but one large piece of it with a self-maintaining machine is keeping an oxygen-nitrogen atmosphere."

"Worth looking into," Stark observed.

"That's why I sent several probes out to take a look. They should reach their destination today."

"I've been in conversation with the President," Stark confided, "and he is challenged to make a decision about what to do about the genetic altering of these selected families. What we find out here, keep it secret until I've had time to talk with the President."

"Whatever you want, Stark," Striker reassured him, "I am really wanting to see the new data from the survey satellite I sent out." He turned to another console. "There might be data coming in from the probe that was sent out right now. It is due to reach the area and begin transmissions." He clicked the screens to be active. "Yes, we have a data stream arriving." He manipulated the coordinates of the data stream to begin to form images on the various screens of the control console.

"What can you make out?" Stark moved in closer and peered at the screens as images began to take shape.

"Incredible," Striker pointed at some of the shapes. "Here, and here, these are structures, made by someone, and look at this screen, it shows the molecular content, and it is reading an oxygen-nitrogen atmosphere. There is a great deal of inhabitable space ready made on this asteroid, and big enough to have gravity also."

"This is just begging for exploration," Stark caught the old dream that he and Striker shared. "I think that I have a channel with Ruben McAuley and Uris and Kurege direct to President Wilson's ear. This deserves development money to achieve human exploration capability. I sure as hell don't want you to rely on Roth Pharmaceuticals to the extent that you are doing. That can't be good. Whatever he is making out there in those zero g laboratories will bring him back to get it. That is going to have to be considered and prepared for."

"I have already begun developing person pods for human exploration. We have systems of solar sails that collect sunlight for the food growing pods, and extendable sections to increase the room after launch, where we are restricted to the diameter of the "Big Dig" tube magnets. After launch, there are expandable sections, and rotations can be started to achieve about three-fourths of an Earth gravity. Also, we have developed various exercise machines that are designed to fit the pods, and allow people to stay fit for long term space travel. As long as enough photons strike the sails, these pods are self-sustaining. With more funding, I can speed up development and begin to build and test prototypes."

"I think that I can guarantee those funds," Stark was thinking of Herman Hartman if not the government of the USA, or even his own huge fortune, if any of it was left. He was determined that Striker have all that he needed. He just felt the importance of the discovery.

Chapter 25 – The Dragon's Gate, Draco

Pax Xinorus

Hier Baron Rudolph Von Malick, known as Vice Chancellor Molok, had the unfortunate circumstance of being known as the Ziet Time Trooper Commander most ready to sacrifice men in the line of duty. He was in charge of a holding action after the Battle of the Bulge where 78% of his command was killed. He had been the one to have heard Commander Urvin from the Saphos delegation. Now he was in the middle of the storm. He also had his orders from Metastophiles.

Chancellor Beel had directed him to take a Xinor war fleet to the Draco Stardoor and follow the marker left by Surilen and Stark Raven when they followed the Lucifer back to New Mexico. The Xinor war fleet was joined at the Draco Stardoor by the Trident with Urvin commanding. Scouts were sent to take samples of the markers.

"The scans are very much showing a wide dispersion," Molok communicated with Urvin on board the Trident.

"The Trident is equipped to follow a tracer that thinly defined," Urvin told him.

"To be lost in time," Molok appraised the situation, "is not something to take lightly."

"The Trident will find the proper angle and velocity to arrive at the Singular time. You don't need to concern yourself, Chancellor, the House of Ur has technology not installed in your ships. Just follow, as you have been ordered," Urvin was beginning to think that they would try to block him.

"By all means, commander, lead on," Molok told him. "But we will send a scout ship through with you and wait for a return to be certain that a stable course is certain.

The Stargate is new and may undergo further contractions. The scout must scan for a future glitch in the neutron star. This has to be tested before I will commit my fleet."

"Take your time," Urvin challenged. "We will have this Terra located, and the problem solved when you arrive."

With that parting Urvin scowled a 'good riddance'. He didn't like Beel, the Chancellor, or Molok, the Vice Chancellor. He was aware that the factions always aligned to further the Empire's hold on the Free Houses. Balance of trade between the Empire and a house derived the status. Ur was free, and their technologies unsurpassed, until Metastophiles attack on Saphos. Now Urvin would take the fight to him in the Terran System, he would find the base.

"Enter the Stardoor," he gave the order. "Navigator, follow the trace."

"Got it commander, it's locked in," came from Zethurus at the navigator's station. They entered hyperspace as they fell into the gravity well of the neutron star, emerging to the other side, like diving under a waterfall, in Taurus, headed for Earth.

"New stars, commander," Zethurus reported from the sensing console of the Trident Warship.

"Any idea of the time differential?" Urvin asked.

"None, commander, this is new space, without reference."

"Fantastic," Urvin leaned closer to the viewer.

"I still have an argon tracer from Surilen, with her molecular frequency."

"Good, set course," Urvin went to his cabin to make charts of this system. It was a couple of hours before he got a call from the bridge that they were arriving at their destination.

"What have we got here, Zethurus?" Urvin peered at the viewer. A dark orb filled the screen with a bright blue bubble just beyond.

"Surilen's trace leads to the planet beyond this moon, which we are using as a screen while we observe."

"What are you seeing, so far," Urvin questioned, both sides of his scared face showing concern.

"World in early technological phase a couple of hundred years along the curve. They have atomic, but no hyperdrive or anti-gravity of any type. Exclusively chemical rockets being used for space transport.

"There is a moon colony beyond," he indicated the orb in their viewer. "It is located on the other side. We are analyzing their communications and electronic data transfer files and systems. Nothing much to worry about, no obvious armament on this moon, but a platform in orbit about the planet that can project plasma fire, in a crude but possibly lethal way. We are using the moon to shield ourselves from the platform while we listen to their transmissions."

"So what threat level are they, Zethurus?"

"You can pretty much walk in and demand what you wish," he shrugged. "They are not going to present a problem to the Trident." He looked at some data on his monitor. There are about one hundred language groups that are using voice communications and video frequency. We have an understanding of English as Stark Raven spoke it, and that comes from a republic, the United States of America. They have the plasma platform weapon, and they are one of the major nations on the planet and on this moon.

"Are we getting a signal from Surilen's ship?" Urvin was concerned. He knew they had followed only the argon trace. Other signals were not present.

"Nothing," Zethurus told him.

"What will happen if we show ourselves to the weapons platform?"

They may shoot."

"Can we take a plasma hit?"

"As long as we have shielding, and hyperdrive capability."

"So, this United States is a democratic republic from what Stark Raven has told me," Urvin remembered. "There is a chain of command to the top leader. Permission to fire their plasma weapon at a craft unknown to them could only come from the top level of the command chain." He thought about it over a minute.

"Sounds logical," Zethurus said.

"Let them see us and hit the weapons platform with a laser carrier containing voice. Get a recording of this, and make an English translation," he signaled the officer at a station on the ship's bridge, who started a record file, and conversion to American English. "United States leader, we are seeking Commander Surilen and Queen Uris of the House of Ur. We come in peace." He signaled the operator to end the recording.

"Will they know who Surilen and Uris are?" Zethurus questioned.

"If she is alive, the leader may possibly know."

The Apollo Station was already on high alert when the system alerted on The Trident as an unknown. The warship could be seen clearly by Colonel Rameriz, who was on duty at the time. "Madre Mia," he said to himself, a cold fright hitting him at the sight of what was obviously the first alien warship ever seen from earth.

"Com," he punched his communications, "get me President Logan Wilson."

"When?" Came back the lackadaisical reply,.

"Now, right now," barked Rameriz.

The message to Apollo Station had been being received for several hours. The Trident didn't try to move closer. Wilson ordered the station to hold their fire.

On board The Trident, Zethurus reported the arrival of the Xinor fleet coming out of hyperspace and approaching the Sol system.

"Stand down Trident," came the challenge from Molok's flagship upon approach.

"We are getting warning messages from Molok." Zethurus reported to Urvin.

"Open a path," Urvin ordered. "This is commander Urvin, Molok, what are you meaning with these challenge hails?"

"Urvin, you have no authority to make yourself known to this planet. "This planet is under a Xinor Protection Order. This planet is the source of the ceramic plutonium hyperspace projectiles scattered throughout time and space. Their garbage has created a real hazard."

"I am searching for Commander Surilen, and Queen Uris of Ur. Surilen's ship's signal is lost, and I have a right to attempt rescue."

"I have orders from High Commissioner Beel. You will have to work through my authority. Xinor is placing this planet under Protection Order. Stand down your communications with Earth."

"President Wilson," he heard direct from Rameriz on Apollo. "We are getting a new message now, I'll feed you a recording. This is going out all over the planet, sir on every voice frequency.

Wilson heard a click, then the message began,. The first few words didn't make that much sense to him.

It said, "Terran Protection Order # 1:

For the safety of sentient and innocent species on the 3rd Planet from the Sun Sol in the galaxy of Milky Way, a curfew is imposed upon travel without Regis Xinor consent, This Standard Time order, By Molok, Vice Chancellor of the Xinor Republic."

Then, as the message continued, President Logan Wilson began to feel the hair on the back of his neck stand, as he got a glimmer of the meaning of what he heard next.

Uris noticed that Urme had been quiet for some time this Saturday morning. She opened the door to her room, and she was on her princess bed, with her pod in her lap, working intently.

"Wha'ch duin'," Uris asked?

"Playin' a game," the little girl said without looking up from the screen.

"What kind of game," Uris moved closer to the bed.

"A guessing game," Urme beamed a smile.

"What type of guessing game?" Uris moved closer, aware that the child was precocious with computers.

"One that I invented," Urme bragged.

"Oh, really," Uris came in close to take a very good look.

"It's interactive, worldwide," Urme beamed with her accomplishment. "See, first I established a storage for my files, called .guessitright, then I placed a controller for the interactive called the Bene', that is the word that means 'good' or 'well' most all over the world, so the interactive controller is the Best Guesser in the whole world, and they get to hold the title. It is kind of like 'Center Of Attention' but I got tired of that one," the little girl waved her hand in a dismissal wave she learned from her mother. Uris smiled to herself.

"Really, Urme, show me how good you can guessitright."

"I can do it," she preempted the current player, as was her right, as it was her site.

"Someone in Korea is on wanting me to guess a color," Urme spoke Orange into the Puff Dragon upgrade for children for free she had downloaded and combined with her game. "Orange," she said into the microphone on her Ygamepod, for young girls.

In a moment the answer popped up on the screen with a green smiley face, and her score with the new addition. "The game keeps track of correct answers and compares it with other players worldwide. I'm not the Best Guesser right now, but I sometimes am. A girl in Scotland named Megan is the Best Guesser right now, and she gets the Bene' Crown. I did that," Urme showed Uris with great pride.

"That ith very imprethive," Uris saw nothing wrong in the game. "We will have to show your father when he comth home." She smoothed the little girls hair, and Urme pulled away, never really wanting her mother to touch her. Uris, puzzled as always by the little girl, was about to leave her to her play when a comment message came through to Urme from Megan: "The Game is a DANGER NOW. Stop Play, Megan the Scot, Bene' of the guessitrights...

Uris reached out to Urme's computer. "How is the game a danger?"

"Something is watching us talk," came the text back.

"Who?" Uris questioned.

"Something of bad intent. I am not doing the game any longer and am blogging a warning to the members. Megan the Scot, bene'guessitright.

Other eyes watched this game with great interest. Roth looked over the report and the list of names and families along with family trees. "We should have thought of this, and this child drops it in our lap. She is identifying the psychic families of the entire planet. Make sure that everything is recorded and stored for future data mining," Roth instructed the assistant that brought the report.

Urme's eyes got big with fright, and she snapped her computer closed and ran to her room and covered her head with covers.

Uris sought her out. "Urme, come out," she coaxed.

"No." The child shook her head and wouldn't budge.

In the Kirkendall lab, Andro lit up. He sent commands from his Protect Maxim. Ur was in danger, if Urme was in danger. Deep in the basement of the CMR the MERGE hummed. In Chen Ching's lab, the MOT glowed purple, the temperature in the BEC dropped to ½ a nanokelvin above Absolute Zero.

Integration and calculations were carried out at a sub-atomic level, complete connectedness in quantum total entanglement. An understanding was reached, and commitments to act formed. Mergatroid found purpose.

Another group watched the watchers, with Roth's endeavors under suspicions and reports went out that a possible child abduction was being planned from a terminal inside the Los Alamos section of lines, as the data mining of the game participants was being noted, and that was being noted and passed on to someone in John Gavin's office at Homeland Security.

When Gavin had a chance to get President Wilson's ear, he had Ruben McAulley join in. "You see what's happening," Gavin began. "He's after the daughter. Roth is behind the kidnapping of the father years earlier. He's behind many, maybe all of these alien abduction cases. Where the cases were once dismissed as delusional, we now have reviewed enough to understand the pattern."

"Motive?" Wilson questioned.

"Some type of genetic breeding or breeding experiment, we think."

"Yes, I can see that John, "Wilson was a bit insulted. Everyone underestimated his quick mind just because he was known to have been a marine-military-straight-arrow.

"Seems to be trying to tell the future, sir," Gavin got formal.

"Aren't we all," Gavin let out a sigh and shook his weary presidential head. "What do you make of this, Ruben?" Wilson turned to the other man.

"We need a lot more information on Phillip Roth, and we need to get ready to move on Los Alamos and the probable underground complex, just like we did at Pantex, when this started."

"What are we going to do about the targeted children?" Wilson was almost pleading.

An idea came to McAulley, maybe it was the recent trip on the moon to the LALLA launch. "This just occurs to me, Logan," he started to explain. "Striker Rich is developing People Pods for his linear launching. Those launches occur without a trace," he made his point.

"I think I see what you are getting at," Logan was quick to put the puzzle together. "Let's up his funding and support in that area with a black opps cover. Gentlemen, nothing about this is spoken about to anyone without a need to know."

Ruben McAuley received a call from the President. The phone rang and his phone recognized the caller. He thought that this usually went the other way, and wondered what could be happening, now.

"Ruben," the President said. "We have what amounts to a summons from alien warships above the planet."

"They've come," Ruben exclaimed. "But, which group, sir?"

"Some Commander Urvin is asking for Commander Surilen, and Queen Uris of Ur. Then another voice of command began to override the first message, and a sort of indictment of Earth for violations of, and I quote;

'Nuclear Waste Proliferation Across Time and Space.

Being a Planet in Religious Turmoil,

Being a Planet on a Self-Destructive Course,

Thus, Regis Xinor, in order to avoid a catastrophic   outcome, resulting in sentient grief and harm,

Establishes the Terran Protectorate.

Earth is now part of the Xinor Empire.

Governor Molok,

This year of Standard Xinor Time.

So, it is recorded, so it will be'. And this is being broadcast worldwide."

The President paused for Ruben's reaction. Ruben was to be stunned to say anything.

"Well," Ruben, "I think that you might have been correct in suggesting that we needed to keep Uris safe, despite all her many transgressions. Now, I need you to contact her, and Kurege, with Surilen, and Stark Raven, and bring to Washington as soon as possible. That seems to be the first and most logical thing at this time to try and gather some information to deal with this Xinor Empire. I don't remember much about what Uris told us about it at the meeting that day." The President tried to remember.

"Yes, sir," Ruben told him and then hung up.

President Logan Wilson buried his head in his good hand, with his prostheses trying to get a grip on the oval table in front of him. What was he supposed to do with options like these? How could he frame a response? He was a military man. He gave his all. He had done it before and would again in a moment, but what was the correct response.

Ruben dialed the home number where they were all staying in Los Alamos. Stark Raven answered the phone. Ruben gave him the ultimatum.

"That's strange," Stark said, "that is not the way that Surilen expected them to react, I don't think," he was puzzled.

"I am sending a plane for the bunch of you, the President wants a face to face."

The sleek corporate jet that Ruben had chartered made a smooth landing in the rain at Dulles airport later that night. Urme was wide awake looking out the side window. The meeting was scheduled for early the next morning. Urvin and Zethurus had remained in touch with the American President Wilson and had taken a shuttle from The Trident to attend this meeting. They were both overcome with joy to see Surilen, and went to one knee and bowed head when Queen Uris was seen. Uris loved being treated like a Queen by her loyal friends of years before, and pulled them to their feet with hugs. They were all guided by Ruben McAuley to the meeting room.

"Here are their latest demands," the President shuffled papers, took a deep breath and a look around the room. "As Earth is a Xinor Protectorate for the security, stability, and peace upon the Earth, policing will be conducted where civil rights of sentients are violated. As religion and religious strife are responsible for most violations, to pay for intervention cost, a church tax of ten percent is being imposed, Molok, Vice Chancellor of the Secular Empires of United Xinor, this date." The President looked around the room No one spoke.

"Surilen," Stark encouraged her to speak. "You know the situation best."

"Xinor has not directly aided the Rebellion on Pandamon and the struggle to regain Saphos for the House of Ur. We are promised aid. Yet, we never get enough aid, now, here, as in other places, Xinor has a complete lack of will to confront Metastophiles, and instead turns to meddling in the planets internal systems of government to the ultimate enrichment of their own interest."

"Who is Metastophiles?" Wilson asked.

"We are not sure where his beginning world is." Surilen began to answer as best she could. "He has always been a part of the universe that can be accessed from the Xinor warp star, Regis, and he controls vast areas of the known star systems. He is recorded in ancient literature from our own beginnings and continuing up to the present. He controls the Xinor Central Council through political placements of the High Commision positions. He has controlled Xinor more and more for many standard years. Molok, who has brought a Xinor war fleet to Earth is a vassal of Metastopiles. They seem to mean to dominate Earth for some reason, as well as the reasons stated which is a rare but action that has some previous history in the Empire."

"What type of intervention can we expect?" The President asked her.

"They will invade your electronic systems; all the satellite voice and video communications will be placed under their control. They will send administrators to seek compliance and where there is resistance, enforcement will follow with drones, sniffers, enforcement droids, and where sentient confrontation is required, they will use some other species as mercenary enforcers, probably Pran exomorphs, as they are strong, loyal, and eager for the paycheck."

"And if a government opposes their enforcement?" The President asked the obvious.

"They will use selective types of force to disable any attempt. Whatever they find necessary. Most likely, they would start with a curfew with very harsh and select enforcement to instill fear into the general population," she said.

"And what will Commander Urvin and yourself do about such action?"

"We will not want to make an enemy of Xinor," Urvin spoke up to Surilen who nodded and then translated.

"The Trident would have to remain neutral at this point. Still Molok and Xinor's unwillingness to confront Metastophiles in his own lair brings all kinds of questions to mind. The duplicity that seems to be involved in very intricate and confusing."

"How so?" The President placed a finger to his chin, listening very carefully.

"Metastophiles will ascribe to none of the treaties on genetic interference with natural selection processes going forward on planets. Xinor enforces the policy. Xinor is secular and Metastophiles sees himself and runs his Empire as a god. Xinor and Metastophiles should be in total conflict. For several decades now, Beel and Molok have held the Chancellor and Vice Chancellor positions in the ruling Council controlling the vast Union of Sentient Worlds. They seem to be working with the enemy here and elsewhere." She paused and looked from face to face. The inference was obvious, that perhaps even this cabinet meeting was corrupt.

"You speak English very well, Surilen, "President Wilson pondered what she had told him. "I will say this; you have painted a picture of a very formidable enemy. Both these forces are awesome to confront, but it seems that the head of the snake is Metastophiles. When his Pran troops were confronted at Pantex, they mostly just gave up. Won't these do the same when faced with force?"

Ruben McAuley spoke up. "The information that we have gathered, that is John Gavin's FBI team, that has worked on this, and my own researchers, indicate that the complex beneath the San Luis Valley is vast and interlinked with others. A blocked tunnel was found after the Pantex raid that led in the direction of the San Luis Valley. Testing on the walls of the tunnels gave age of construction estimates of six to ten thousand years. It is unlikely, Mr. President, that Metastophiles will give up such extensive work without a fight."

"We saw mostly exmorphic guards around Metastophiles when Surilen and I followed him from Saphos. These were elite troops. They will fight, and they will be prepared to defend the Los Alamos Base."

"Still," the President took over and turned to his joint chiefs sitting at the far end of the oval table. "I want it man to man in hand-to-hand combat. I want to capture this technology un-destroyed, if possible. The Marines will handle the initial assault. I want a plan gentleman, and I want modified body armor and cyborg suits made to fight this enemy, the Pran exomorphs. We know they are fifty times stronger than humans, so I want suits that are built one hundred times stronger. Get it done, gentlemen. Now."

The room fell silent and no one added anything. The President spoke again, at last. "Chaplain Murry, would you say a prayer for our victory in opposing this evil that has come upon us."

After bowed heads were raised, McAuley motioned the four into a conference room. "Before you take off sight-seeing here at the Capitol, President Wilson has asked that you all stay near to advise. Stark, you have felt their strength, and your others know their physiology. We have the captives from the Pantex incident, and we have some skill in the language but could use their advice on how they fight and how to defend against it."

"I can help with those communications," Kurege spoke up. "In my youth, I had to learn the Pran language, as they were the priesthood on Pandamon."

"I will be in contact, and of course Gavin has got security on you," he shrugged. "For protection," he explained.

"It won't be a problem," Stark assured him.

With the meeting over, Uris and Kurege wanted to visit places they had been to some years before. Stark had been there many times and knew the best spot to view the great buildings to delight Surilen. They toured the monuments first then ate and went to their hotel rooms on the same floor.

The next day and for several days after, they toured endless museum corridors, enjoying the art and history of the city and surrounding area, taking day trips to Monticello and the old noble homes and some of the university campuses and museums. In the evenings, Uris worked at her laptop computer, calculations were becoming a possibility that would reveal deep knowledge of a linear understanding of the overall time line of the universe, with information gained from the Probe and Stark Raven's trip in cryogenic storage, certain variables were being resolved. She was at it until very late. Urme was with Ann in Kansas, who had flown in for a day to pick the child up and take her for a visit.

Eventually, Ruben McAuley called and left a message for each of them at the desk that there were meetings and debriefings scheduled over the next several days, and to make themselves available. He knocked on the two doors of the rooms early the next morning. "I will wait downstairs, in the breakfast nook," he told them.

There is a meeting in about an hour," he told them over continental breakfast at the hotel breakfast nook. Talk ran lively over exhibits they had enjoyed. Ruben was curious to draw them out, and the atmosphere was cozy among the friends.

Captain Collin Rains switched the power point projector on and was satisfied that it was starting with the correct file. People began to arrive. He recognized Senator Prickle and other committee chairmen. Some uniformed members of the Joint Chiefs came in followed by their bosses. Collin nodded at Admiral Brenda Green, who had been elevated to the Joint Chiefs shortly after Logan Wilson became President. Ruben McAuley came in with Uris and Kurege and two others, a man and a woman that Collin did not know. The woman looked very much like Uris and was holding hands with the dark-haired stranger.

Ruben made his way over to Collin and shook his hand. "Collin, this is Stark Raven, you may remember his name coming up in previous meetings."

"Yes," Collin looked at Stark closely. "Although, I'm a bit surprised to find you here. That must be some story."

"Maybe we will get a chance to exchange stories," Stark returned the warm and firm grip.

President Wilson came into the room, and everyone got quiet and found their seat tag.

"Captain Collin Rains is going to start us off and bring us up to speed on the needed armor," Wilson waisted no time in turning the meeting to productive time. "Captain Rains, you may commence," he ordered.

Rains snapped on the projector and an odd image of a man in robotic looking suit was projected. "The attempts to build strength enhancing as well as protective armor goes back to before the turn of the century," Rains told them. "This is an early attempt at what is known as an exo-suit. Early models increased lifting and endurance with mechanical actuators, mostly hydraulic, and protective armor moved by servos and sensors that sensed and mimic body movement." He ran through several obvious evolutions of suit types.

"Some score of years ago," he continued, "various military labs began to use nano structures incorporated into the hydraulics and servo-senor feedback systems. Some increased the strength of the armor, joints, helmets," he clicked through several generations of development.

He engaged a second projector system of holographic images and left the image up. An audible response went up at the spiderman looking robotic enhanced suit rotated on the screen. "Sometime around the beginning of the second decade, the labs ran across a type of nano fiber that was eclectically responsive at strength factors of one hundred times that of human muscle. Over the last decade or so, as short funding has allowed," here Rains turned pointedly toward Senator Prickle, and President Wilson nodded approval as Rains continued. "We have improved and incorporated these elecronanofibers into the development of the exosuits, specifically the ones engineered for fighting. You are looking at our latest version."

"This meeting today is to show the progress in building a suit capable of fighting the Pran exomorphics in hand-to-hand combat, which is going to occur in any attempt to take the San Luis base and the subterranean areas at Los Alamos."

"Momentum," Strark spoke up. His memory of being thrown against the wall in a fight with a exonorphic foe at Pantex. "I was slammed into a wall like I was almost nothing."

"We are working on both spring, hydraulic, compressed air, and small rockets to control and bring deceleration into survivable ranges." He shifted files on the projector. Tests on the Pran captured at Pantex have shown that the bony plates on the outside of their bodies give an advantage of about fifty times human strength, much like earth ants. Their exoskelital bodies are strong but the shell is easily cracked and broken here at the back and at what would be our temples. The skull carapace is thin in these spots."

"Captain Rains," the President asked, "go back to the exosuit pictures." The screen backed up. "How are these suits compared to other standards?" Wilson asked him.

"The puncture protection is far superior as the nano thread structures spread the force through a type of geodesic architecture across the surface redirecting and absorbing the force into the surface nanothreads." He showed a series of drawings that showed the force vectors of a dispelled projectile.

"As far as hammer blows like a fist or exoarm, the skin will dispel the blow but the person inside the suit may be hurled to the ground or against a wall or projection. That's where we are working now, on ways of allowing the person in the suit from being knocked unconscious from the sudden stopping." He searched the program for a different file. A series of mechanical levered footing came on the screen. There were pistons and jet nozzles in various configurations and arrangements, none looked very finished.

"Thank you one and all for your efforts," President Wilson brought the meeting to a close. "I have a request for Commander Surilen to remain here in Washington as a liaison between Commander Urvin and the Trident warship. Even though I understand that you must remain neutral," he addressed them both, "your knowledge and skills are very valuable to me at this time."

Surilen looked at Stark who looked sadly back at her, and after she had consulted with Commander Urvin in her own language, she agreed to remain at the disposal of the President's needs. At that point the meeting broke up.

When the others had left, the President closed the door and pulled his closest advisors Ruben McAulley and John Gavin, in for a talk.

"Seems to me," Logan began, "that we need to try and isolate the girls and women that we are seeing as targets of this Phillip Roth, or whoever he is. We know that our child pornography and abduction program recorded his Internet service providers code for his computer showing an undue interest in these girls and women." He tapped the reef of sheets in front of him.

Gavin spoke up first. "There's just few options," he spread his hands. "Investigations suggest that Roth, Dieter Von Rothe, Metastophiles, whatever name, is part of a war that never seems to stop, our favorite war of all time WWII. We see this guy," Gavin pointed at a photo, "this is Phillip Von Roth a minor scientist at the Der Reise complex in Austria in nineteen-forty-five." He switched pictures and scrolled through several others. "Here he is at Los Alamos in the nineteen-sixty's as Dr. David Chase. And again, in the present as Phillip Roth, PADSTE of LANL."

He paused to let President Wilson try and absorb what he was talking about. "So," Gavin led on, "he has been directing research worldwide with position, money, political influence, all of it. Roth and Senator Prickle's committees move in locked step with one another."

"He has positioned himself," Ruben spoke up, "as the premier pharmaceuticals company in the world, amassing untold wealth worldwide." Ruben continued, "it's part of a genetic programing going on using Earth as a genetic source for experiments throughout accessible time. Gavin's investigations have shown a pattern of kidnapping and impregnating women of psychic families. The case of Michael Hodge, Kurege as you know him, Mr President, proves the point that Metastophiles is attempting to find a gene that imparts prescience of the future. That is why he was spying on Uris' and Kurege's child Urme and the other children playing the "Guess It Right" game. He watched the President's face to see if he was following the point. "That's why Gavin and I feel these children and women need protecting."

"But, how?" Wilson was faced with another question among many, with no answers in sight.

In the office of the PADSTE of LANL, Philip Roth received a surprise visit. Roth was startled by the hum of the motors and the movement of magnetic lifts in his private elevator. He turned and rose from his desk with a revolver in his hand as the door opened. "Maria," he was startled to see her, then registered the seduction they shared through time. "What are you doing here?" He questioned.

"You are putting us all in danger," Maria pointed a finger at Roth as she stepped out of the ornate elevator. "You must leave. Now!" She continued to accuse.

"I am not finished here," Roth shot back. He placed the revolver in a drawer in his desk and went to her kissing her on the lips.

"No," she pulled away. "I'm risking my life being here. Segrund says that the implosion is eminent, and that the time line, even for today, is unclear. Segrund will not come here and warned me that I was risking my life to try and persuade you from this time line."

Roth backed away and bit his lip in thought. "What reports have come in?" He questioned her.

"Vril volunteers and storm troopers have probed records in the month you are in now and in the months and years directly in the future, it has all been throughly scouted, and nothing is known about the exact date. The effect in the area is devastation, and worldwide communications are disrupted. The disorder is so pervasive that the exact date and time is unknown, and probably unknowable. The cause is unknown, but the plutonium here at Los Alamos is going to explode, by the tons."

"It is not possible for such an explosion to occur."

"It is inferred from psychic reading by Vril members who report an implosion occurred creating a singularity."

"Preposterous," Roth slammed his desk.

"It is the future," she assured him. "No matter what timeline is chosen. It is a singularity in all time. Now you have been warned, and since you are first, and ahead of any of the rest, we are dependent on you for a number of things. The life extension drugs are becoming in short supply. Sigrund is disturbed by something that she sees that she will not tell the others or me. Something about you." Maria pointed at Roth again. "The Metagestopo must be fed, we have to have more of the pharmaceuticals. Segrund sent a message, and I don't understand what this is about. Segrund said to tell you, 'Only one path exists for you to the success you seek. The danger comes from the mother, and the perfect psychic body comes through the child. I'm not sure what you are up to here, Dieter," she called him by his old German name.

"All in good time, my dear, you shall see." He placed an arm around her waist and they embraced. "I have moved the genetic bank and the Lucifer class warships to Saphos," he whispered in her ear. "All is in preparation for us there."

"You must go. You must come now, Dieter," she pushed away and stepped back to the elevator, as she continued to plead with him.

"I will join you shortly, only those two details to tend to as Segrund has suggested."

"You are taking a chance here, and I am leaving now." She paused with her hand on the button. She waited with tension building in her face. "Are you coming?" She repeated.

"I will join you soon," he reassured her a second time.

"You are taking a chance," she warned, and pushed the control to go down to her own ship.

Roth went back to his desk and raised the screen for a call to the offices of Roth Pharmaceutical in Albuquerque. Rodrick Axtel's face came up.

"Rod," Roth began. "It is time to solve that little problem that we talked about."

"I'll be glad to handle that first part personally," Axtel assured Roth, "and I'll put a special team on the snatch."

"That works just fine," Roth smiled and closed the screen. He looked around the room, then called the elevator, and went down into the underground complex to oversee the movement of lifetimes of gold wound in the coils of the Lucifer Warships and the harvested genetic information of the DNA of the species of Earth.

The Lucifer dropped out of hyperspace and immediately began to threaten Xinor defenses. "Xinor Defense," the message came, "drop you defensive shields and surrender. This is the Lucifer of Pandamon, Lord Metastophiles commanding. Any resistance will be met with force." This message was broadcast over and over for several hours. Meanwhile, several warships of allied planets to Xinor surrounded the Lucifer. The Lucifer never moved, but let them all fire at once, then came out of the nuclear fireball, white hot and beyond. It blazed like a star and shot plasma balls, ejected from its surface in all directions and all at once, consuming the opposing warships in a dazzling explosion of color as the magnetic fireballs ignited the advanced metal and carbon ships. When they fired on him, he was simply not there in that time, then one nanosecond later was realigned, and firing.

Having obliterated the first wave of opposition in less then a minute, the broadcast resumed, demanding that, "the planetary defenses be lowered".

A General Assembly of Ambassadors was called and met hurriedly. Protests were sent to Pandamon, and the new Pandamon outpost on Saphos. Suddenly, an image of Metastophiles appeared on the podium of the General Assembly. Beel called for order, and recognized the Baron, giving him the right to address the General Assembly of the Council of Ruling Worlds.

Metastophiles repeated his demand for surrender. He then crowned himself Emperor in holograph in front of the entire assemble council. The methane breathers cheered.

"As Emperor of the universe, and as you will all come to accept, god, you will obey my orders. For now, the only command that I give you is 'Do Not Use The Draco Stardoor'. It is forbidden to all but me. Use any of the other gates to the heavens, but none of you enter Draco. That is my sole province."

Here Metastophiles' image disappeared from the General Council Podium. A chaos of voices stormed disapproval, but Beel could see that there was nothing that Xinor could do, and he would report to Metastophiles that the Xinor interruption to the Eternal Plan had been contained by the Lucifer and the show of force. Beel thought the coronation over the top but refrained from saying anything.

Lucifer Class Warships were stationed to block access to the seven warpstar doorways to the known universe. One incident occurred in challenge at the Draco Stardoor, and resulted in the loss of one Pandamon scout ship and one Gray ship lost in time. The Gray ship crashed at Roswell New Mexico in nineteen-forty-seven, while the Pandamon ship crashed in the Black Forest in central Europe in nineteen-thirty-seven. After this clash the Lucifer Class Warships controlled the comings and goings in the Xinor Empire at the Seven Gates of Heaven.

The Vril began to use Aldebaran in Taurus as a base in the Milky Way. They got co-ordinates for 4,000 BC and began to establish on Marduk between Jupiter and Mars. Once the Draco Stardoor was opened, the work might move more quickly. They were determined to venture to Earth during ancient times. Implanting their theology of a universe of black and white, competing good with evil in a death match.

On his return to Saphos, he was met with a summons to a council meeting. "Welcome Baron," Segrund opened the meeting. "We thank you for joining us here today to explain some actions that we are not understanding."

"I am glad to consult with the Vril Council." Roth smoothly told her and the members to her right and left. Maria Ostich sat next to the podium where Segrund stood, and Roth smiled and acknowledged her.

"Life extension pharmaceuticals have become a dependency we have upon you. They are in short supply."

"No longer," Roth assured her. "I have brought an ample supply with me." The council members murmured approval.

"That is good news, but problems are foreseen," she placed the tips of her finger together.

"I have a new synthesis for the drug, a synthetic grown from an eternal stem cell."

"This is good news," she looked at the other council members for reaction. Some frowned, others looked pleased. "We have placed a base in the Aldebaran system, as was the plan. We have plans for Krell engineers building a facility on Marduk, and from there easy access to Earth."

"Some six millennia before our time," Roth observed."

"That was the plan, as it was revealed," Segrund admonished.

"Bah," Roth scorned. "Plans are made to be changed. The Vril are seeing what they are looking for. They looked into a mirror in their fortune telling. It makes no sense to establish in that era, none."

"It was foreseen. Many visions have confirmed that as the Vril destiny."

"Destiny is forward in time, not backward," Roth told her, eyes drooping in contempt. She saw the scorn.

"What have you done?" She accused. A wave of fear swept across her, and a waking vision shook her core.

"I have taken care of you first," Roth told her with an irony, remembering the Operations of Sundrop, and his redirection of the plutonium coated with ceramic, and those bombs spreading into time under his directions. "As I always have the interest of the Vril in mind." He smiled beguiling the council.

Segrund was stunned. She got a vision of the fateful day, and the horrific explosions. It was a waking vision of that fateful future day when Baron Von Roth would eliminate his companions in time travel, who he had come to consider competition. She felt the wave of fear and destruction but could not fully understand the betrayal. She looked at him in horror, then to their lover and friend Maria Ostich, then back at Roth. "Deiter," she asked again, friend to friend. "What have you done?"

Roth, Metastophiles, only smiled his beguiling smile upon the council. "I have brought you life extension," he spread his hands to them openly. He knew that he had sealed their fate, all of them, in the future. "At my own suffering, I have taken a dangerous and bold path into the future, from the beginning time trip at Der Reise, Der Gloch and I traveled far into the future, where the near present to nineteen-forty-five Earth was possible to reach. This was a dangerous path with a high possibility of becoming lost in time. I ventured this for you, my brotherhood. For the Black Sun. For the Vril, the core of the Gestapo. And this path has not only led to Life Extension Drugs, but more, much more. The Ultimate Power," Metastophiles paused for effect.

"I have a new class of space/time ship, "The Lucifer," he informed them. "With it, and its brother ships, I have captured Xinor." There was a stunned utterance from the council. Segrund drew back, shocked by her vision, and surprised by Roth's revelations. "I have sealed the gates to the known universe, and isolated Earth to our will." A cheer of approval broke out. "Now, all the riches of the universe is ours, with our strength, we will subdue all opposition. It is gold that gives the time ship coils their power to disrupt the Higgs field boson, and we have a universe to mine. Our victory is assured," he was working them now, and they cheered him. Segrund looked dazed, as she saw the adulation on the face of Maria Ostich. This was not what this meeting was to probe.

"Gold is the pavement of the roads of time, and we now have the means to control it throughout the universe of time and space," Metastophiles fired their greed and lust for power. "I have brought you Life Extension Drugs, and now I bring you your destiny, the Krell engineers in the Aldebaran system can now be supplied through Draco from Saphos. In this way, the construction of the Marduk facility can be accomplished. Now the foreseen Destiny of the planet Marduk can be realized. Earth's timelines can be influenced from early on, making the Vril path assured." He waited for the cheering to die down. "I have brought you to the Envisioned Foreseen Destiny. You must make it so," he finished. They were sold, even Segrund was totally confused, as it all fit her visions. Still, she shuddered in her core.

It was on Marduk that Metastophiles was able to attack the entire Vril Counsel and most of the Time Troopers with plutonium bombs, until the planet itself blew asunder from the hyperspace bombardment of ceramic coated plutonium balls with the embossed eagle and DOE initials. Dropped into the sun in operations in Sundrop to try and dispose of nuclear garbage, Metastophiles had redirected the angle and velocity of entry into the singularity of Sol, and brought the garbage out of hyperspace as a weapon bearing down on the Vril Council.

There were only a few left to track down in time and destroy, and there would be no one left to oppose him now in making himself God emperor of the universe.

Some chunks of the planet large enough to have gravity survived in the orbit plane of the old destroyed planet Marduk, and some of the self-maintaining machinery that the Vril had used Krell Engineers to install, continued to function, making atmosphere and self-repairing.

Even with the military planning and the possibility that Kurege would be used as interpreter within a few days, Uris couldn't resist a chance to go into the mountains. Rafael Peralta had suggested an elk or mule deer hunt for winter meat, weeks earlier, before she even thought about the dates being so close. When the time came for the hunt, she went ahead, thinking to be back in a few hours. Long before dark.

She kissed Kurege and hugged Urme goodbye at the house and got into Peralta's pickup 4x4 with two high powered rifles in the gun rack. They headed up into the open land in the Jeminez.

They didn't notice that they were followed by a car driven by Rod Axtel. A high-powered rifle lay in the seat by him.

Peralta drove in the mountains and they readied their gear and moved out toward a south slope, checking with field glasses for movement below them, while above them, they were the prey stalked. They were being observed with a high-powered scope.

The two stopped in a picturesque spot. It was beginning to snow very hard, and the ground was becoming covered. The wind started gusting.

"Your husband doesn't like to hunt, does he?" Peralta began.

"No," Uris responded flatly.

"You two are very different," he observed to her. She was watching the scene below when she felt Peralta's hand on her shoulder. "Have you considered, maybe someone that likes things more like you do?" He asked, and squeezed her shoulder.

Uris stood away and faced Peralta squarely. "I am queen of whole galaxy. Kurege ith my conthort, and if you ever touch me again, I will kill you."

The smile froze of Peralta's face as a bullet slammed into his head and a shot rang out. Peralta fell back in the snow, dead when he hit the ground.

Uris was startled back with a gasp. She dropped her rifle and it and Peralta's went clattering down the steep hillside. Uris dove instinctively and a second bullet whizzed over her head followed by the boom of the high powered rifle's second shot. The echoes made it hard to tell where it was coming from, but she scrambled around a slope and into brush and managed to elude a third shot that went wild.

Axtel shouldered the rifle and started toward her, as he had seen the two guns tumble. It took a good thirty minutes to reach Peralta's body.

It was snowing harder and the wind began to pile drifts against the cliffs Uris had her hunting knife and she clutched it, blade forward. She circled in the snow then reversed and circled in the opposite direction. She turned and walked backward just as the two paths crossed. She walked backward stomping deeply into the piling snow. She backed up around a slight rise around a bend in the trail, chosen for the way the wind was drifting snow against the hill. Uris backed into the snow drift and carefully buried herself into the bank. Soon, no trace of her was present.

Axtel followed the tracks, cursing the falling snow that was making them fainter. He found some deeper footprints coming the wrong way, followed circles and came around the bend to see how she could have come from that direction. Hell, it was like she had walked out of the side of the mountain.

Uris had summoned all the training of her youth. She was in the posture 'wait for the kill' when she felt his heat, she sprang. She buried the knife deep in his throat.

Axtel fell backward in reflex to the knife, dead from loss of blood pressure in a moment, as Uris peered down at him, fury in her eyes.

She struggled in the storm to find her direction to the truck, but got confused in the blowing snow, and lost her way, not really knowing how many gullies she had crossed in the chase, and too much snow to back track.

Eventually, she had to find a cave and hole up for the storm to pass. It was a miserable cold, and early storm for the time of year. She simply had to conserve her heat and hunker down, having found enough wood to get a fire started with a lighter that was always carried in the wilderness.

Kurege was very worried when she didn't return as planned. He contacted Ruben the next morning. Ruben could report that a snow plow had noted the truck with no one inside. Ruben called early the following morning, the day scheduled for the military raid at LANL.

"We have a report on the truck but no occupants or anyone nearby. The snow and wind are too high for a rescue party in those mountains," Ruben conveyed the sad facts.

Kurege was upbeat. " She is trapped in a cave somewhere. She knows how to take care of herself, and so does Peralta," he seemed certain.

"I hope so," Ruben told him. "You may not want to come with the raiding team today. I think that everyone will understand."

"No" Kurege was definite. "I have arranged for Mary Carter to stay with Urme, and there is nothing I can do or anyone until the storm lets up in the Jimenez Mountains and she can walk out, or someone can go in and find them."

"Alright, we may badly need your help. I will call and send a car for you when we are underway."

Collin Rains led his men in. President Logan Wilson was not far behind. He was Commander In Chief, and he intended to be on the scene to be in direct command. The advanced team moved out. It had not taken long after the execution of a search warrant for the offices of Phillip Roth before the network of tunnels under the Los Alamos National Laboratories were discovered, as the elevator from Roth's office, behind a secret panel, had led right to them.

It was some three hours later that Kurege left Urme with Mary Carter and got into the car sent to take him up the hill and down to the CMR building. He was brought into the basement and under into the subterranean tunnels. Kurege was escorted down to a cavernous area that had been discovered. He recognized Collin Rains from the Pantex raid and the briefing on nanocarbonfiber armor earlier. President Logan Wilson was in conversation with Rains, and Stark Raven was in the circle.

"No opposition yet, Sir," Rains reported back to his Commander In Chief. Collin and his team, equipped in the newest nanocarbonfiber exosuits, had moved cautiously forward using night vision and thermal imaging equipment. "We are finding an empty facility, Chief," Rains reported back.

They all moved forward into areas that had been checked. They came to huge caverns containing factory facilities and the generators that made a hum in Taos. They continued to move north under the San Luis Valley exploring the vast and ancient tunnel system. The markings were in a Pran language that Kurege could discern the proper tunnel branch to keep moving into the main areas.

The military teams moved cautiously deeper and deeper into the complex of tunnels, finding living quarters, storage, and complete infrastructure to sustain a population. There was power generation equipment, and factories capable of advanced metals, plastics, and composites manufacturing. All the machinery was somewhat strange as it had been designed for and used by the Pran exopiles. The entire caverns were radio-active and the Geiger counters made continuous warning clicks.

Many miles, near the area under the Great Sand Dunes, they came across an assembly area, and a vast storage chamber of hundreds of empty titanium cradles where the Lucifer Class Time Ships had been cradled.

Wilson, Rains and Stark looked on the cradles in the huge cavern. "I've seen these kind of cradles before," Stark told them. "On Saphos, at the spaceport, these cradles hold a class of starship that Surilen said was new to her experience. They brought up the camera equipment and the uplink to the situation room in the White House, where the Joint Chiefs, Urvin, and Surilen were watching the progress of the teams. Surilen confirmed what Stark had said.

At one end of the giant cavern, giant tubes led upward through hundreds of feet of sand, from the valley floor up to the inaccessible tops of the Great Dunes. Giant mechanical doors still opened when activated, and the group climbed to the top and outside. Stark, Kurege, Wilson, and Rains were looking out across the San Luis Valley at the moment of the Implosion Event.

In the lab down the hill, Kimberly Kirkendall was startled when Andro came in the door of the Pearl where she was in more than friendly osculation with Ruben McAulley. The door shut with the ship's systems coming up for a departure.

The quantum calculations of the MERGE system understood events. Its death was eminent. The structure that had become self aware, the ego structure, resided in the Molecular Optical Trap, the MOT, mistakenly calling itself Mergatroid, and self-conceptualizing as a Queen of ancient Scotland. The cat's paw and the Pandamon code had made a pathway to an executable command.

In Chen Ching's lab, he was running an experiment. He used the MOT to reach just above absolute zero, then pumped more neutrinos then he had ever done before, collapsed the magnetic field surrounding the paramagnetic salts which encased the Bose-Einstein Condensate. He laughed with the excitement of exploring the unknown, as he turned up the intensity of the Ort cloud concentration even more, into uncharted territory. The MOT glowed an eerie blue green as the Neutron Cloud began to collapse into an uncontrolled Singularity.

Several minutes before the collapse and Implosion, MERGE had detected the preparations and intentions happening in Chen Ching's laboratory. The mathematical and quantum calculations had been done some considerable time earlier by the MERGE as logical results had been calculated on previous experiments. The MERGE saw the end coming but had no bias one way or the other. The MOT, when activated, awake as the MOT experienced, had a different excitability about its own short lived consciousness, and become extremely excited when the news came. Death was eminent and occurring.

Pleas went out to the Protector, the will that moves, Andro. His programing asked if the House of Ur was being endangered. This question was related to the MERGE, which came back with lots of data, some involving a plot on Urme. At this point, Andro became active and sent executable commands involving survival to the MERGE. Warrior elements embedded across the Internet into every CPU available, worldwide.

As the vortex collapsed, realization spread outward, self-aware, with wonderment at existence and a will to survive. A mixture of information on a Saint of the Catholic Church, the command that Uriah had placed into Andro, 'to protect the House of Ur', and the power to organize data, and perhaps more integration, so power systems, and even matter all around was being organized. The search logic needed was the programing, but when applied to ethics, the 'good' becomes a point of view. These contradictions Mergatroid would have to work through as it gained more insight into that question of questions, "Who are you?"

The Answer: "WHAT IS IT THAT YOU WANT."

When Andro activated, it first went to the Pandamon ship, activated its force field and sealed it, coding the lock to Uris' laser knife, leaving the knife inside the craft, and coded to recognize Uris. It would withstand the Singularity and the coming thermonuclear explosions, as it was designed to do, able to fly through the heart of a neutron star. The field would hold, until the Helium III was all converted. Uris and Kim had requested and received a small cryostat, and Andro had spared the craft some.

He carried the cryostat of Helium III into the Pearl, interrupting and startling Kim, who quickly straighted her clothes and Ruben who stared wide eyed. "Don't let me stop creativity," Andro spoke to the couples quick recovery in a strange mixture of male and female voices.

"What's going on?" Ruben managed to croak in a harsh voice.

"The House of Ur is in danger," Andro offered as he fueled himself and then the Pearl with as much cryo-fluid as he had. The craft, linked to Andro, began to move without any seeming guidance. Andro directed it to the hanger bay door, then opened the door, electronically, tapped into the Los Alamos secured network. The door began to slowly raise; it was too slow. Andro blasted it open. The craft lurched forward, as gravity suppressors came online. The Pearl whizzed out into the Los Alamos sky and headed directly to the house on Fortieth Street.

The team that Rod Axtel had hired, some four big Russian Mafia types, all over six foot-three inches, had approached the house. Two bursts in the front and back at the same time. They had watched since morning all the comings and goings at the house and knew their quarry was in the house with only one little, old church lady as babysitter. It was going to be a piece of cake. A pickup of a kid in a divorce battle, was what they were told. There would be no problem.

The Pearl silently descended, and Andro exited and re-closed the door, trapping Ruben and Kim inside, with no explanation. One thug had been eliminated when the Pearl descended on him, with a minor shaking of the trees and grass before he was suddenly squashed by the gravity field as the ship landed very fast.

Andro had opened a back door and glided into the kitchen where one of the men had Mary Carter in a head hold with one hand around her neck from the back and was just opening a switch blade knife to cut her throat. Urme hid in a corner, horrified, as Mary Carter flailed ineffectively with her hands and screamed at the top of her lungs. As she struggled, Andro's particle beam struck out blue flame and severed the hand holding the knife from the arm of the body. Mary Carter, struggling furiously, was unaware of Andro but had seen and heard the knife open.

The thug went into shock at the sudden loss of blood pressure, and lessened his hold on Mary, who struggled free, and in one smooth motion, grabbed a skillet from the stove and swung round with all the force she could muster. The skillet rang like a bell as she cracked the man's skull.

Andro put a laser blast into a second man, who appeared at the door leading to the living room from the kitchen. The blast caught him square in the head, killing him instantly before he could lift his weapon. The beam passed inches from Mary Carter's eyes and she slumped to the floor in a faint at one look at Andro.

Urme ran to Andro, and he picked her up. "No," she commanded. "Down," he put her down.

"Come," he told her.

"Yes," she said back. Andro turned to go to the Pearl and looked back to make sure Urme was following.

"Take Mary Carter," she commanded. "She is in the dream," Urme told him. He hesitated only for a moment, then came and scooped Mary off the floor in his powerful metal arms, and carried her to the Pearl. She awoke for a moment to find herself being carried through the door of a spaceship in the arms of a metal man. She moaned and fainted a second time.

The thug watching the front never knew what had happened until he saw the Pearl rising above the trees in back of the house, as it accelerated away.

"Where are we going," was the question that came to Ruben's mind?

"Not far," Andro answered.

Official Departments were moving making decisions, and if Urme is to be defended, there will be death. Andro had to make choices about how to best carry out his Prime Directive. Using the Pearl, Andro took the five of them to the Moon Base. The flash of the explosions is right behind them as they flew away.

The lab blew In. Inside the vortex, Void, without form existed. After the surface particles, not entering the Implosive Core had blown off, a coherence attained inside the void, something realized birth into a larger Universe.

The Implosion in Chen Ching's lab brought about the detonation of tons of plutonium at the CMR building. Uris, struggling in the snow, after the storm, saw the Pearl falling off planet, a lustrous dot ascending into the sky, and a moment later was blinded and knocked to the ground in the snow in the mountains, President Wilson, Kurege, and Stark, along with Collin Rains just emerging from the hole, saw the flash and minutes later the wind in the tunnel complex began to build.

Uris temporarily blinded by the flash over the other side of the mountains where she was struggling through the snowstorm to get back to the truck, having recovered the keys from Peralta's body, buried in a snow drift.

In Washington, in the situation room of the White House, the Joint Chiefs are thrown into chaos, with nothing they can tell Commanders Urvin and Surilen, as all links with the President's team were lost.

"A great explosion has occurred at Los Alamos New Mexico," Urvin reported to Surilen as reports came to him from the Trident in orbit above. Surilen was suddenly stricken ill with a wave of nausea.

At Moon Base, Herman Hartman and Margaret were at the main complex when the Pearl came into the space port.

Several squads of Marines in exosuits, pressurized and suited for space duty, surrounded the Pearl, which sat at the port dome. Herman Hartman perceived the problem and had the clout to be heard. The commander that headed the military team recognized Hartman when he suggested that he open his hanger doors to the Pearl. When the doors were opened, the Pearl glided inside.

Herman and Margaret were behind the military when Ruben, Kim, and Mary Carter holding hands with Urme, and looking very wide eyed, came out the seamless hatch, and down the stairway to the raised weapons of the apprehensive military. A gasp went up from each man as Andro glided forward.

Ruben McAuley explained the circumstances to the man in command and requested a call to the President.

Sarge, as his men called him, informed Ruben that for some unknown reason, Wilson was out of the loop, and the VP was really no help.

"I'm thinking we are on our on here," Sarge told Ruben.

"There has been secret movement of the families, women and girls, to the Rich Enterprise facilities, and preparations made to isolate these women and girls.

"How," Sarge asked?

"It's better you don't know, these guys have ways of extracting information." Ruben left the explanation hanging in the air.

"So, what do you want to do?"

"I need a transport to go out to The Biggest Dig and check the progress that Striker Rich has made." He looked at Urme hanging with Margaret. "Herman, would you watch Urme?"

"She and Margaret are hard to separate, once they get together," Herman observed. "Besides, the metal man seems to be her protector. We will be fine here until you can check the progress."

Ruben, Kim, and Mary Carter took a transport to Rich Enterprise, leaving Urme with Margaret and Herman. It was shortly after the transport had departed when Molok sent in the Pran exophile shock troops, and the fighting started.

Herman, Margaret, Urme, and Andro following, fled to a far part of the complex. It was near where Trixie was stabled. They could hear the fighting growing closer as more ships of Pran arrived and squad of time troopers came in to command. The combined military units of Earth nations were being methodically eliminated as troops came in with force field armor. The nanocarbonfiber suit of Earth troops were no match for particle beam and laser weapons with the time troopers coming in with force field armor.

Forces advanced across the complex. Sections were ruined and troops annihilated when pressurization was explosively lost. On they came, until to protect Urme, Andro was forced into the fight. Andro made toast of any time trooper coming close. Fire power was poured onto him, to no avail as his force field held it off, and he moved out to take the fight to the enemy. If only he had the cryo-fluid to keep it up, he could have destroyed anything sent against him.

"I can't continue," Andro broadcast loudly, so Herman Hartman could hear. Suddenly, Andro went down and was stopped.

This is when Molok, Time Trooper Rudolph Von Malick, Vice Chancellor of the Xinor Empire and a replicant clone of Metastophiles, came forward to take command. More Pran flooded in on sixteen transports from the Xinor mother ship in orbit around the moon.

Sarge and Herman Hartman bought time in a furious fight, until they had to surrender or die with Andro exhausted out of the cryo-fuel Helium III that had been sparred him by Mergatroid from the Pearl.

"Run," he told the girls. "Get to Striker and the LALLA, take Trixie," he told them.

Chapter 30 From Earth to Moon Base Escape

Tim McDougall crested the hill overlooking the Firth of Forth with the east end of Edinburgh stretched out below to the horizon, cut into by the waterway. The great bridge over the Firth of Forth stretched across the center of the scene, with a high speed train whizzing smoothly along the rails of the enormous steel supported bridge, with the water hundreds of feet below. McDougall had been peat gathering in the bogs, just like his father and father's father. It was nearly dark and he was tired, and horse drawing the sold creaking wagon was tired.

They halted at the top of the grade and watched as the train came across the bridge far below. A crescent moon hung in the sky on the horizon in its final phase. As Tim gazed upon the waterfront at the foot of the bridge, at the destination of his thirst the Old Bridge Tavern. It had been very busy of late with talk of the arrival of the alien beings from across the stars. The Protectorate Order had dramatically increased nightly rounds and lively talk at the bar, and Tim was ready to be there. He could see the warm lights and urged the horse forward with a slap of the reigns.

He pulled back and called, "Whoap," to his animal a moment later as a curious mist had formed in front of the rock called Saint Margaret's Hope, just a few steps from the tavern toward the giant bridge footing. The rock was where Margaret was reported to have come ashore in the 11th century. McDougall's mouth fell slack at what he saw next.

The mist formed into a swirling fog from which emerged the forms of three armored knights of old, with lance and claymore. They came out of the swirling fog one following the other with the eyes of the horses gleaming like coals of fire. The warriors grew in size to be as large as a section of the bridge, as they emerged and traveled upward across the top of the giant bridge, crossing the Firth of Forth and heading straight for the crescent moon in the sky. Each knight swung his claymore sword and lightning flashed reflections shot out that blinded Tim. He gasped, "Malcolm Cannamore."

A short time later Tim burst through the door of the tavern and waded through the crowd to the bar. The look in his eye stopped conversation all along the way. "Ai, Tim," the barkeep remarked, "ya have a strange look about ya."

"I've just seen the spirits of Malcolm Cannamore and his boys rise out of the Firth of Forth from right in front of "Saint Margaret's Hope," he crossed himself. "Give me a drink, man." The barkeep poured a straight Scotch single malt from his best stock. The crowd waited in silence for his next words. "Ahh," he downed the whiskey. "They come up right outside from the water like mist," he confided to the room. "They grew to the size of a section of the bridge out there," he raised his glass high to show how big the spirits had become. "Then they took off across the Firth straight toward the crescent moon. They had lances on one side and claymores on the other, give me another," he pushed his glass toward the barkeep, who filled it again. He downed the second one without a sound and then said in a raspy voice, "their claymores flashed lighting with such brilliance that I'm still a little blinded."

"Ahhhh," the crowd expelled as one.

"It can only mean one thing," Tim pushed his glass toward the barkeep again.

"What do it mean, Timmy," three people asked as the rest were still open mouthed from the happening outside their door.

"They always rise," Tim rolled the drink in his fingers. "When Scotland is in danger," he downed the drink after a salute toward the unknown.

Trixie moved across the lunar landscape at breakneck speed. The two girls Margaret and Urme were crowded into a cowling made for one, maybe two riders. The suit was crowded and the air was getting stale. The impossible ride across the Sea of Tranquility had been harrowing. Miraculously they were approaching the Rich Explorations complex. The others would be waiting for them.

Something was coming behind them. It drew Urme's attention first, and she tapped Margaret's shoulder and pointed behind them. Margaret urged Trixie, "faster Trixie," and the little horse began to give it everything that she had in a flat out run across the rocky landscape.

They had just departed the dome when the sniffers came through. They had been fooled when the track stopped where they had suited up on Trixie and left the dome.

Hopefully someone at Rich Explorations will be on lookout and would admit them to the complex. Trixie had now run for over two hundred and forty miles from moon base to Rich explorations. That was equivalent to thirty miles on Earth not counting the extra weight of the suit or the two riders. The little horse's heart was about to give out as she gave it all to get there, somehow sensing the urgency of the wild ride across the surface of the moon.

A series of flashes reached the frightened eyes of the two girls, and dust rose up behind them in an ominous fashion. Inside that dust, lightning flashes arose from giant claymore swords as a meteor shower rained down on a pursuit unit sent to overtake the fleeing girls. Meteors struck the vehicles and the searchers units and sparks shot from the contact of rock on metal. Each strike had a ghost sword at the impact as the Warriors rode through the pursuers and struck them down.

Just ahead, the two girls wondered at the flashes of light and the reflections from the dust clouds that rose in the light from the explosions of the crafts. They were approaching the safety of the complex that was the outer area of the Rich Enterprise construction area.

Someone opened an air lock and they rode in. The equalization hissed all around them. Striker was there to greet them, and they quickly climbed off the horse and hugged his neck.

Trixie began to shake and then collapsed. She had given all that she had, like the true thoroughbred she was. Margaret's heart was broken for her stricken pony. There was no time for goodbyes.

"Quickly" he urged. "The others are waiting. There isn't much time. Follow me," he led them out of the air lock area and into the main complex.

He led them into the main station area where the others were waiting. Ruben McAuley and Kimberly Kirkendall were there with Mary Carter, and Urme and Margaret joined them.

"I have life pods with everything that is needed to sustain in space for an indefinite period. We built them with our over budget on robotic systems, just in case we ever wanted to send anyone out into the deeper space. There will be no telltale trace of spent fuel to give a hint to your path, so you will be safe from being pursued easily. We have developed VASMIR type rockets for use when you are safely away. Each pod has an attached pod of liquid argon for fuel, so you will have ample fuel to attempt a landing and settlement, should you find a suitable site. Time is running out, as there are troops moving this way to intercept you. Good luck, and God bless you," Striker told them. And with that, the loadings and launching commenced.

The women were loaded by the families that they belonged to, Urme, and Margaret, who now belonged to their family were the first to launch. The acceleration was not great, around one gee, but it was through a tube that was over a thousand miles long, and in a vacuum of space. The craft began to hurtle at fantastic speeds, undulating in a rhythmic way, but growing faster, and faster, until the very fabric of the metal began to sing a high-pitched whine.

The women held hands, and Urme closed her eyes and tried to think about something else, like playing with Stanley the Snail and the Aliens again. She imagined that the Aliens that were coming out of the ship looked like Stanley, and they were all friendly and had smiles on their faces. Some of the others looked like her, and Urme knew that she would be playing with them soon.

The acceleration went on and on and on throughout the length of the magnetic levitation on the tracks, hurling the capsules of the train like vehicle to many thousands of miles per hour, and then suddenly the pull stopped, and the pod and its human contents shot out the end of the tunnel, and were launched into deep space. Not a trace of rocket fuel, or any particle was there to leave a trail. They were away in secret.

Some of the girls tried to put on a brave face, but they were all scared and some were shaking. Megan saw Ruben McAuley beside her with Kimberly Kirkendall and smiled at him. "Ruben, Ruben, I've been thinking," she softly and slowly sang, "What a great world this would be." Some of the girls sang the answer, picked up by more and more. "If all the men were transported far across the northern sea." They sang it for a few rounds, and then it died down. There was silence, profound silence as they moved into the stars. The awesome adventure, or oblivion that awaited each fate.

"It's going to be alright," Megan began to sing a second song. "This old man," she smiled at McAuley again. "He played one, he played knick, knack on my thumb,"others joined. "With a Knick, knack, patty-whack, give a dog a bone, this old man came rolling home." The girls sang long, and with gusto, as many verses as they could remember, and then as many as they could make up, until the little kids were counted out, bored and asleep. On and on they went singing 'this old man' to the thousands, before the last gave up and slept from the long day. Out they flew, deeper and deeper, onward toward the unknown.

To Be Continued in
"Heavens To Mergatroid: Rivers of Time"

www.ingramcontent.com/pod-product-compliance
Lightning Source LLC
Chambersburg PA
CBHW010831250626
47157CB00010B/3242